THE MAN FROM OUTBACK

When Mari was whisked off to Australia,
the idea was that a holiday there would
help to mend her broken heart. However,
as soon as she got to Ninna-Warra Station
she encountered Kane Manners, the manager, and her heart was soon in trouble
again. Nobody on Ninna-Warra Station
was used to girls, or any white women at
all, in fact, and Kane Manners didn't
exactly welcome her. "No white woman
has been on this station for twenty years,"
he told her angrily. But Mari stood her
ground. "One always has to make a start,"
she said bravely. "I mean about having
a white woman here. You might
marry one—one day."

NOBODY READS JUST *ONE* LUCY WALKER!

The Other Girl
Heaven Is Here
The Distant Hills
Sweet and Faraway
The Call of the Pines
Come Home, Dear
Love in a Cloud
Follow Your Star
Home at Sundown
Reaching for the Stars
A Man Called Masters
The Stranger from the North
The River Is Down
The One Who Kisses
The Man from Outback
Down in the Forest
The Moonshiner
Wife to Order
The Ranger in the Hills
Shining River
Six for Heaven
The Gone-away Man
Kingdom of the Heart
The Loving Heart
Master of Ransome
Joyday for Jodi

Available in Beagle editions

The Man from Outback

Lucy Walker

BEAGLE BOOKS • NEW YORK

An Intext Publisher

Published by arrangement with the author and the
author's agent, Paul R. Reynolds, Inc.

First printing: May 1971
Second printing: September 1971
Third printing: April 1972

Printed in the United States of America

BEAGLE BOOKS, INC.
101 Fifth Avenue, New York, NY 10003

CHAPTER ONE

Mari Curtis sat in the back of the dust-covered car while her Uncle Ralph sat in the front seat by the driver. They bowled at a terrific pace over bumpy trackless ground, the steering-wheel sometimes spinning free in Bob's hands.

Already Mari thought of the little wizened brown-faced driver as "Bob." That was all Uncle Ralph had called him when they had arrived at the landing strip.

"This is Bob, Mari," Uncle Ralph had said, then looking at the quaint little man he had added laconically: "My niece, Mariana Curtis, from England, Bob. Come for a holiday."

Bob's expression said he was seeing a mirage. For one moment his eyes had widened, looked affrighted, then quickly hooded had recaptured that former dead-pan expression. It struck Mari as a cross between the comical and the odd.

"G' day," Bob said, then not waiting to hear what kind of reply the pretty dark-haired girl in the ice-blue dress might make, he picked up two cases and began to stow them away in the boot of the car.

"Not used to girls!" Uncle Ralph explained to Mari. He did not add that nobody on Ninna-Warra Station was used to girls, or to any white women at all, in fact. There was every good reason for Bob's staggered reaction to the sight of Mari. Uncle Ralph, back from his holiday in England, had not bothered to tell anyone on the station he had brought Mari with him.

If the driver didn't know about her—hadn't prepared to meet her—then what about Kane Manners, Mari wondered.

For the first time in all that long trip—three days by jet airliner to Darwin, then one day by a vintage DC3 out to Ninna-Warra Station—Mari began to think about Kane Manners.

Uncle Ralph had told her the bare facts, but they were very bare indeed. Kane Manners was his partner and, now that Uncle Ralph was nearing retiring age, was also his station manager. In addition to this job, Kane Manners owned another station called Half Moon which he had leased out to other people.

"Uncle Ralph," Mari said, veiling her sea-blue eyes against the glare of the light. The clear pale colour of the sky was so pure, yet it hurt her eyes. "Uncle Ralph, what does Kane Manners look like?"

Bob, in the driver's seat, moved his hat forward over his brow. Uncle Ralph took his pipe out of his mouth and coughed.

I wonder if he's bossy and they're scared of him, she wondered to herself. Something about her question had put both Uncle Ralph and Bob off their beat.

"Well . . ." Uncle Ralph drawled. He was once again the outback man, now that he was on home territory. "He's a big fellow. Well, tall, anyway. He's quiet. Likes to do things his own way." He turned and looked over his shoulder at Mari. "You don't have to worry about Kane, Mari," he said. "He's quite a nice fellow—when you get to know him. Just carry on out here at the homestead the same as you did at home in England. That's all there is to it. . . ."

What prophetic words, had Mari only known!

At home she had housekept for her father, and even now, driving fast over a dusty and pitiless landscape, Uncle Ralph's words tinkled like a little bell of warning. At that moment she didn't heed it.

Instead, she thought of Robert Alton, her erstwhile dear "steady" from next door, back there in England. How scornful Robert would have been of this dead-pan driver; this noncommittal uncle. He loved to probe, draw people out and look at them through a microscope. That was because he was studying to be a scientist.

Mari was seventeen, rising eighteen, and Robert Alton was twenty-one. One day, during Uncle Ralph's visit to England, Mari and Robert had had the wonderful idea they would marry. Straight away! All they had had to have, they thought, was the idea. It was as simple as that. Two could live as cheaply as one; they knew, because Robert had worked it all out on paper. If the worst came to the worst Mari could get a job—in addition to looking after Robert and her father, of course.

Mari had been thrilled. She would be engaged, then married. It was a wonderful idea and all quite easy. Everyone was doing it.

"On a starvation ration?" her father had snorted.

That had been the end of Robert Alton for the time being. His parents had whisked their son away to an uncle in Edinburgh for the vacation, and Uncle Ralph had decided to give Mari a "holiday" in Australia.

Robert whisked off to Edinburgh, and not even writing to Mari, had broken her heart. At nearly eighteen Mari knew that a broken heart is a very sore thing indeed. In fact, all the way to Australia, through all the exotic countries *en route*, she had looked out of the windows of the jet liner with sadly clouded eyes—until she landed in Darwin.

There in the palatial, tropical hotel, she met Allen Webster.

They had been waiting in the cool palm-decorated lounge for the trans-country plane, and he came in. He was tall, extra good-looking in a slightly fun-making wicked way, and he had come across the lounge and smiled at Mari. He knew Uncle Ralph and somehow wangled an invitation to sit down with them.

"If you don't like it out there at Ninna-Warra, Mari," Allen Webster had said, half an hour later and smiling in a you-know-how way right into Mari's eyes and using her Christian name, just as easily as that, "we'd like to have you here." Then grinning wickedly he had added, "That is—I would."

"Why shouldn't she like Ninna-Warra?" Uncle Ralph had growled ferociously over his long drink of ice-cold lager. He had disapproved of Allen Webster buying Mari a gin and tonic, and had looked it. "There's everything a girl wants out there at Ninna-Warra."

Allen Webster had flicked up one eyebrow in an engaging way.

"Including that ogre Kane Manners?" he asked. "By the way, does he know this charming young girl is about to be landed on his plate for dinner to-night?"

Now, hours later, driving in the car from the airstrip to Ninna-Warra Station, Mari thought of Kane Manners. A flock of emus raced past the car as they neared the scrub

banks of a creek bed. The car swerved round the first big
clump of trees Mari had seen since they left the landing strip.

Why had Allen Webster in Darwin called Kane Manners
an " ogre "?

Mari took off her white hat and put it on the seat beside
her. What did it matter anyway? She was here and nothing
could alter that. She leaned her head back and closed her
eyes. Her pretty dark brown hair, swathed round her head,
caught the lights of the sun in it. She was a very pretty girl,
very young, and though she didn't know it, very inexperienced.
Yet she had spirit. Canny old Uncle Ralph, when back there
in England, had seen that.

Once in Australia, he had thought, this little heartache
about the boy next door would soon pass. He had seen the
first signs when Mari had lifted her delicate pointed chin and
widened her eyes when Allen Webster in Darwin had put on
his Lothario act. Uncle Ralph did not know that anything or
anyone that was kind and gay would have lifted Mari's heart
at that moment. She needed a little gaiety very badly, for she
had been sad for quite a long time. Several weeks, in fact.
Uncle Ralph, who thought Allen Webster had had more
success than was necessary, wasn't very pleased with him.

The landscape was changing, growing more interesting, yet
Mari sitting back in her corner seat was thinking more of
Darwin than of England or the creek bed outside the window ;
more of Allen Webster than of Robert Alton.

" If you don't like it at Ninna-Warra," Allen Webster had
said, " we'd like to have you here."

" There you are, lass," Uncle Ralph said from the front
seat. " Home at last!"

Mari opened her eyes.

They had mounted a rise. Stretching away below them the
track fell into a rocky decline like a gash in the hillside. At
the bottom of the gash, trees grew thick and high, some of
them reaching right up as if to find the sky with their long
slim leafy arms. The car passed through a gorge and the
walls on the far side were red and blue and green, shining as
if wet with water. There were ferns, thick bushes, and more
of the tall slim trees whose arms sought the sky.

"But where is home?" she asked, without noticing she had called it *home*.

The car slid past the straining posts of the cross-fences, and there was the homestead. It was a low rambling house, surrounded by a veranda and standing in a nest of trees. There was a wire fence around the house but no garden to speak of. The car stopped at the wire fence. Mari read the words " *Ninna-Warra* " on a rectangle of board attached to the gate.

"Right here," Uncle Ralph said, answering the question Mari had asked quite five minutes before. He seemed pleased with this homestead, even proud of it.

"It has a nice name," Mari said, a little wistfully.

Bob and Uncle Ralph got out of either side of the driving seat.

"Well, this is it, lass," Uncle Ralph said. He beamed at Mari as she extricated herself from the back seat. "First duty you've got, my girl, is to go right in and make the tea. I'll help Bob bring in the cases. You see if you can live up to your home standards. Wonderful cup of tea you could make there, Mari."

Mari was dazed.

"You mean . . . you mean I'm to go right into the kitchen? Won't somebody mind?"

Ralph Curtis hooted.

"There's men hereabouts and we need a woman to look after us, Mariana. Go right ahead. No one will stop you, and the three of us will just love it."

The three of us! Bob and Kane Manners and Uncle Ralph! Mari's heart dropped. Was there no one else?

Uncle Ralph gently patted her shoulder as he propelled her in the direction of the veranda steps and the wire-screen door that protected the open doorway beyond.

Bob, straightening himself after depositing a case on the ground, could now stare his fill. Uncle Ralph and the girl had their backs to him. His burned, weathered face wore no expression, but the very stillness of his stance betrayed the fact that he was seeing something the like of which he had never seen before. A white woman come to live on Ninna-Warra Station.

Mari mounted the steps—her instinct told her dry rot was in the boards, but she did not think about it then. A dog had his brown and black nose around the corner, but he did not stir. Uncle Ralph let go her arm and returned to the car. Mari looked back, but neither he nor Bob was taking any notice of what she did now.

Delicately she put out her hand and opened the screen. She looked down a long, narrow, linoleum-covered passage, scrupulously clean but, except for the floor cover, bare.

She went inside and took one step, then stood still and listened. There was only silence.

She walked, carrying her hat in her hand, a little way down the passage. The doors to the left and right were open, and on the far side of them, on the outside walls, the windows were wide open too.

There was a sitting-room, with leather-upholstered chairs and a gun-rack in the corner. There was a heap of harness on a small table, and a case of books in that room. Other rooms were bedrooms, and one that looked like an office, another a dining-room. It was all clean, bare and masculine as a hospital ward, for there was no carpeting, only linoleum on the floors.

She went eerily, because of her tiptoeing, down the passage, looking in one door after another. There was a small room near the end of the passage, opposite the dining-room, that was clearly unused. The mattress stood on its side on the bed as if it had been there many a long day.

Where, Mari thought, is the kitchen?

She went out on to the wire-screen veranda at the end of the passage and saw the open door leading into the kitchen. In its dim recesses she could see the gleam of something white where the light from a window fell on it.

She took a step into the kitchen.

There across the wide linoleum-covered floor was a huge refrigerator against the far wall and beside it a " deep freeze." Mari's eyes widened and her heart leaped. Even at home in England she hadn't had those.

Under the window was a stainless steel sink, and farther along a shining-topped table with matching chairs around it. There was an electric stove, and on another bench, beside the stove, there was a kettle, a coffee percolator and a frying-pan—all gleaming silver-steel, and all electric.

In this strange land, in this empty homestead—was Mari's dream of a kitchen! It was like magic.

She put her hat down on the table and walked softly over to the bench and let her fingers stroke the lovely blue and silver gleam of the electric kettle.

This great barn of a homestead, her fingers seemed to say. And this lovely kitchen. Oh, I would like very much to cook in this kitchen.

There were heavy footsteps coming down the inside passage, out on the back veranda and then to the kitchen door. Mari had turned her head, and saw with relief that it was Uncle Ralph.

"Leave the tea half an hour, lass," he said. "Seems Kane's not in from the muster yards yet and I've got to turn the engine on. No engine—no electricity. That's the way it works!"

He beamed at her as if he too knew this was magic and expected Mari to appreciate it as he did.

Uncle Ralph had exchanged his nice London felt hat for a fearful brown one that had a brim like a dusty veranda. He stumped off—through the back-veranda screen door, on to the gravel path and then away around the corner of the house.

If Kane wasn't in *yet*, it meant he would be in soon.

Mari wished, unexpectedly, that she was back in London.

Then that spirit which Uncle Ralph had admired so much came to her aid.

So Uncle Ralph and Kane Manners would come in presently to find their tea nicely prepared and served up to them by the latest thing *in housekeepers*, would they?

Well, it *would* be the latest thing in housekeepers too. Uncle Ralph at least was going to have a shock.

Mari picked up her hat and went out of the kitchen, through the house to the front where her case sat waiting for someone to lift it in. Clearly that someone had to be Mari herself.

She carried it to the room where she had seen the mattress up-ended on the bedstead. She put her hat on top of the wardrobe, then, finding the bathroom, had a quick wash.

Back in her room she opened her case. Out came her " trews," her flattest flatties, her cotton print over-blouse.

Down came the swathe of hair, and with two strokes it hung, shining, to her shoulders.

The make-up box came next, and on went the dash of eyebrow pencil, and the dash of mascara—things Mari hadn't dared to use in her father's presence. She managed to put the lipstick on with the kind of quick flick that made her mouth look like a rich peony.

" The very latest edition of *housekeepers*! That's me," she told her image in the shabby dressing-table mirror. " That's me! "

Without realising it she was arming herself against indignation, and also against Kane Manners. In a fore-warned way, she knew he knew nothing of her presence in the homestead. That " ogre " appellation of Allen Webster's back there in Darwin sounded to Mari as if Kane Manners wouldn't like her being here either. So she armed herself with mascara and lipstick and a lovely red mouth. Unconscious of beguilement, she let her shining soft brown hair lie, ambassador to herself, around her shoulders.

All the time, she told herself encouragingly that she was very angry.

" Now for that cup of tea, if only Uncle Ralph has got that engine—whatever it is—going."

She went light-footed out of the door of her room, down the passage and through the door that led to the veranda.

There she came to a stop. Through the wire screen she saw Kane Manners coming towards the house. She knew it was he, for bells rang in the far-off world of her imagination.

He had come from the stables. Around those stables, in a mute spindly group, stood tall shade trees, and in the paddock beside them two horses were rolling in a sandy patch.

All this Mari saw without looking, for her eyes were on the man coming to the house. He was carrying a stockwhip in his hand and was winding the long, long leash around the handle. He was very tall and his clothes were khaki cotton drill, and his hat, like Uncle Ralph's, had a veranda for a brim. He was looking down at the stockwhip in his hand, yet strangely, Mari was aware of someone with a considerable power of silence ; a silence that made itself felt. She *knew*, without diagnosing it, that here was someone who shared only part of himself with other people. The greater part, the powerful part, was for himself alone.

Then suddenly the picture of the man coming towards her was broken by the dog with the black and brown nose. It raced around the side of the house and came up to the man, skidding to a stop, as the man stopped, and stood still, ears pricked, waiting for Kane Manners to do or say something.

His face creased in a smile and his white teeth flashed in the brown of his face. He put out one hand and the dog sprang up to meet it. Then the dog was back on his four feet again, standing still, waiting. The man bent and patted his head, then he straightened up and came on towards the house, finishing winding his whip.

He's more than thirty, Mari thought. Perhaps a lot more. She could see all his face now and the colour of his eyes and the fine lines radiating from the corners of his eyes.

He came up to the screen door, and as he put up his hand to push it open he looked up and saw Mari framed in the passage doorway.

Quietly Kane pushed the door open and took one step up on to the veranda. He closed the door behind him without turning, so that he still looked at Mari.

" I beg your pardon," he said. Then after an æon of silence he added, " I don't think we have met?"

The grey eyes in the brown face looked at her with a searching, penetrating, inimical look.

Mari, who had never been shy, was astounded to find that that was what she now was.

" I'm Mari Curtis," she said. Her voice sounded like a schoolgirl's to her own ears. Then she flushed, but quickly lifted her chin to combat the effect of that slowly rising colour.

" Uncle Ralph brought me with him," she finished.

" Uncle Ralph?"

" Yes, my Uncle Ralph. My father's brother."

He took off his hat. None of his movements were quick, yet they conveyed the capacity to be very quick indeed if he wanted it that way. His hair was dark brown and very thick, and he was very good-looking.

"Have you come to stay?" he asked. They stood and looked at each other in a battle of silence.

"For a long time," Mari said.

His shoulders relaxed and his mouth eased into a smile. It was a good smile in spite of the fact he had had a shock, and as the nature of this shock began to reveal itself he became coldly angry.

"No white woman has been on this station for twenty years," he said. "And there is no other white woman here."

"One always has to make a start," Mari said. "I mean, about having a white woman here. You might marry one—one day."

He lifted his chin with a jerk, then let his grey eyes travel over her, taking in the slim youthful figure, the print blouse, her white oval face with its rich peony-red lips and above her short straight nose the sea-blue eyes. He took it all in, specially that shining dark brown hair, falling across one temple and down on to her shoulders.

"I beg your pardon," he said for the second time. There was a formidable dislike in his voice.

He wasn't going to like her! There wasn't very much she could do about it, she supposed . . . a little sadly.

"Excuse me," she said. "I'll go and make the tea."

CHAPTER TWO

Mari, out in the kitchen, heard Kane Manners's heavy footsteps striding down the inside passage. He had probably gone into the office, or outside to the front veranda in search of Uncle Ralph—and an explanation.

Once in that dream of a kitchen Mari had regained her spirits. She wouldn't think about Kane Manners. After all, she had spent all the former years of her life *not* thinking about him. Why start now?

She smiled, tossed the vagrant lock of dark hair out of her left eye and plugged in the electric kettle. A small red light went on, so Mari knew that Uncle Ralph had the engine working.

The red light fascinated her. She tried the electric frying-

pan in another plug, then the coffee percolator. They all had
red lights. For a moment they seemed magic playthings.

Mari with a certain naïve delight perceived she now had
three men at her mercy. She would give them for breakfast,
lunch and dinner what she liked. Her own father had been
a food fad, and a stickler for punctuality. He had never
allowed Mari to be absent from a meal. Twice a day, seven
days a week, she had had to be there to serve the kind of
meals her father liked, and at the time he prescribed. Her
mother had died five years ago and when she was sixteen she
had left school to housekeep for her father.

Now she had her own house—in the middle of a desert,
true, but *hers*—and the kitchen full of things that shone and
had red lights when they were turned on.

When the tea was ready Mari carried the tray through the
house. They were on the front veranda: she thought she
could hear Uncle Ralph's voice.

With one foot she eased open the screen door on to the
veranda. She stood, the tray in her hands, and looked at
Uncle Ralph sitting nonchalantly in the easy-chair; and
Bob, pretending to be occupied with distant vistas, sitting on
the veranda step.

They had been waiting for her to bring the tea to them!
She hadn't been in the house two hours, and they were
waiting to be waited upon. They hadn't even shown her
where anything was kept.

Men! Mari said scornfully to herself.

She put the tea-tray down on the cane table near Uncle
Ralph and ignored the look of astonishment on his face as he
saw her hair down to her shoulders, her lipstick, the mascara
on her lashes, the slim slacks and the little pointed shoes. He
half got up out of his chair, and then, putting one hand
behind him to support his weight as he sank back, closed his
eyes, then opened them again to make sure he was seeing what
he did see.

In England he had never seen Mari in anything but a neat
dress and with her hair done up. In this rig-out Mariana
looked little more than a child. He had a sense of misgiving.
He couldn't think of anything to say.

Bob had stolen one look over his shoulder and quickly

turned his gaze and his expressionless face back to the distant horizon.

Mari, turning from the table, caught him sneak another half-look; and she smiled.

"Tea?" she said. "That's what you're waiting for, isn't it?"

She looked innocently at Uncle Ralph.

"Where's Kane?" she asked, as if it was of no real importance. "Doesn't he drink tea?"

This galvanised Bob into action. With an unexpected speed he stood up, stepped up on to the veranda and came towards the tray.

"I'll take it to him," he said. "He's in no way for company. Gets moods, you know. Terrible prickly fellow when he gets that way. I'll take his tea to him."

While he was speaking he looked everywhere but at Mari. She rocked herself from heels to toes and back again, and glanced again at Uncle Ralph.

"Does he mind my being here, do you think?" she asked casually.

"Certainly not," said Uncle Ralph, but Mari noticed there was an uneasy note in his voice. He looked at Mari—so childlike in those clothes—and wondered who on earth he had brought to Ninna-Warra Station.

Mari had two voices. One would have told him—" Me out of prison. Me out of those nice suburban clothes. Me here, where nobody, not even you, dear Uncle Ralph, will tell me what to cook."

The other voice, a little frightened, not so certain now, queried—"Won't I do, after all?"

Bob had finished pouring a large cup of black tea for Kane, put a slice of the toast Mari had made from the stale damper on to a plate—after looking at it with appreciative bewilderment—and stumped away, through the front door and down a few yards of the passage.

So that was where Kane had buried himself. In the office!

"Hadn't you better do your hair, Mari?" Uncle Ralph said.

"You mean put it up? It is rather hot for long hair, isn't it?"

She fished three hairpins out of the pocket of her slacks

and with a flick and a twist had her hair in a knob on the crown of her head. Uncannily, the bewildered Uncle Ralph thought, the knob was smooth, and what was more, it stayed there. At least she looked a little *older*.

"Is that better?" asked Mari, bending her head sideways and looking at Uncle Ralph as if he were a mirror and she could examine in his eyes to see if her hair was indeed right.

Uncle Ralph imagined for a moment he was looking at a French gamine, and wondered where he had seen her like before. It had been on posters advertising a film, in the London Underground, but he didn't remember that.

"Milk and sugar, Uncle Ralph?" Mari asked as she lifted the teapot and glanced at him again.

"Where'd you get the milk? Anyway, we don't drink milk. Soft way to drink tea—*with milk*."

"Powder in a tin," Mari said, being very cheerful. "I mixed it with an egg whisk."

She poured the tea and took it to him. She offered him the sugar. There were no comments about sugar; he simply helped himself to six spoonfuls.

Mari poured her own tea, and then another cup of milkless tea for Bob, who came back to the veranda. He didn't dare look at her, as he carried it with a plate of toast to the veranda step. He also had put six spoons of sugar in his cup. He hadn't put any sugar in Kane's tea, Mari noticed.

She sat in a cane chair beside the table and leaned back and contemplated the roof.

"Galvanised iron," she said softly. "And look at the cobwebs."

"Eh, what?" said Uncle Ralph, munching toast. Bob kept an implacable back turned to the veranda.

Mari sat up and picked up her own cup of tea.

"That's what you brought me here for, wasn't it, Uncle Ralph? To clean away the cobwebs from the veranda ceiling, and to make tea—and possibly cook dinner? It wasn't just for a holiday. It was to make life comfortable for you and Bob—and particularly for . . . for *Kane*."

"Psst!" hissed Uncle Ralph, nodding in the direction of Bob. Mari shook her head. As if Bob didn't *know*. That silence, that dead-pan face, that race to take Kane's tea to him, were all eloquent of protection of Kane!

What would that wizened, weathered, bow-legged horse-man be protecting Kane from? A girl in the homestead, of course.

"Well, it was the cobwebs then, was it?" said Mari innocently.

"Cobwebs be damned," said Uncle Ralph, swallowing tea in a gulp. Then he mumbled something about—"A nice holiday for you. A change from that drizzly cold climate. Come out and see how your relations this end of the world get on. Not many girls 'ud get a trip across the world in an aeroplane. Not to mention the fine clothes——"

He broke off and stole a glance at Mari's colourful over-blouse and the slacks. He winced.

"You wouldn't know what to do with yourself, Mari," he finished lamely, "if you didn't make a cup of tea, now and again."

A little sorrow like a small snow-clad hand touched Mari's heart for a minute.

You helped send Robert away from me, she thought. And fooled my father.

She shook herself and the cold hand fell away.

"Who cooks your dinner for you generally, Uncle Ralph?" she asked aloud.

"Now listen here," said Uncle Ralph, putting down his empty cup on the floor. "Ada—she was a lubra—she cooked better'n any professional cook ever did. Well, she died. Got old and died like anybody does. Sooner or later. Then there was one lubra after another. 'Pon my word, they never knew whether to put the peas in the porridge or the oatmeal in the soup. No one here to teach 'em."

"You mean you and Kane, and Bob, didn't feel like teaching them?" Mari asked, innocently.

"We've got this whole station to run, lass. It's not the same as it was when I came on this place thirty years ago. Then it was just horses and cattle. Now it's all mechanised. Me and Kane have got to put bores down everywhere. Have you any idea, girl, what it means to put down a bore? If we don't put 'em down and run cattle on every inch of this lease then the Government will take whole slices of it and give it to new settlers. Fellers that don't know the north from their left hands."

"Why shouldn't they have some of it, if it's as big as all that?" asked Mari, who had very much been bred in the Welfare State.

"Because we're closed-in here. North is Half Moon. That's Kane's station. Can't get through there. South of us is the rocky region. Can't drive cattle through that. The only way out is west and east. We've got to hold it all."

Mari looked at her uncle in surprise.

"Why can't you drive cattle through Half Moon if Kane owns it?" she asked. "It must have a way out?"

"Not now since Kane leased it out to that Raywood crowd. They've closed the boundaries to everyone."

"Then can't Kane unlease it?"

"You don't know what you're talking about, Mari. What's more, don't talk about it in front of Kane. He's apt to get annoyed."

"Why did Kane lease it?" persisted Mari.

"Women shouldn't talk about men's affairs," Bob said unexpectedly, without turning round.

Mari drew in a breath ready to tell Bob all about modern women, but Uncle Ralph cut in quickly.

"Talking about Kane," he said in a mollifying voice, "maybe you'd like to get him another cup of tea?"

Mari sat up straight.

"I suppose if Kane wants another cup of tea he'll come and get it," she said. "Besides . . . do you know what, Uncle Ralph? I don't think I even like Kane, though I'm willing to give him another chance about being polite to me. What's much more important, Kane doesn't like me. I thought you'd better know right from the start."

"Psst!" said Uncle Ralph again, nodding his head in the direction of Bob's back.

Bob, intuitively aware of that glance, moved his hat farther forward on his head and gave more concentration to far horizons.

At that moment Kane himself came down the passage and out of the front door. The sound of his powerful stride announced him in advance.

Mari leaned back in her chair again, and like both Uncle Ralph and Bob became suddenly absorbed in the distant view. It was no more than brown stubble paddock and pale clear sky, yet for the moment it totally absorbed the attention of the three people sitting by their emptied cups on the veranda.

Kane closed the screen door behind him and stood silently contemplating the group. No one felt exactly inclined to turn and look at him.

It was Mari, in the end, who first turned her head. She looked up at him, trying not to be shy, just curious. What had he come out on the veranda for? Another cup of tea?

Kane looked at her.

She was struck by his masculine silence—masculine, yet benevolent. And his eyes had a touch of mystery in them.

"That was a very good cup of tea," he said quietly, politely, yet only half of him speaking; the other half critical, aloof and not to be drawn.

"Would you like some more?" Mari found herself asking.

The sound of their voices broke the battle of silence on the veranda. Bob moved his hat to another angle and Uncle Ralph stirred and began doing things with his pipe again.

"No thank you," Kane said. "I have work to do."

Mari could almost hear Uncle Ralph and Bob expelling breaths of relief. There hadn't been an explosion!

Kane put his empty cup and saucer on the table and walked towards the veranda steps. Bob, without turning, moved over a few inches so Kane wouldn't trample him in the process of going away.

On the gravel pathway Kane changed his mind about his speed of departure. He stopped, and turned. Then he caught sight of the brown and black dog who had been lying on the side veranda, only his nose poking around the corner. Kane's stern, unbroken face suddenly creased. He smiled, the edge of his white teeth showing very white and his eyes creasing and wrinkling at the corners. He flicked his fingers, and the dog was a black and brown streak as it shot across the veranda, leaped over the low balustrade, skidded to a stop on the path in front of Kane, then stood statue-still, his ears pricked.

Kane smiled down on the dog—said something with his eyes which only he and the dog understood—and the dog leaped in the air to touch his hand. Kane bent down and patted him.

" Back, Laddie!" he said.

The dog turned and walked quietly and sedately up the veranda steps round to the side and with a flop and a sigh sank back to his former position. Only his paws, with the brown and black nose resting on them, could be seen round that corner.

Kane looked up at the older man on the veranda.

" You'd better come down and look at that stallion, Ralph. He'll ride tough and he's got a hard mouth, but I think I'll tame him."

Ralph Curtis loosened himself from his chair with pretended enthusiasm. Kane meticulously took the makings for a cigarette from the pocket of his shirt. He was intent on *not* looking at Mari.

Mari, leaning back in her chair, had been surprised and just a little thrilled by that change in Kane when he had smiled at the dog, then spoken to him. It was as if a brilliant light had switched on inside him. Now, as he stood there, waiting for Uncle Ralph, it had gone out again. Mari suspected he was about to take Uncle Ralph out of earshot where he could continue with the business of saying, " This girl must be got out of here as quickly as possible."

It wasn't the done thing, in Kane Manners's directory, to have *girls* on Ninna-Warra Station!

" One good thing about the stallion," Uncle Ralph was saying as he walked stiffly, and a little stooped, to the veranda step. " That'll be the end of losing mares. That stallion's caused a lot of mischief round the hills this last year. . . ."

Kane's back, and the hot afternoon sun on it, the tilt of his hat where he had clapped it on his head, made Mari feel small-girlish indeed—and just a little wistful.

Was it girls in general he didn't like? Or this one, Mariana Curtis, in particular?

" Bob," she said to the broad brown back, " doesn't Kane know any girls at all?"

" Not young girls," Bob said in his even toneless voice, not turning his head. " There's the young woman up at Half Moon. He goes there——"

Oh does he? thought Mari. I wonder what she's like. Older than me, but is she better?

She jumped up and began gathering together the cups and saucers, including Uncle Ralph's, which had been left on the floor beside his chair.

"What were you thinking of for dinner, Bob? And who was going to cook it?" she asked.

"Steaks." When Bob spoke, which was not often, it was always through half-closed lips. "We have it every night," he added. "Kane likes it that way. Men outback eat mostly steaks."

"Does he cook them himself?"

"Sometimes. Sometimes me. Sometimes Ralph."

There were no honours for Ralph Curtis because he was older than the others. On her uncle's behalf Mari felt indignant.

"Who was to be the cook to-night?" she persisted.

"M'self, I suppose."

He hadn't once turned round, and information had to be dragged from him. Mari crossed the veranda and picked up his cup and saucer from the step above him. He was pre-occupied with rolling a cigarette.

"Well, I'll give you a shock," Mari said softly, very near his ear. "I'll cook them for you." Privately she was thinking that when Kane Manners found out what a good cook she was he wouldn't be hasty about sending her away.

Bob turned and glanced at her, then quickly away.

"Right," he said. "Steak's in the meat-house."

Mari stood up straight and looked at his back coldly.

"You expected me to cook them, didn't you?"

"That's what Ralph said," Bob drawled. "'My niece,' he said, 'she's a good cook and housekeeper. You boys'll be all right from now on. Time we got a woman in the house to do for us.'"

"Oh, did he?" said Mari.

She felt childish enough to want to pour the dregs of Bob's teacup on the top of his faded, dusty, wide-brimmed hat. He hadn't once taken it off since Mari had first seen him arriving in a cloud of dust at the airstrip.

"That's it," said Bob, turning away. On second thoughts he turned back to her. "House is all cleaned and washed. Natives all away, walkabout; so I did it myself. Nothing to complain about." He got up from the step, moved his hat forward on his head by an inch, hitched his pants with one hand, and added: "Like I said—steak's in the meat-house."

He walked away down the gravel path in the wake of Ralph Curtis and Kane.

Mari stood at the top of the steps and watched him go. Way down towards the stables and the horse paddock she could see the diminished figures of Uncle Ralph and Kane leaning over the stockrails, talking.

So much for looking at the stallion, Mari thought. They weren't looking at anything. They were talking about sending Mariana Curtis back to England. At least Kane would be talking about that.

Perhaps he was afraid that young woman he went to see up at Half Moon would be jealous of another female appearing on Kane Manners's horizon.

"She just might have something to be jealous about, too," said Mari, tossing her head.

She put the teacups on the tray and took them back to the kitchen. There she sat on the edge of the table and pulled the pins out of her hair so that it fell in waves down to her shoulders again. She shook her hair out, then lifting one knee so she could rest her chin on it, she wrapped her arms round it and *thought*. She was sorry she had that unkind wish about the somebody at Half Moon. All she wanted Kane Manners to do was like her well enough to get by—as it were. Or so she told herself. No girl likes to feel an utter failure in the eyes of any man.

"Even Bob, for that matter," said Mari.

After that, her thinking was mainly to do with what she herself dreamed life on Ninna-Warra might be. Strictly, she kept Kane Manners out of that consideration.

I like this kitchen, she decided at length, releasing her knee and letting her foot descend to the floor. I wonder where the meat-house is.

She went outside and looked for it.

By the time the men came in, had their baths, and were ready for dinner, Mari had had two very busy hours. She knew every nook and cranny of the house by then.

She was quite sure it had been many a long day, probably many a long year, since a linen tablecloth had been used in the dining-room, let alone a bowl of flowers put on the table. She guessed the Ninna-Warra household usually ate at the polished kitchen table.

It had taken her an hour of fossicking to find, stacked away in the bottom of a huge wooden trunk in the spare room—her room—a whole covey of linen cloths, bathtowels and sheets.

She had forthwith changed all the dreary fawn-coloured towels she found in the bathroom, and the shower-house which was under one of the tank-stands, for fresh white ones. She had changed the brown workaday bedcovers for some white quilts which she found in the trunk with the other linen. They were old-fashioned quilts, but they were white and fresh and brought light into the bedrooms.

She made up her own bed and used for a cover a gay chintz curtain. Tucked in at head and foot, no one would know it was a curtain, and it brought dancing colour into the room.

Mari had had a bath before she cooked the steaks and emptied a tin of tomato purée into a saucepan with some herbs, pepper and salt, and thickening to make a vegetable for the steak. By this time she felt fatigue like a hot wind pressing at a door, but she pushed it back. Time enough to sleep later. To-night had to be a success.

When she heard the men in the bathroom and the shower-house she slipped across the passage from the dining-room into her own room and began quickly to dress. On went the ice-blue dress that had stunned Allen Webster. Fine micro-mesh stockings were pulled over slim legs, and the neat high-heeled shoes that went with the dress were slipped on her feet.

A brush and a swish and a curl and her hair was up in that enchanting swathe on top of her head. The make-up went on carefully but quickly.

She had to time that entrance. Kane Manners was really going to look at her this time!

Then she was ready.

As the men went into the dining-room Mari went, tap-tap with her high-heeled shoes, to retrieve the steaks from the oven.

She picked up the dish with a warmed towel, and, manœuvring herself through the screen doors of the kitchen and passage, presented herself in the doorway of the dining-room.

The three men were standing at the head of the table talking, their sundowners in their hands.

Mari's entrance brought a sudden silence, then Uncle Ralph put his glass down and moved round to draw out a chair for Mari. Bob looked at his glass fixedly, but Kane looked at Mari.

For a moment Mari was pleased, until she saw that the expression in Kane's eyes was no more than one of restrained formal politeness.

If they had never had a white woman there before, she couldn't believe she didn't make more impact on Kane than that.

He leaned forward and put his glass on the table as Mari came round with her dish to the head of the table.

"I think you had better sit there—on your uncle's right hand," Kane said quietly, still unsmiling. He remained at the head of the table himself, and Mari could see, by this disposition of places, he really was the head of this particular family.

As she put the dish down he said, "Thank you"—in a way that he might have said it to anyone on earth. Or so Mari thought.

Her heart sank.

Her tablecloth, the shining silver, the glorious aroma from the dish on the table, the blue dress, and her hair on the top of her head, made no impact on him. He was as distant as a snowbound peak in the Alps.

Uncle Ralph broke the ice.

"Why, Mari, that's splendid," he said as she moved round and took the chair he was holding for her. Clearly he meant that she now wore the right clothes; and not that dinner was cooked and beautifully served. That he took for granted.

Also, she thought, because he's not tired after that long journey he assumes I'm not tired. Well, he's wrong.

Very quietly she sat down and looked at Ralph Curtis.

"I'm glad you like it, Uncle Ralph."

Kane was sitting down now; he picked up the serving knife and fork and looked at Mari.

"You will have some steak?" he asked. He didn't call her

Mari, Mariana, or even Miss Curtis. He only looked at her in a way that suddenly and unexpectedly broke down all Mari's defences.

Where was all her confidence now?

She was tired—tired—*tired*. Tiredness had come over her, just like that. It was the sole cause of the tears at the back of her eyes.

"Excuse me, please," she said, pushing back her chair. "If you don't mind . . ." She could say no more. She ran from the room, across the passage, into what she now admitted was the most hideous little spare room in the world. Her room.

She closed the door, and leaning against it, let the tears stream unchecked down her face. She thought of Robert Alton, of Allen Webster, and her father. And she was dreadfully, overwhelmingly—homesick.

I've tried to pretend—and find a substitute. But I can't do it any more.

She flung herself face down on the chintz curtain that was her bedcover, and there, dressed in the blue frock and the high-heeled shoes, and with her hair still pinned gracefully on top of her head, she cried herself into exhaustion, then sleep.

"I hate him, I hate him," was what she wanted to say of Kane Manners. Yet she could not quite frame those words. That other secret voice that was inside Mari and which so often had so much to say unbidden was interrupting: "That's not the truth, Mariana Curtis, and you know it."

She was nearly asleep and could only just hear that tiny insistent voice. It made her think of Kane Manners walking away into the afternoon sun, his hat at that angle—someone strangely important who was walking right away from her— away, away into the distance, perhaps to be lost for ever.

Mari drifted into sleep, and in it could still hear those footsteps.

They stopped outside her door, but she was too deep in the sleep world now to hear that tap.

Two strange brown outback men came in, creakily and one at a time, to see if she was all right. The third strode impatiently up the passage and then down again.

Two men looked down at her, the ruffled hair, the tear-stains still on her face, and then creaked back to the door.

"Ssh!" said Uncle Ralph. "She'll be all right by morning. Just worn out. I guess we kinda asked too much of her."

"Maybe," said Bob, noncommittal but his dark eyes astonished. He had never seen anything as lovely as a young girl lying on a bed covered with a gay chintz curtain. There were still mysteries in this world to present Bob with the gift of wonder.

Ralph left the door ajar so there would be plenty of airflow through the night for the sleeper.

Kane Manners came back from his third stomp up the passage and pushed open the door. The passage light shed a glow inside and over the bed.

Kane went away to his own room and brought back a light cover from his own bed.

Brusquely, matter-of-factly, he crossed Mari's room; but very gently he put the cover over her.

Mari felt its light comfort and stirred. Her face was no longer sad, only dreamy.

Uncle Ralph and Bob were very busy in the kitchen when Kane came out of Mari's room. Not for a whole world of sunshine and rain, things very precious in the outback, would they have let Kane know, or each other, they had noticed that act of kindness.

Half an hour later Kane, in his office with the door shut, was talking on the private interval wave-length to Daphne Raywood at Half Moon Station.

"Ralph arrived back from England to-day," he said, drawling a little. "He brought his niece with him."

There was a long silence, then Daphne's cool clear voice— one that was faintly touched with a special female kind of authority—came back.

"Young, or not so young?" she asked.

"Young, I'm afraid." Kane's voice was strictly impersonal.

Again there was a long silence and neither hurried the other. Daphne's cool voice broke the silence again.

"It won't do, you know," she said. "You will have to do something about it, Kane." She paused, then added, "Will you come over and see me about it? Too late to-night, of course. But when can you come?"

"I'll manage it," Kane replied. "I'll call you to-morrow."

CHAPTER THREE

It was half past five in the morning when elderly Ralph Curtis tapped at the door and brought in a cup of tea. Mari, in spite of her heartache, had slept deeply and had hardly moved all night. Somehow the shoes had come off. A hairpin or two had fallen out and Mari's pretty hair was wispy and she had to brush it out of her eyes as she sat up. She was sorry about her crushed dress, but the chintz curtain covered that. She hadn't remembered putting that *thing* over herself.

"Here you are, lass," the elderly man said kindly. "Drink this and it will improve the state of your immortal soul. I looked in last night but you were sound asleep—I let you be."

"Thank you," Mari said. Actually it was the first time in her life, so far as Mari could remember, anybody had brought her a cup of tea. It had been she who had done the tea-taking to others.

"Now take this cup and the sugar. There you are. I'll go fetch the toast."

"Toast?" said Mari, taking the cup and saucer in one hand, balancing them carefully as she straightened her dress with her spare hand.

"Yes. I made you some. Marmalade too. You like toast and marmalade?"

"Oh, yes, please."

Ralph Curtis had gone through the door and not waited to read the surprise, and the slightly shamefaced expression, in Mari's eyes.

She was ashamed of her performance last night and she was surprised that anyone still felt kindly enough towards her to bring her tea and toast.

She had behaved like a schoolgirl.

Ralph came back with somewhat badly made, soggy toast, but the state of the toast didn't worry Mari, who was sipping the tea and beginning to take a less jaundiced view of her room. Her father used to say, when she took in the early morning cup of tea: "Ha! This will improve my view on the state of the nation."

Mari now understood what he meant. The tea was heavenly. It filled Mari with the same kind of pleasure that a man near death with thirst felt when he found water at last.

She took a wedge of the toast, and Ralph Curtis sat down on the end of the bed.

"We're all sorry about last night, Mari. We're just three selfish men. . . ."

"Is Kane sorry too?" asked Mari sceptically.

"Of course he is. He doesn't say so, but then you've got to know Kane. Give him a chance, lass. . . ."

Mari opened her eyes wide. She give Kane a chance? Shouldn't it be the other way round?

"When you went down to the stables with him yesterday he told you to send me back home, didn't he, Uncle Ralph?" she said accusingly.

"He certainly did, but that wasn't because he doesn't like you, Mari. He just doesn't think this is a fit place for you."

Mari took another sip of tea.

"He doesn't like me," she disagreed, looking at him over the rim of the cup. "He doesn't talk to me. He *glares*."

"The whole thing's taken him by surprise. Give him a chance, Mari. For our sakes. . . ."

"You mean you and Bob? Uncle Ralph, don't you mean that you and Bob want a housekeeper?"

Ralph Curtis uncrossed his legs and recrossed them the other way round.

"Maybe I do," he said, with the kind of flat dignified truth she associated with her father. "But then, so does Kane."

"Want a housekeeper!" finished Mari, thoughtfully munching toast. She lifted her blue eyes to Ralph again. "Don't you think I'm too *young* for such a responsibility?"

For a moment mischief lurked in her eyes.

"Well, we'll ride along and see," said Ralph cautiously. "Anyone can ride out to a boundary week after week and know every inch of it. But one never knows—one never knows for sure "—and after a pause—" what'll happen."

"I know for sure," said Mari. "I'll be reminded I have a return ticket."

Ralph Curtis dodged that remark. How simple he really was, Mari thought.

These men!

Oddly enough this voiceless exclamation cheered Mari up. She put the empty teacup with its saucer on the table beside her bed and swung her legs over the edge.

" That's the girl. Strange thing how one takes a new view of life in the morning," said Ralph, getting up from the end of the bed. " Now you get along and have a bath and come along to the office as quick as you can. I'll show you how to use the transceiver set before I go out. No woman in a homestead is ever lonely these days. There's the open session and you can join in with all the other ladies on stations hundreds of miles away. A regular tea-party they have, even though it's early in the morning. Then there's another session to-night."

Mari hurried with her bath and dressing. It wasn't only that it would be fun to talk to other people on other stations, it was that in the process of going to and from the bathroom, of dressing in her own room, she could see the kind of things about that homestead that were screaming for attention.

Bob had said he had washed and cleaned the homestead. That was just what it looked like. Bare, scrubbed and masculine.

It wanted beautifying, Mari decided, for want of a better word. Whatever else its shortcomings, the spaciousness of that house pleased her. She wasn't intimidated by the acres of floorboard and linoleum needing the polishing cloth. She felt she wanted to dance in the passage, the rooms, the veranda and even the bathroom—they were so big. One could dance and dance, she thought, without knocking anything over. Meanwhile she had to hurry, for Uncle Ralph was about to show her how to use the magical transceiver set.

" Quite simple—see," Ralph Curtis said later, as they both stood in front of the narrow bench behind the door in Kane's office where the transceiver stood. It was a large box with a panel board with inset dials.

" Plug it in here," said Ralph. " She works on the generator. If the engine blows, then we use an old pedal set out in the store. Now turn this knob and you can hear. Got it? Turn it off and you're out ; now turn this knob and you can speak—

if they've opened the air to you. Mustn't speak till they open the air. Got it?"

Yes, Mari had got it. It was quite simple. When she turned the " in " dial she could hear a man telling a woman how to treat a rash on a baby's legs.

" Flying Doctor," said Ralph succinctly. " When he tunes out there's open session. You can all have a go. He'll tell you when. Now I've got to get out on the run. Six weeks is too long for anyone to leave the cattle. Anything could have happened."

He made for the door, then turned with a last word of advice.

" Don't do too much, lass. We'll be home at sundown, and a nice hot dinner for the men is about all we ask of you the first day or two."

He clattered the short distance down the passage to the front door, let the wire screen bang behind him, and was gone.

Nice hot dinner is all they want, thought Mari, a little ruffled.

Really! Those men!

She cradled her arms around herself and rocked gently backwards and forwards on her feet as she listened to the Flying Doctor calling another station and saying in a friendly voice, " Good morning, Sara, how's Reg this morning? Did he respond to those inhalations?"

How funny! They were hundreds of miles away from one another yet they talked to one another as if it was across a breakfast table.

The thought of breakfast tables sent Mari flying down the passage and out to the kitchen. She, too, let the wire door bang behind her. She had better wash-up before she began to play with that intriguing transceiver set.

Inside the kitchen door she stood quite still and opened her eyes wide. There was not a dish in sight. The sink, the table, the benches were bare. There wasn't a crumb under the toaster, and the teapot which must have made her own tea was emptied of tea leaves.

They'd washed up! Ralph must have washed her cup and saucer and plate while she was dressing.

They were sorry, then. Ralph had told the truth.

Mari wrapped her arms around herself again and did that dance she had promised herself in all this space. So they were sorry! She had resorted—though she hadn't meant to do it—to the meanest of all women's tricks, she had shed tears. Their hearts weren't cast iron. They did have feelings. They were sorry.

Maybe Kane Manners hadn't washed up, but he would have known that Bob and Ralph were doing it. Well, that was as good as being a party to it, wasn't it?

She forgot her grievances of last night and set to, with a will, to find polish and polishing cloths.

The passage and the kitchen would be enough for to-day. But oh, how she would make them shine! All because they'd done something for *her*.

She couldn't find any polish anywhere, then she remembered Ralph had mentioned the store.

The store! In the store must be stores.

In her enthusiasm Mari forgot the time and forgot the transceiver set. Quite a lot of outbuildings had to be looked at before she found one that might be the store, but alas, it was locked. It had an iron grille over the two windows, so there was no temptation to try and prise one of them open.

Fancy locking anything up here, she thought. Why, there isn't anyone for miles and miles and miles.

She looked out over the grey-brown vista of paddocks. How vast they were! Out there beyond the homestead garden there was nothing but a sea of plain.

She lifted up her head and looked at a flock of white cockatoos flying overhead.

They must have come from somewhere and be going somewhere, she thought. And of course Ralph and Bob and Kane must have gone somewhere too. . . .

Thinking of those three men riding out on their horses made Mari remember the harness she had seen in the top room— the sitting-room-cum-harness-and-gunroom. That's where there would be polish. Somebody had been polishing harness when she had looked at that room yesterday.

She ran back to the homestead, up the three wooden steps on to the veranda and into the passage, once again letting the wire door bang behind her.

Now I know why they bang the door, she thought. It's company. There's so much space—and nobody to hear—and it's fun. Next time I go through there I'll bang it twice.

She found the polish and cloths as she had expected, and was going back down the passage with them when she heard the sound of a woman's laugh in Kane's room. Then the voice said: " Oh really, what fun! I can't believe it. Do tell us all more."

Another voice said, " Joyce are you sure 7KY is not listening in? Do try again. We can't talk about them if they're not listening in."

The transceiver set!

Mari tiptoed into the office with the feeling that she was intruding, uninvited, on someone else's party. She stood, the huge tin of polish and the cloths huddled against her, and gazed with awed fascination at the box.

" Well, I've tried," the voice was saying.

" Let's try again. Come in 7KY, if you're listening. Come in."

Mari shook her head in regret for the speaker's disappointment. 7KY didn't answer.

" You see," said the first voice. " There's no answer. The girl can't be there. They couldn't possibly take her out on the run the first day. She wouldn't be able to stand it."

" Oh, I don't know," said another voice. " Some of those English girls can really ride. . . ."

" Yes, but not in the blistering Australian sun—and the dust—on the *first* day."

" Joyce . . . what did you say her name was?"

" It's only what Bill Connell said. One of the horse buyers was in Darwin day before yesterday and he said Allen Webster saw her with Ralph Curtis. Bill Connell picked it up on the pedal wireless from Donovan's station last night. That's right, isn't it, Beryl?"

Mari, still holding the polish and cloths, found herself sinking gradually down on the swivel-chair in front of the transceiver set.

Why? she thought. *Why . . . ?*

" Yes, that's right," said someone called Beryl. " Allen is supposed to have had lunch or tea, or something with them.

The girl's terribly shy, apparently, but very pretty. Ralph Curtis told Allen——"

Another voice cut in.

"We're dying to hear, darling, but let's try 7ky again. They might have tuned in by now. 7ky, come in. Please come in 7ky. We're all listening for you."

The voices, like those of chirping birds, died into a minute's silence.

"There you are," a voice said at last. "They're not on the air. Do go on and tell us, Beryl. We're dying to know, and you can't keep a secret from the transceiver these days."

The voices, like a choir of birds, all chirped with their laughter again and another voice begged Beryl to go on.

"I only know what Bill Connell picked up on the pedal set from the buyer on Donovan's. He said Allen Webster met her and her name's the same as Ralph's. Curtis. Mary Curtis."

"*Mari*," Mari corrected them, then sat up shocked. "*Good heavens, they're talking about me.*"

Suddenly she remembered what Ralph had said about everyone joining in on the open session. It was on now.

"Hallo, hallo! It's me," she said in a voice not much above a whisper, partly from alarm at the magic of this instrument and partly because she was frightened of interrupting uninvited. "I mean I'm Mari Curtis."

But the voices were going on even when she was speaking.

"I wish someone could rouse Half Moon," someone said. "You bet they'd know over there. They say Kane rides over there at least once a week."

"The only person who ever does," another voice said with a touch of sarcasm.

"If you're listening, Half Moon," the first speaker said, "we don't wish to be unkind. We just wish you'd join in."

Half Moon, thought Mari. That was Kane's own station, the one he had leased to someone else. So he rode over there once a week!

"You're wasting your time, Katy. They never answer."

"Sometimes a girl talks on the air to Darwin post office."

"Another mystery girl."

"Well, let's stick to this one. Go on about Mary Curtis, Beryl."

Mari turned the " in " knob off and turned the " out " knob on. The voices were all silent and suddenly the whole homestead stood still in silence. Mari had never heard such a silence before. It was as if she had cut off a choir of angels.

She juggled knobs furiously and at last could hear the voices and the laughter again.

" Can you hear me? " she asked helplessly and loudly, but clearly they couldn't for they were talking gaily to one another again. She had not turned on the " out " knob.

I wonder what they're like? Mari thought. That's an old voice and that's a young one. And oh, that one is not very kind.

The unkind voice said: " Any girl who goes to Ninna-Warra and thinks she can crack Kane Manners's steel-bound heart is in for a disappointment."

" Oh, I don't know. He used to be such a dear. Something happened. Did anyone ever find out? "

" Hard not to, on this air," a voice laughed.

" Well, maybe it's that mystery voice over at Half Moon. He's the only person who ever goes there. And she has got a nice voice."

Someone imitated an excessively polite and rather haughty voice: " Calling Darwin Post Office. This is Half Moon. Have you a cablegram for Raywood of Half Moon? If so, please post through ordinary letter mail. Do not relay by air. Have you got my message, Darwin Post Office? Over to you."

" Look out, Kay," a voice on the open session said. " They may be listening."

" I don't care if they are. No one has ever been unfriendly in the centre or north since Robin Doherty shot one of the Burtons. And that was ninety years ago."

" Well, they're not unfriendly to Kane Manners. He goes over there."

" Well, he's got another girl to contend with now. . . ."

Mari leaned forward and pulled the connecting plug from the wall.

So! He used to be such a dear, did he? And now she, Mariana Curtis, was just another girl he had to contend with!

Well, she would show all those voices she had other things

to do than just listen to transceiver sets. It was like sitting down in front of the radio in the mornings at home . . . and letting the housework pile up for the afternoon.

There were things to do about this house and Mariana Curtis was not just another girl to contend with. She was a girl who loved a nice house.

She remembered that when she left school the neighbours all advised her father that keeping house was too much to expect of a young sixteen-year-old. She wouldn't know anything about it.

Mari had been holding the polishing cloths and the tin of polish all this time. She looked at them lovingly, and at the transceiver balefully.

"Just see what we can do!" she addressed her bundle. She jumped up and went through the door into the passage.

Just another girl to contend with!

What about these passages? Clean—certainly. But had they ever seen polish?

This house would shine—and not a thing out of place—before Kane Manners or Uncle Ralph or that dead-pan Bob knew what had struck them.

Uncle Ralph wasn't the only person who blitz-drafted things in this world!

Mari polished. She had so many conversations in her head with voices on the air, Kane Manners, Uncle Ralph, and even the neighbours next door in Leander Lane, eleven thousand miles away, that she had put the first coat of shine on the long passage, the dining-room and kitchen before she knew she had really started.

By the time she had reached the kitchen door the fact that she was hotter than she had ever been in her life told her she had done enough of that for the time being.

The thing to do now, she thought, was wash and tidy up, have a well-earned rest while she thought about what she would give them for dinner to-night.

After she had washed, Mari changed into a lighter pair of slacks and put on a clean blouse.

She wandered out on the front veranda to look at the scenery. The part of it that's not desert, she thought.

Then she remembered a packet of cigarettes on the office table. Mari soft-footed back to the office at great pace and retrieved the cigarettes and a box of matches. She bestowed her second baleful glance for the day at the transceiver set and went back to the veranda. She sat down in the cane chair, lit a cigarette with a flourish, and leaned back. She felt queen of all she surveyed.

The house behind her and the great cattle run in front of her—was all hers. And there was no one to tell her what to do.

Mari sat bolt upright and coughed.

There wasn't much in smoking cigarettes. The smoke caught in her throat and the taste in her mouth was awful. Regretfully, she stubbed out the cigarette on the table ashtray. She would wait to take up smoking till another day.

It was midday and she thought she might make herself some sandwiches and a cup of tea for lunch.

It was at that moment she realised her ear had caught a sound that was foreign in all the surrounding silence. She sat up straight and listened. It was a motor car and it was coming up the track at the side of the house. Mari stood up, and at that moment an enormous overlanding car, like the ones the Americans drove in London, swung round the side of the house and came to a standstill outside the enclosure gate. A girl in a sun-dress with a wide-brimmed hat on her head got out of the car. She looked slim and smart.

She opened the garden gate as Mari walked to the edge of the veranda. She looked up, smiled in an arranged kind of way, and came on. She was dusting a big leather gauntleted driving glove against her right leg.

" Do come in," Mari said as the girl came to the foot of the steps. " I expect you're a friend of Kane's—or of Uncle Ralph. . . ."

The girl put one foot on the lower step and looked up at Mari. She took in Mari's form-fitting slacks and the little flattie shoes that Mari thought were such darlings. She even paid particular attention to Mari's colourful blouse and the lovely pile of dark brown hair on her head.

" My!" she said at last, still with that arranged smile. " Ralph Curtis did bring a surprise packet back from London. I had hardly believed it. . . ."

" You can touch me," Mari said gently. " I'm real."

"I can hear you, that's proof enough," the girl said, and she came up the three steps on to the veranda.

She was very pretty. Her skin was a smooth tan, and her hair, where it showed under the brim of that big hat, was a kind of straw gold. Her eyes were a grey-blue, but they weren't terribly nice at the moment because they were so clearly summing Mari up in a curiouser-than-thou kind of way.

"Oh, are you the girl from Half Moon?" Mari said with a sudden gleam of enlightenment. The girl the voices on the air had been talking about, she thought.

"I am not," the visitor said coldly. "I'm a neighbour of Half Moon. Kane used to be very friendly with us—till he leased out Half Moon. Didn't old Ralph Curtis mention us? I'm Alice Whitford from White Trees."

"Well, you see, I haven't been here long enough to hear about the neighbours," Mari said, trying not to be hurtful with the truth.

Alice leaned back against the veranda post and watched Mari with measuring eyes.

"You will," she said. "From me. I used to know Kane very well till Miss Icy-voice from Half Moon took over. I'm sorry to be so blunt, but you might as well know the truth. By the way, we've all heard about you already. The transceiver set, you know."

Mari's eyes opened wide.

She thought of all the voices on the air hinting at what they had heard about her but not one of them actually saying what they had heard.

This girl, Alice Whitford, would have heard too. The "air" was so lacking in secrets. That was why Alice had come over. She must have driven a long, long way.

Alice removed her left shoulder from the veranda post and stood up straight.

"Now we've cleared the air," she said, "shall we have some tea? I'm famished. And we might get around to talking of other things."

Mari longed to hear more about Miss Icy-voice but didn't judge this an opportune moment to ask.

"Yes, let's make tea," she said in a friendly way. "I was

on the point of making some sandwiches when I heard your car." Then, because her ear was attuned to the great silence of the station, she realised there was a noise somewhere out there beyond the garden homestead. It was a horse galloping, and a minute later it came into view. Kane had come back to the homestead.

He slowed to a canter, then trot, swung himself out of the saddle as the horse reached the gate, and threw the reins over the horse's head where they dangled to the ground.

Alice had heard too, and like Mari she stood and watched as Kane swung open the small gate and came up the path.

Coming towards them, he had the same effect on Mari as his back had had yesterday when he had walked away. She had a feeling that was something wistful, and just a little sad. He was really very nice. He had the kind of face . . . No, Mari could not diagnose it.

His brown face was dark under the brim of his hat and his eyes gave nothing of his thoughts away as he came towards the two girls who were standing watching him from the veranda.

He came up the three steps and took off his hat.

"Hallo, Kane," Alice said quietly. A little tight smile played round her mouth but it was a smile that only a girl who knew a man very well could offer to him. "Long time no see!" she finished.

"It has been a long time, Alice," he said. "I'm sorry. I've been very busy. Leaving Half Moon and taking over this place was quite a job."

"Yes, I know," said Alice. "You've had to live a hermit's life—except, of course, for your tenants on Half Moon?"

After the first glance, which for some reason seemed anxious, Kane had not looked at Mari, and now, vaguely, she felt she was intruding in this conversation.

"I'm just about to make some sandwiches and tea," she said, turning towards the screen door.

Unexpectedly Kane spoke to her.

"That would be nice, Mari," he said. His voice was soft and not quite so impersonal as yesterday.

It was some time before Mari took the tea-tray out on to

the veranda where Kane and Alice were now sitting in two easy-chairs. They were talking to each other, but not exactly comfortably, Mari thought.

" If I leave the tea here . . ." she began, as she put the tray on the table and the sandwiches round at the side. She meant to slip away and give them more time together.

Kane had risen to his feet.

" Sit down, Mari," he said quietly, holding a chair for her. " I'm sure there can't be anything inside that can't wait for you," he added.

Curious, but in those few minutes he made Mari feel as if she belonged to the homestead.

Mari sat down and drew the tray towards her and began to pour the tea. Alice, though silent, was not still. She was thwacking the side of her chair with her gauntleted gloves ; her eyes moved from Kane's face and his far-away eyes that were looking out over the paddocks, to Mari's absorbed face as she performed the tea rites.

"I suppose you know why I'm here, Kane," Alice said suddenly. " Those damn' transceivers leave nothing unsaid in the north these days. The air is electric with talk. You might as well know about it."

Mari, passing Alice her tea and then offering her sugar and the sandwiches, had a feeling the other girl was trying not to hurt. She longed to tell Alice not to do this. It didn't matter about herself. She didn't know any of these people in the north and on the air. It mattered about Alice herself. Kane would not be hurt. Mari knew this instinctively. He was, in some respects, cast iron.

His answer was unexpected.

" That's why I came up to the homestead. The old pedal set at the hut out at the muster yards has been working over-time this morning."

Mari was so surprised she burnt her mouth with hot tea. She looked quickly at Kane, but he was not looking at her. He had put his teacup, like Ralph and Bob yesterday, on the floor and was rolling a cigarette.

" So the rumours are true?" Alice asked with an edge to her voice. " Does Mari know . . .?"

Kane looked at Alice gravely. His eyes were not exactly

expressionless. In a way they were kindly, but at the same time not inviting any further comment from Alice.

"Shall we talk of something else?" he said with a studied noncommittal note in his voice. "To begin with, how is everyone on White Trees? How's Bill? Your father?"

Alice looked at Mari, then, making an effort, turned back to Kane.

"As if you really care how we are, Kane," she said, sipping her tea. "When you leased Half Moon to the Raywoods, you doubled the cost of our droving cattle. It takes two months now when it took us one month to drove through Half Moon. You made no explanations, no apologies. . . ." She turned her face and looked directly at him. "Do you know you lost every friend in the north that day, Kane?"

Mari still had a feeling Alice was talking at random; uneasily searching for something to talk about.

Kane was silent for a fleeting moment.

"I'm sorry about that," he said. He lit his cigarette, and then bending over picked up his cup of tea. Evidently he liked to smoke and drink tea at the same time.

"But you know it?" Alice persisted.

"Yes, I know it," he replied gravely. Suddenly his eyes were on Mari. "What have you been doing this morning?" he asked. "Other than receiving visitors on the front veranda?"

Mari was still suffering from a muffled kind of shock which was because Kane was speaking to her at all, let alone in a normal kind of way, as if he'd been doing it ever since he'd met her.

Mari felt it would be unkind to say, "Listening to the open session." He had listened to it, or someone who had listened to it had told him about it, and he had come home. It was an unwise subject to dwell on just now.

"Looking around," Mari said. "Kane, why do you lock up the storeroom and put iron bars over the window? There isn't anyone for miles around."

"People sometimes pass through," Kane said lightly. "And often the homestead is empty."

"Not any more," Alice said pointedly.

"It's mainly because of the natives," Kane went on.

"They don't understand possessions. Part of their tribal law. Everything yours is mine and everything I have I share with you, is their creed. Everything that's given to them they give away, or share. By the same token they're given to sharing my things too. They've all gone walkabout now but the store and the machinery shed are locked as a matter of course."

Alice had finished her tea, and had nibbled only one sandwich, and she now stood up.

"I think I'll go walkabout too," she said.

Kane stood up.

"You can't do that, Alice," he said quietly. "You must have a proper lunch. You must have been driving since the early morning."

"Nine o'clock," she said to him. "Quite a compliment to Ninna-Warra, isn't it? Of course, it was only curiosity that brought me, you know. Please don't think it was anything else, Kane. But I'll be on my way. . . ."

"You can't drive straight back to White Trees now," said Kane firmly.

"Then I shall have a further lunch down at the muster yards. I'm not ready for it now. Do you mind if I look over your bullock mob, Kane?"

"Not at all, Alice. Do that. I'll be down presently myself."

A small gleam came into Alice Whitford's eyes as she turned away. The tension in her figure eased, and she smiled.

"See you later," she said and ran down the steps of the veranda. She had not looked at Mari, nor said "good-bye" to her. Perhaps the nonchalant wave of the gauntlet glove was meant to include Mari.

Kane stood at the top of the steps and watched Alice get into her car and swing round in a swirl of dust and drive away.

Presently he turned to Mari, who was looking at him, perplexed.

"I think, Mari," he said quietly, "you and I had better have a talk."

For a long time he looked at her sea-blue eyes.

CHAPTER FOUR

" There's too much space on the veranda," Kane said. " The office might be a better place."

He held open the screen door for her and she went through the doorway, down the passage to the office.

Mari sat down in the chair near the transceiver set. She decided not to think about the expression on Kane's face when Alice Whitford had walked away. He had looked after Alice, sorry she was going, anxious because she had gone without a proper lunch. Perhaps he was sorry that Mari was there and he couldn't say freely what was in his mind.

His firm leisured step followed Mari down the passage and into the room. He crossed to his own chair in front of his desk, and because it was a swivel-chair he spun it round with his hand and sat down, facing Mari.

He looked at her with serious intentness.

He took his cigarette-makings from the pocket of his shirt and began to roll a cigarette.

" I was very sorry Ralph brought you here, Mari," he said slowly, watching his own fingers and not Mari's reactions to his words.

Mari put her head on the side and looked at the toes of her shoes.

They are nice shoes, she thought. Better to look at them than at Kane. With great misgiving she wondered why looking at Kane did something odd to her. There was something different about him this morning; almost as if something had happened to make him different.

There had been quite a silence in the office. Kane had finished making his cigarette and he now lit it. Mari lifted her eyes and watched him exhale a slow stream of smoke.

It doesn't choke *him*, she thought. Her blue eyes were serious and just a little sad. Kane watched them through a veil of smoke.

" You haven't said anything, Mari," he said quietly.

" About Uncle Ralph bringing me here? *I'm* not sorry." She tilted her chin. " I like it here."

43

"You will find it very lonely, I'm afraid."

"Not in this big house. There's too much to do. What with all the conversation on the transceiver this morning, and Alice Whitford coming——" Mari suddenly relaxed and smiled at Kane. He was being different this morning so she would be different too. He was still remote, not exactly friendly, but he had a look in the back of his eyes, almost as if he was sorry for her. Well, she must do something about *that*. No one was going to be sorry for Mariana Curtis.

"It was nice—your coming home for lunch too. I'm glad you came. Well, it hasn't been very lonely to-day. That open session's terrific fun. . . ." She wavered before the sudden veiled enigmatical look in his eyes. She drew in her breath and went on: "Besides, there's cockatoos flying over, now and again ; and some horses down in those yards. If I get the plants to grow in the garden there'll be all the flowers . . ."

Kane interrupted her.

"Was the open session the only thing you listened to this morning, Mari?"

"'Fraid so," said Mari cheerfully. "There's lots to do around a house, you know. . . ."

Again he interrupted her.

"What do you miss most in England?" he asked unexpectedly.

"The coffee bars," Mari answered promptly. She smiled. "That's where we all meet. I mean my friends. And we talk. . . ."

"And drink coffee?"

"Yes, of course. But that's only part of it." She suddenly warmed to her description and her eyes lit up. She drew her feet up under her chair and pressed her hands together between her knees. Mari always thought this was the nicest part about wearing slacks. You could do anything with your feet. You weren't showing bare knees.

"It's the dim lights and brown walls and blue smoke in the air. All lurky-loomy, if you know what I mean. There's onions hanging from the ceilings and empty wine bottles. . . ."

She stopped. Kane Manners was watching her. It occurred to her that he was playing for time as if waiting for something. He was very different from the man she had met on the back veranda.

" All the same, I don't want to go back, just yet," she finished. She decided that pride was an important thing and she wasn't going to let Kane Manners rule her comings and goings across hemispheres. " Uncle Ralph asked me to come," she said firmly. " And he does own this station, doesn't he?"

" He does," said Kane. " But he can't run it without me. He's getting on now."

" You're really the boss?" Mari asked quickly.

For a brief moment a smile flickered round Kane's mouth. It was something Mari would have liked to capture—just long enough to see what it was really like.

His eyes flicked towards the door and his head moved sideways as if he was listening for something.

Mari had a sudden intuitive feeling that something was wrong. Come to think of it, she'd had it ever since Kane came in. She just hadn't diagnosed it.

Kane was looking at her steadily.

" Just now . . ." he said, " when you told me that about your friends, and the coffee bars, your eyes lit up and you smiled. Is that what home in England means to you? Would that be enough if . . .?"

He didn't finish, for he heard the sound that Mari heard and for which she too had now been listening. A horse had galloped up to the garden gate. The gate slammed, footsteps came stumping fast and heavy up the path on to the veranda. The wire door slammed behind someone and the footsteps came down the passage.

Before he came into the doorway, Mari knew it was Uncle Ralph.

He stood there a minute, looked at Mari and then at Kane. Imperceptibly Kane moved his head, making some kind of negative sign to the older man.

" What is the matter?" said Mari. " Why have you all come home? I suppose Bob is bringing up his own rear-guard. . . ."

Her words died away because she knew by the bleak look in Uncle Ralph's eyes that this was not funny. Something *had* happened.

Not Bob . . . she tried to say.

Uncle Ralph came right into the room. He stood by the mantelshelf, his back to it, turning the brim of his dusty ancient hat between his fingers.

" I showed you how to use that blasted transceiver set, Mari," he said. He sounded as if he had a frog in his throat. " You didn't hear . . .?"

" I heard the voices talking about me," said Mari, tilting her chin. " I turned them off. Flat! Is that what you're both worrying about?"

Uncle Ralph made no attempt to meet Kane's eyes but Mari knew that somehow their thoughts had communicated with each other's.

" A little thing like that didn't upset *me* . . ." she began, yet knowing with a sudden thudding drop of her heart it wasn't just women's gossip that had brought Kane and Uncle Ralph galloping home. Nor even Alice Whitford's visit.

" Please tell me, Uncle Ralph," she said.

Kane stood up.

" Would you rather I went, Ralph?"

" No. I guess I need you too. . . ."

" Please tell me," said Mari. Then she knew.

"*Father*," she said. " Something's happened to my father?" Ralph nodded.

" It was his heart, Mari. He told me it wasn't too good, but it had been that way for years. Nothing much wrong with it . . . just had to take care. . . ."

He's dead, thought Mari.

Uncle Ralph had hit her a blow straight between the eyes, yet she couldn't feel it.

Why can't I feel it? she asked herself. Of course this is why Daddy wanted me to go to Australia with Uncle Ralph . . . for a *holiday*. And I only kissed him once when I said good-bye . . . because I was cross with him . . . about Robert . . . not letting me marry Robert. . . .

She shook her head slowly from side to side, then she looked up at Uncle Ralph pleadingly.

" Did you say he was dead?" she asked. Her face was a dying white and her hands and feet were cold.

Uncle Ralph nodded.

" I didn't say it, Mari lass. But you're right. A message came over the air this morning. One of the men picked it up on the old pedal set."

" I see," said Mari, nodding her head sagely. She didn't see, and she didn't feel anything, either.

She looked up at her uncle.

" I'm funny inside," she said. " I don't sort of feel anything. . . ."

It was Kane who moved. He stood up and came across the room. He took hold of Mari's hand and jerked her to her feet.

" Your father died in his sleep, Mari," he said, looking her straight in the eyes. " You now have no parents . . . no home in England. . . ."

Mari's face creased like a distraught child's.

" *Don't!*" she cried, dragging her hand away from Kane. In a minute she was across the room and into Uncle Ralph's arms. Sobs shook her as she pressed her head against his shoulder.

" You shouldn't have done it that way, Kane," Uncle Ralph said over Mari's head.

" I had to do it that way," Kane said. " She was suffering from shock. There are times when one knows one has to be cruel to be kind. She's crying now . . . that's the best thing that could happen, for a woman."

" And for a man?" Uncle Ralph's voice had that frog in it again.

" I'm sorry, old man!" Kane said, relenting, suddenly grieved himself. " He was your brother as well as Mari's father. If I can do anything for you both please let me."

Mari drew herself away from her uncle's arms. She pulled a handkerchief from the pocket of her slacks and wiped her eyes.

" Thank you, Kane," she said. She went towards the door, thinking that her legs were strangely stiff and that in a minute she would really understand what had happened.

She had to face her grief alone . . . her own way.

A week later Uncle Ralph and Kane went down to the stock-rails to have their usual confab after dinner. Mari noticed they did this whenever they wanted to talk about things in a leisurely way.

Sundown was a leisurely time, for all the world was gradually quietening and darkness was stealing, a wraith, over the land. On the trees by the tank-stands the white cockatoos, already sleeping, clustered on the top branches like a thousand flowers. Mari guessed there would be about a thousand cockatoos there and wondered why, with all the miles of empty bush beyond the homestead, they had to come here to roost.

Home. That was it. Even the birds had to have a home at sundown.

She sat on the veranda, leaning back in the chair, wondering if her face was still as frighteningly white as it had been in the mirror all the week.

She looked at Bob's back where he sat on the top step, staring out to the western sky as Mari did and as Uncle Ralph and Kane were doing as they stood, one foot each on the lowest rail, talking.

Dear Bob, Mari thought. He had helped her cook the dinner on that awful night after she had heard of her father's death. He hadn't spoken. He hadn't said anything at all about the news. He had just done things. It was Bob's way.

She had cooked the dinner and gone on with her planned chores because Kane's words in the office, sledgehammer-hard though they had been, had communicated their own message. She had to stand on her two feet and *take it*. She had to cry, and grieve, but get on with life.

Down at the stockrails Kane and Uncle Ralph were indeed talking. Uncle Ralph knew more about his brother's affairs than Mari had known, and he was now telling Kane.

" His business was slumping down to nothing. The big stores growing like mushrooms soon dwarf those little shows. I was financing him to start again in a new town. He told me his heart was wonky. He didn't want to take too much money. . . ."

" Did he think he might go any minute when he let you bring Mari out here?"

" No, I don't think he did," said Uncle Ralph thoughtfully. " He just wanted to get her away from that young chap next door. Alton, his name was. Robert Alton. A nice-looking youngster, you know, and plenty of brains. But only a puppy 'ud want to get married on brains and nothing more."

" It has been known to come off successfully," Kane said

dryly. He took out a cigarette and lit it, then added slowly:
" Mari didn't strike me as broken-hearted when I saw her
standing there—" he paused, then went on—" standing there
on the veranda, the night she came."

" Like I said. Puppy love!" Uncle Ralph said. " There's
never much in that. Not as much as the kids think." He blew
clouds of smoke from his pipe. " She'll marry sooner or later,
Kane. Lovely girl! And talking of marriage, I've had something else on my mind." He pointed the stem of his pipe at
Kane. " If you don't do something about getting married
sooner than later you'll find yourself an old bachelor like me.
Only you haven't got a young niece you can bring out from
England to housekeep for you in your old age."

" Thank you for the idea," Kane said even more dryly.
" As you remarked, Mari is not much more than a child.
Puppy love means puppy marriage. Yes? By the way,
Ralph," he said, deliberately changing the topic, " looking at
those clouds over there it seems like a blister to-morrow.
Much more of this heat and the grass'll be burnt out round
the bores."

Ralph leaned his arms on the stockrail. Every now and
again in the ensuing silence he took his pipe from his mouth
and blew thoughtful clouds of smoke westwards towards that
same burnt-out paddock grass.

" It's no good her going back to England," Ralph said
quietly, persistently. " She's got no home. She's not even got
any real friends. When these kids start going together . . .
steady, they call it . . . they lose their other friends."

" I suppose this is a roundabout way of telling me she can
tear up the return half of her ticket and make Ninna-Warra
her home . . . for life," Kane said.

Ralph straightened up and turned his head towards Kane.

" That's about it, Kane," he said. " She's got no home. I'm
her only living relative, and what's more to the point—she's
here."

Kane remained silent.

" She's got to have a stake in the future," Uncle Ralph went
on doggedly. " If she doesn't stay here it'll be because she
marries one day. If we find someone suitable around, that
is. . . ." Uncle Ralph broke off. His pipe had gone out, so he
packed it down again with his thumb and relit it. For the

first time in a week a smile crept round the corners of his mouth. He turned back to the stockrails and leaned on them again so Kane couldn't see his face.

"Take Allen Webster now," he said thoughtfully. "What's your opinion of that chap? A bit brash, I'd say, but you know he's the best judge of horseflesh in the north. He kind of took a shine to Mari. He even suggested she got back to Darwin if she got sick and tired of being out here."

He stopped, waiting for some remark to come from Kane, but there was only a grim silence.

"A girl with as much nous as Mari's got could get a useful job in Darwin. She wouldn't be so far away. I could keep an eye on her," Ralph went on.

"And Allen Webster keep an eye on her too? He uses the same eye to judge women as he does to judge horses, Ralph."

"Yes?" said Ralph. "I guess you're right. If she goes to Darwin——"

"What you really mean, Ralph, is this. Mari stays here to keep her out of the way of Webster and his like."

"She stays here because it's her home," said Ralph. "Now don't wall yourself up in that steel heart of yours, Kane. I know you don't take much to the female of the species, though I kinda remember the time when you were pretty friendly with the Whitfords over at White Trees. And you don't show any sign of being against that young Raywood woman over at Half Moon. It's only since you've leased out Half Moon you've been like this."

"We won't speak of Half Moon, nor the Raywoods, if you don't mind, Ralph," Kane said a little tersely. "I think you're insisting that Mari's future is the topic at the moment. If she makes her home here—it's going to create a slightly ridiculous situation. To begin with she is used to, and attached, to, the life of a big city—the cinemas, coffee-bars, that sort of thing. Then, well, think it out for yourself, Ralph. One girl and three men on a lonely homestead!"

"It won't last that way for ever. She's young, I know. But she likes it here. Give her time. Don't rush her. Let her grow up a bit."

He took his foot off the rail and turned to go. Then he looked back at Kane.

"You know what?" he said. "She's a lovely girl. You've

noticed that, Kane? Thought you would. Ah well, guess I'd better go and oil up the engine. I've missed that out this last day or two."

He walked away along the side path leading to the engine-house, a small round-shouldered stump of a man whose hair had turned a shade greyer in the last seven days. He grieved for his dead brother and now he was thinking about Mari. In spite of his optimistic talk he was worrying about her.

Old Ralph knew as well as Kane that a lonely cattle station was no place to imprison a girl of Mari's vitality. All right for a few months . . . a year or two. That was what he had intended when he brought her out to Australia. Now, all was changed.

Kane watched his figure disappearing in the gathering darkness. Old Ralph Curtis had been a fine cattleman in his day, Kane thought. He was still a fine judge. Kane did not like to see that extra stoop and those extra grey hairs.

He turned his head and looked towards the homestead veranda where Mari had put on the light. The girl sat in her chair, now leaning forward, her chin cupped in her hands as her white oval of a face looked out towards the night.

Thoughtfully, Kane turned and followed Ralph Curtis in the direction of the engine-house.

CHAPTER FIVE

Days passed and Mari's colour came back; also some of her spirit. She began now to be thankful her father had died so peacefully, and a little grateful to him that he had thought of her future and placed her in Uncle Ralph's hands. She had thought that this holiday to Australia had only been because of Robert Alton.

Kane Manners and Uncle Ralph were in the office, listening to the news of the cattle market when Mari, her kitchen cleaned up, her bread rising in the tins by the hot-wall, put her head round the door.

" Please, are women allowed in here for five minutes?" she asked politely. The air was heavy with pipe and cigarette smoke.

Nearly as nice as the coffee-bars, she thought, but she had no wild nostalgic yearning to go home just yet. All the same she felt she had better ask Uncle Ralph—what next?

"Come right in, lass," Uncle Ralph said. He began to get up, but Kane was already on his feet. He turned a chair so that Mari could sit down.

They made a half-circle in front of the transceiver set and Uncle Ralph leaned forward and turned it off.

"Please, Uncle," Mari said hastily. "I didn't mean to interrupt. Besides, I might learn something."

She linked her fingers and rested her hands in her lap. Ralph Curtis looked at her quizzically and Kane looked back at the tip of his cigarette.

"No good living on a cattle station if you don't know everything about it," Mari said brightly. She stole a glance at Kane. His expression had not changed.

That one fell on stony ground, thought Mari. Yet somehow she knew she wasn't quite doing justice to Kane. Ever since the two men had come in with that terrible news about her father, Kane had been very nice to her. He hadn't said much —that was true—but his manner had been gentler, almost kind. It had shown in the little things like the *way* in which he held open the door for her, placed a chair for her.

He knew that when she swaggered a little in those enchanting slacks, threw back her head at the challenge of the kitchen and those endless polished floors, put a dash of mascara on her lashes, she was also throwing about herself a camouflage so no one else would suffer because there was a sad Sally in the house just now.

Yes, Kane knew, and minute by minute her heart was going out to him.

In the meantime she had to resolve the first problem, which was . . . where did she live from now on?

"I suppose," she said, looking at her cat's-cradle fingers, changing their pattern and looking at them again, "I suppose, Uncle Ralph, you would like me to stay here a little bit longer?"

She looked up at her uncle quickly, innocent-eyed yet with something behind their sea-blueness that showed she was anxious.

"Stay here a little longer?" blustered Uncle Ralph, really indignant. "You're not thinking of leaving us? This home's your home. For good and all. . . ." He paused, and lowering his voice to normal tones added, "You haven't got any home in England now, lass. You have to face that. You see, your father had a business, and business always has some debts. The house now—it'll have to be sold. . . ."

"I know," Mari said. "You don't have to tell me, Uncle Ralph. Daddy didn't have any money, did he?"

"Well . . ."

Uncle Ralph cast an uneasy glance at Kane as the latter stirred.

"Now sit there, Kane," Ralph said. "Don't get that look in your eye that says it isn't dignified to discuss Mari's business in public. Mari doesn't mind. All she wants to know is, is this her home now? Am I right, lass?"

It's Kane's home too, thought Mari. Unless he goes back to Half Moon some time. Surprisingly the thought depressed her. Of course if he didn't want her to stay . . .

"I could go to Darwin and get a job there . . ." she said tentatively, hoping neither Uncle Ralph nor Kane would believe her.

"What sort of a job?" Kane said unexpectedly.

Ah, at last he was taking a vital interest in her future.

"Housekeeping, I suppose," she said. Then suddenly she smiled, showing her lovely white teeth and letting the anxiousness in her eyes resolve into a clear, sparkling light. "I'm pretty good at housekeeping, aren't I, Uncle Ralph? That's why you gave me such a rip-roaring round-ticket holiday to Australia?"

"Certainly not," said Uncle Ralph in as big a voice as the size of the office would permit without offence to ears. "I wanted you to have a holiday—see what this country's like. What would you do, Mari, without something to do round the house? You'd be bored to death—a young girl like you."

"Go horse-riding," Mari said, with her old touch of mischief. "Bob took me yesterday morning. I liked it, and I was good at it, too."

Uncle Ralph's bristling brows nearly stood on end, but Mari had a feeling he was managing this on purpose. What was Uncle Ralph up to now?

" All the same," she went on, " if I did go to Darwin I'm sure Allen Webster would help me get a job. He——"

Kane spoke abruptly.

" I think, Ralph, if you leave Mari and me to have a talk we might thrash this thing out together. Under no circumstances would I be a party to her going to Darwin."

Kane was on his feet, as if expecting Uncle Ralph to go. There was a silence in the room, then Kane finished what he was saying. His voice was very even as he added, " Neither would I be a party to Mari leaving the station just now."

Uncle Ralph ceased to look surprised. He stood up and blustered about looking for his pipe, which he had knocked out and put in a pocket and now couldn't remember in which pocket.

" All right," he said, having found his treasure. " Get some sense into her head while you're about it, Kane."

He went to the door. Mari, catching a glimpse of his reflection in the glass of a wall-picture, thought she saw a *smug* look in his face. She was mistaken, of course. After all, reflections in the glass fronts of pictures were very misleading.

She watched her uncle go, and then turned to Kane. He walked over to Ralph's chair and set it straight against the wall. Then he walked back to the swivel-chair by the desk and, sitting down, turned it to face Mari. By this time his face had become thoughtful, his eyes trying to be kind. Or were they, too, trying to hide something?

She began to wish she hadn't overplayed her hand like that about going to Darwin. Kane was a man of integrity. He wouldn't like her stirring up Uncle Ralph.

" You would like to stay on the station, wouldn't you, Mari?" he asked, his voice quiet but with just a hint of a man more than thirty years of age talking to a misguided school-girl.

She decided that truth and open frankness was the only answer for Kane. He would see through anything else.

She nodded.

" Yes. I don't want to go away from Ninna-Warra."

" You know it's no life for a young girl, bushed in here with three men." He paused, then added very slowly, " All three of them very much older than you."

" You really mean I'm very much younger. There's a difference, isn't there? But I'm not really young, you know, Kane. After all, our great-grandmothers married when they were sixteen, and at home everyone's getting married young now. . . ."

He was looking at her, straight into her eyes, in a way that made her hesitate.

" But of course we weren't talking about marriage . . ." she said apologetically.

" Perhaps we might," Kane said slowly, still looking at her in that strange, searching, half-concerned, half-thoughtful way and not altering his voice at all.

She opened her eyes wide and looked at him.

" The three of us, carrying on this way indefinitely, is an impossible situation, Mari. You should have the prospects of some kind of future. If you put some of your life . . . some of your spirit and youth . . . into Ninna-Warra, then some of Ninna-Warra should be yours. Yes, I know Ralph would be thinking of that too, but when I took over the managership of Ninna-Warra I also took over the option of purchase. It will be mine when Ralph goes, though there will be a big sum paid over to his legatees."

Mari said nothing. She could not drag her eyes away from Kane. He wasn't looking at her now but only at the cigarette he was rolling between his fingers. He finished the job and, putting the cigarette between his lips, struck a match to light it. He looked up through the smoke haze at Mari.

" Would you . . . marry me, Mari?" he said. He spoke very quietly.

Mari blinked. She would like to ask him to say that again. She couldn't possibly have heard right. Then she knew by the way Kane looked at her, so still and inquiring, that she had heard right. Those words had been said.

" Marry you?" Mari said, bewildered. " Why—why, I haven't thought of . . ."

But hadn't she? Hadn't she cried that first night because he hadn't noticed her dress? Hadn't she lain awake on other nights, and hadn't she, just as she was on that edge of sleep, fading out from the living world, thought of a tall man who looked like Kane? Hadn't she, on the verge of that sleep-world, seen his face come a little closer, so very close, until, falling asleep, she had been dreamily happy?

And come to think of it, why did she like big bare floors and cooking for three men on a lonely cattle station?

Yes, just why did she?

Mari felt the colour slowly mounting to her face.

" I didn't think you liked me that much," she said lamely.

He smiled, a touch of irony in his eyes.

" I like you very much, Mari," he said.

Like? Well, that was something. But not *love*?

" People ought to get married for love," Mari reminded him a little primly, faintly hopeful.

Kane really smiled this time. It was a beautiful smile and Mari wanted badly to take it and hold it to her. His teeth gleamed in his brown face, there were crinkled lines at the corners of his eyes and those same grey eyes were suddenly kind and amused.

Then he turned a little in his swivel-chair to knock the ash from his cigarette into the ashtray.

" If I don't watch out I'll become a habitual bachelor," he said. He turned back and looked at her again. " I would like a home and children of my own." He paused. " And I would like you to stay here on Ninna-Warra. With me."

" But you have a home of your own," said Mari, still longing for him to say something more, something personal. " You have Half Moon."

His face suddenly shadowed; his mouth drew into a straight line, and only with an effort did he relax it.

" We won't talk about Half Moon," he said shortly. " I have leased it out and the people up there don't want any social contacts. They've closed the stock routes and don't welcome visitors. I have to tell you this now, Mari, because you will have to know Half Moon is out of bounds."

" For everyone?" queried Mari, remembering those voices on the air had said only Kane went to Half Moon to visit. There was someone up there on Half Moon they called Miss Icy-voice and only Kane called on her.

" For everyone," Kane said briefly. " That is except myself, and I go there occasionally for business. They are my tenants and they've still got a lot of my cattle roving the scrub and hills. From time to time I have to muster them out."

" I see," said Mari thoughtfully. That shadow in his face wouldn't have anything to do with Miss Icy-voice, would it?

If he was bothered about *her* he would marry her, not Mari, wouldn't he?

" You haven't answered me, Mari," Kane said quietly. He was looking at her again with grave, thoughtful eyes.

No—she hadn't answered him when he had asked that all-time record-smashing question. *Would you . . . marry me, Mari?*

Not *will* you, but *would* you? Was there a difference in meaning?

Mari looked at him, her eyes steady, which was strange because her head was spinning and her heart kept stopping, then starting again, with nothing disastrous happening to her. With such strange goings-on in the upper part of her body she ought to have dropped dead minutes ago.

Marry him? Marry Kane?

Mari was aware of the long silence and that Kane did nothing to break it. He wanted her head to make the decision, not her heart.

Why did she have this wonderful feeling of a sun rising in another inner, better world? Could it be possible . . .?

Yet he had said it. *Would you . . . marry me, Mari?*

Now is my chance, Mari thought, just a little wildly. If I don't take it now it might never come again. I'm in love with him. I am. I am. Other people take mad chances in life, but this isn't mad. It's right.

All the time she was thinking, she knew what she would say. She had known it from the moment he had asked that fantastic question. It hadn't required a mental leap at all. The bumps and starts, the stops and goes, with which her heart had been carrying on for minutes, was only that vital thing within her morse-coding what she must say.

" I would like to marry you very much, Kane. If you love me," she said gravely. After all the head did have a say in the matter too. She was half-shocked, half-thrilled, at her audacity in speaking at all.

Now was the time for him to ask her did she love him. But this he did not do. He was silent a minute, then he stubbed out his cigarette, stood up and came towards her. He seemed to tower up there near the ceiling as he put out his hand. A little mesmerised, Mari put her hand in his and he drew her to her feet. Obeying some quite independent will, her other hand came forward. He stood holding both her hands, looking at her.

"I'm a lot older than you, Mari," he said. "It mightn't be simple."

She smiled.

"Oh, that's all right," she said easily. "A few years are neither here nor there, and I'm a lot older than you think, Kane. A lot older than my years——"

The same tantalising half-ironic smile came back into his eyes.

"Go and think about it, Mari," he said. "It's a very big question, and the whole of your future is at stake."

She shook her head slightly, trying to puzzle it out.

"Why did you do that, Mari?" he asked, seeing the movement of her head. "Are you afraid that, after a while, you will miss your London life?"

"No," she said. "I wasn't thinking of London exactly. I was thinking of someone else." That someone was Robert Alton, and she only thought of him because she had remembered that when he first told her he loved her he had kissed her. And what a kiss that was, too!

"Someone in London—whom you will miss?" Kane was looking at her steadily, his eyes critical and a little cold.

"No," said Mari firmly. "Not now. You see, it's too late. . . ." She broke off.

What she really wanted to know was—who kissed who first —if Kane was going to marry her.

Again Kane saw that slight movement of her head . . . felt, because he still held her two hands, a slight tremor go through her body. Unexpectedly she stood on her toes and kissed him on the lips. For less than a second she saw a shadow in his eyes.

Kane dropped her hands and moving past her held the door for her.

"You're like a beguiling child, Mari," he said, the fleeting smile showing the gleam of his teeth. "Go and think about it. It's too big a decision to make in a moment."

Mari walked past him, through the door, then stopping, looked back over her shoulder at him. She smiled. Kane closed his eyes for a minute then turned back into the office.

Mari suddenly had twin aeroplanes under her feet. She

flew down to her room, closed the door behind her and stood looking at herself in the mirror.

" He loves you . . ." she told her image in the mirror. " He didn't say so, but he *must*. He asked you to marry him. Well, don't look so surprised! Perhaps he didn't hate you when he came on to the veranda that day. Perhaps he liked you. He was cross because he had an inkling he was going to lose his old bachelorhood. He had to fight to save it, didn't he? He must have liked me an awful lot, after all."

She spread her hands, and her image in the mirror spread its hands too. They looked at each other. They took a step closer to each other. They were almost touching nose to nose.

" I don't know," she said. " I don't honestly know. I don't think he really loves me yet. But he will. Maybe he will love me differently . . . when he learns." She smiled, and the girl in the mirror smiled. " But I love him."

Suddenly she flung her arms wide as if she could enfold that other self. She leaned her cheek against the mirror and closed her eyes.

" I must be mad . . because I don't know anything about him. But I'm in love with him. I was all the time. How crazy can I be?"

Then a little sadly, a little. thoughtfully, looking down at the delicate pointed toes of her shoes, she repeated:

"*How crazy can I be?*"

CHAPTER SIX

Two weeks later, Mari, dressed once again in her freshly-laundered blue Courtelle dress, her white straw hat on the crown of her carefully swathed hair, set out to cross the great north with Kane.

Ralph Curtis and Bob couldn't come to the wedding. They had to mind the station while Kane was away. Any time now the native stockmen would come back from walkabout, and more than one person had to be on hand to give them directions.

Ralph told Mari how nice she looked.

"That's my girl," he said, patting her arm. "This is a great day for your old uncle."

Mari had seen Kane's eyes soften with the edge of a smile when she came out of her room and stood on the veranda, waiting for Bob to bring up the big car to drive them down to the plane. She didn't mind that he said nothing. She passed muster. What more could she hope from a man like Kane who said very little that was endearing but who had the care-taking qualities of a brother?

Mari had quickly discovered that that was what this court-ship or engagement was going to be from the start. True, he had been very thoughtful and kind to her. He had had a lovely little horse brought up from the muster yards to be her very own. He had taken her to the store so she could pick her own saddle and bridle. He helped her take the dishes out to the kitchen after meals, and Mari was sure that however much batching the three men had done until she came it had never crossed Kane's mind that he would carry dishes to the kitchen for the housekeeper. It had more than crossed his mind now, because he did it. Also, quite often, he kissed her on the forehead . . . and several times on the lips . . . but oh, so gently . . . as if he was being careful and Mari's lips were butterfly's wings that might easily crush.

How did she tell him she knew all about kissing? Hadn't she been going to marry Robert Alton, except that everyone went mad with designs for frustrating this, and Robert had ended up in Edinburgh and Mari in Australia?

Dear Robert, Mari thought, now forgiving him for not having written. Just as well he didn't. She might not have had the heart to fall in love with Kane.

Mari was sure that Kane would come closer to her with marriage, because that was what she herself wanted. One evening, down by the stockrails, she had slipped her arm in his and leaned her head against his shoulder. When they had turned to go back to the homestead her arms were round Kane and his arms were round her. He kissed her. Yes, it was that delicate, careful kiss, but she felt his arms stiffen and for one moment he held her very tight.

Mari's heart soared. As they walked back under the dark-ling sky and the first prick of stars in the sky, they said nothing to each other but Mari talked to herself.

"He thinks I'm too young, and too small and too delicate, or something. Actually it is very nice and chivalrous of him to think that way. When we're married it will be different."

So sure was Mari, she actually skipped every now and again as she walked.

With conscious discipline she made herself forget the first night of their engagement. That night he had showered and dressed and gone over to Half Moon. It had been long after midnight when he came in. Mari knew this because, lying awake on her bed, she had listened to every sound of the night, hoping for only one—Kane's footsteps on the path and veranda.

Why had he gone to Half Moon? To see Miss Icy-voice, the girl the people on the air had talked about? If he liked Miss Icy-voice why didn't he marry *her*? Perhaps she was married already and was really Mrs. Icy-voice.

Perhaps, perhaps, perhaps!

Mari didn't listen in to the transceiver set because in her heart she didn't want to know. Knowing might spoil her happiness.

Standing on the veranda waiting for the car, her head high, her blue dress with its slim skirt making her seem a little taller than she was, Mari was amused at Uncle Ralph's enthusiasm about the manner in which she, Mari, had taken to Kane.

"Who would have thought it 'ud fall out this way." said Uncle Ralph, glowing with something that smacked a little of victory.

"Of course it makes everything all right for you, Uncle Ralph," Mari said, teasing him. "Now you have a house-keeper for ever. She can't walk out on you . . . when she gets mad about the puffing-billy pipe of yours and burnt-out tobacco in ant-hills along the veranda ledge."

"Well, I always was a designing man," said Uncle Ralph, squeezing her arm. "I believe in science, you know. It's a known fact there's a certain chemical reaction males are known to have for the opposite sex."

Mari was watching the cloud of dust made by Bob bringing up the car. She only half-heard Uncle Ralph's words. Then suddenly they made an impact. She turned her head and looked at him, her lovely blue eyes questing.

"What do you mean, Uncle Ralph?"

"Nothing, nothing, child. Look at yourself. You're a lovely girl. Of course Kane would fall in love with you. He'd have to be blind if he didn't."

He spread his hands, then fished in his pocket for the pipe. He began to tamp down the tobacco in the bowl of it with his thumb.

"Sure I gave him a little help," he said with a conscious air of pride in achievement. "Told him there were enough bachelors around the place. After that, he only had to look across the room." Uncle Ralph beamed over the bowl of his pipe as he clenched it with his teeth. "See what I mean?" he said, removing the pipe a minute. "There you were . . . waiting . . . pretty as a picture. I only had to give him the idea. Then he could see for himself. . . ."

Slowly, one by one, like tiny rounded pebbles falling into a clear cold stream, Uncle Ralph's words dropped in.

He gave Kane the idea. It had been a *suitable* idea for all three of them!

The car bowled up to the gate and at that moment Kane came out on to the veranda. He had gone inside to bring Mari's case. He signalled to Bob to come up and help with the load.

Mari looked at him. He stood so tall and straight, his hat already clapped on his head at that careless yet infinitely intriguing angle, his strong profile turned to her because he was looking at Bob, now coming through the gate.

Uncle Ralph had given him the idea.

She shook her head slightly as if to shake cobwebs from her brain. But Kane wasn't a man like that, surely? He had to have other reasons for getting married. Reasons like having a home—and children?

Yes, he had said that about home and children himself. He had never said, in words, that he loved her.

Had she dreamed a meaning into the fact that he wanted to marry her . . . not Miss Icy-voice?

There had been talk of her having a stake in the future—a stake in Ninna-Warra. Kane had said he had an option of purchase over Ninna-Warra when Uncle Ralph gave up. It was easy to marry Mari—whereas Miss Icy-voice might be difficult . . . the kind that had to be wooed ardently ; and Kane was not the wooing kind.

Kane turned to Mari and held out his hand.

" Are you ready, Mari?" he said. He looked straight into her eyes and smiled.

Mari's heart lurched.

I won't believe it. Or if I do, I won't care. I love him and I'm sure he loves me . . . well, just a little bit.

She blinked her eyes, then put her hand in Kane's hand.

" Come down to the gate and see us off, Uncle Ralph," she said.

Kane had made all the marriage arrangements by radio telegram. Mari had wondered why it had to be Dampier and not Darwin. Kane had friends in both places. He didn't seem to like the mention of Darwin after Mari had suggested the idea of going there and getting a job.

Darwin, Mari decided, was definitely *out* as far as Kane was concerned.

Ah well! Perhaps he liked his friends in Dampier better. Meanwhile—not to ask.

Not to ask about Miss Icy-voice and Half Moon either. Perhaps Kane had been rejected and he felt sore in his pride about it, the way Mari felt sore in her pride.

Not her heart, though. How strange! Why had Robert in her gallery of memories dwindled into a very youthful sort of person?

With a light step Mari went down the path, her hand in Kane's, Bob leading the way with the cases.

As Mari got into the car she looked back at the homestead.

" Be waiting for me," she said. " You've no idea of the face-lift you're going to get—when I'm married."

She waved her hand to Uncle Ralph. When Kane tucked her in the back seat she put up her face so that he might kiss her.

Kane took off his hat and kissed her lightly.

" Spare Bob's blushes," he said with a smile.

Dampier was a pearling port on the edge of the cattle country. There were two huge stations lying near it and using the port to export their beef; but mainly the town was preoccupied with pearling and as a store port for the outlying stations.

Mari, as they had flown in over the bay, had thought she had never seen anything more beautiful than the water lying beneath. It was a breathtaking aquamarine blue, edged with gold along the beach edge. To the west the sea was first purple, then fire-red and gold as the sun went down. Against this dazzling scene a pearling lugger, black against the orange sky, was just coming in.

" Oh," said Mari, awed by the scene. " What wonderful colours! Isn't it beautiful!"

" You need to be above it to see it at its best," Kane said. " On land I'm afraid you'll find it grey. The pindan, except for odd spots, is treeless."

All the same Mari was glad they had come to Dampier to be married. Here she couldn't be anything else but happy. In a world so full of colours there could only be happiness. She had forgotten Uncle Ralph's words because she wanted to forget them.

When the plane landed and they were allowed off the port landing-strip, past the silver cyclone wire fences, a man and woman came through the small crowd waiting to greet passengers and the man had his hand outstretched to Kane's hand and the woman was smiling with pleasure as she looked first at Kane and then at Mari.

" Kane, old man!" Kane's hand was being wrung and his back was being slapped affectionately by a tall slim man in white tropical clothes, a panama straw hat on his head. " We were just about knocked sideways with the news." The speaker turned to Mari. " This must be Mariana," he said. " That's what it reads on the notice on the registrar's door. I'm calling you Mariana right from the start. . . ." He wrung Mari's hand as if it was a man's. She tried very hard not to wince.

" Mari, this is Mr. and Mrs. Pollard. Ben Pollard is a pearler and his wife is . . ." Kane smiled at the tall, well-built woman in a pretty sun-dress and not wearing a hat at all. She was looking at Mari with kindness and interest. " I don't know how to describe you, Ann," he said. " Except to say you're a good friend when a man needs just that."

" Oh nonsense, Kane," Ann Pollard said. She was shaking

hands with Mari now. She was looking at Mari and smiling, but talking to Kane. "We didn't do any of the things you asked us to do in your radio telegram except arrange for the special licence. We are not going to let you take your bride to a hotel for your honeymoon. It's all far too public. There's not a window in the place. All open wire. The shutters are all up in this torrid weather."

She dropped Mari's hand and turned her friendly, beaming eyes on Kane.

"You're to have our bungalow," she added. "Now don't protest. It's a glorious excuse for Ben and me to take a few days' holiday up on Thursday Station. We've promised to go for months—and this has jerked us into going. Besides, there's a party and race-meeting on."

"Not another word, old chap," Ben Pollard was saying as Kane attempted to protest. "It's all fixed. As a matter of fact, Ann's cleaned and polished and bedecked already. We're not even going back there to-night for fear we put a mark on the Formica table or a crease on the bedcover. We'll all spend this night in one of the pubs, anyway. Bit of a break for us too, you know."

"You are very kind," Mari found herself saying to Mrs. Pollard. Suddenly she felt shy, very much the stranger, desperately dependent on Kane.

"You put the cases in the car, Ben," Mrs. Pollard said to her husband. "I'll take care of Mariana."

Once again she smiled as she took Mari's arm and guided her to a big landroving car of ancient lineage which was parked in a row with a dozen others, all dust-covered.

Mari looked back at Kane.

"My dear child, he's coming," Mrs. Pollard laughed. "There's nowhere for him to escape to in Dampier." She had meant it as a joke, but seeing Mari's sudden flush, her smile became a little concerned. "Getting married is rather an ordeal, isn't it?" she said brightly.

Mari had the feeling that Mrs. Pollard was one more person who thought she, Mari, was very young. As she stepped into the car she longed to look older. She wished she hadn't been so childishly anxious to stay near Kane.

"Yes, I suppose it is an ordeal," she said. "It's just that I'm such a long way from . . ."

" Home? You've only recently arrived in Australia, haven't you? Well, don't worry. You'll soon learn to love Australia."

" Oh, it isn't that . . ." Mari said, slightly confused.

Suddenly she decided that she was going to abandon being embarrassed, abandon this wild inclination to look round and see where Kane was—to get near him, next to him if possible, as if that way lay sanctuary.

After all, she was grown up. She was definitely tired of people treating her as if she was a slightly overgrown school-girl. Of course Mrs. Pollard meant well, and she was truly kind. But when did people begin to know that anyone over the age of sixteen was *adult*?

And Mari was seventeen. What was the date? Good heavens, she was just on the point of striking eighteen any time the town hall clock chimed.

Mrs. Pollard installed herself with Mari in the back seat of the dusty overlanding car while Mari indulged in these re-habilitating thoughts.

" Are you comfortable?" said Mrs. Pollard. " I always leave the men in the front seat. They like to talk, you know."

" To one another, you mean?" asked Mari. " Don't they like to talk to us?"

Mrs. Pollard laughed.

" You've a lot to learn about outback men, my dear. They never think women know anything about the business of cattle-running or pearl-fishing. We do, of course—but we don't tell them."

Mr. Pollard and Kane were putting the cases in the boot of the car and they now came round, one on each side of the car, and got in without ado. Kane had taken off his hat and Mari could see the damp ring around his head where the crown had pressed its line.

She had a curious burgeoning feeling of being possessed and possessing. She didn't know him very well, but he was her man. She belonged to him, and in this sea of strangers, this strange white shell road lined on either side by wide verges of buffel grass, the white and silver bungalows of the town lying in the near distance, he was her only contact with reality.

She wished she could lean forward and touch him, or that

he would turn his head and speak to her. In her need of Kane, all thought of Uncle Ralph's words was indeed driven from her head.

Kane was listening, his head a little on one side, his right arm flung along the back of the seat, to Mr. Pollard's monologue on the state of the pearl-shell industry.

Mari's spirits lifted and she turned more eagerly to Mrs. Pollard.

"You're being very kind to me," she said.

Mrs. Pollard noticed the sudden lighting of Mari's face.

"Not at all," she said, smiling. "You and Kane are being kind to us. Ben and I were thrilled that Kane turned to us to fix the marriage licence. He's been out of touch for so long, and we've been wondering just what goes on out there at Half Moon and Ninna-Warra."

She smiled and touched Mari's hand.

"The only news we had of Kane was that he had disappeared into some kind of hermit shell and no one and nothing could drag him out. We were quite worried." She looked conspiratorial before she added: "Now, of course, we know the reason. He's been courting someone eleven thousand miles away. Well, my dear, I for one can tell you Kane hasn't looked at another woman for months. He's been keeping himself strictly for you. How did it all happen—a pen-friendship, I suppose?"

"Well, not exactly," Mari said. "Ralph Curtis, his partner in Ninna-Warra, is my uncle, you know. . . ."

"And of course you corresponded with him! Then Kane got interested. I can see it all!"

Mari thought that if that was what Mrs. Pollard could see —and it made her happy—she, Mari, would leave it at that.

The car swung round a corner, passed two bungalows standing well back from the road, sheltered and partly obscured by groves of lovely tropical trees and shrubs, and began running along a wide, grey-white road through the outer fringes of the town.

Kane turned his head and looked at Ann Pollard.

"You've been very good, Ann," he said. "I'm sorry to put you to trouble. I rather think it might be better if we stayed at the hotel. We'll only be in Dampier a day or two and it's not worth turning your home upside down for that."

His words were disarming, and as he spoke he smiled. He seemed much more relaxed in his manner, almost buoyant, in fact. Clearly he liked being with the Pollards.

Mari's spirits were still high, for suddenly she saw another Kane. He was human and there was something fresh about his smile as he spoke to Ann Pollard.

"The house is all fixed, Kane," Mrs. Pollard said emphatically. "The turning of the house upside down, if that is what you call it, is all over. As a matter of fact, I'm a better housekeeper than you think. I hardly had to do a thing."

"Nonsense, old chap," Ben Pollard interrupted without turning his head. The road was a winding one and not very well made. Clearly he knew all the bumps and hollows in it but he still watched how he put his car through these hazards. "Honeymooning in a hotel in Dampier is out of the question. Absolutely no privacy. Besides, we need someone to feed the birds and the dog while we're away. You're doing us a favour too."

The car pulled up with a jerk as Ben Pollard applied his brakes. They were outside a low, rambling, timber-and-iron building. A wide veranda reached out to the pavement and against the buff-coloured walls were several long wooden benches on which sat a number of the residents of Dampier, taking their sundowners in leisurely ease. The wide front door was open, and in place of windows there were very big square openings in the wall, covered with a fine mesh wire. Mari could see at once that the mesh wire was to keep out the insects, not the view, for she could see right into the hotel and everything that everyone was doing there. Like the front veranda, the rooms, the bar and the big reception-room were decorated with indoor plants of every size and shade of green. It was a very spacious cool-looking place, but it was clear that the Pollards had told the truth. There would be no privacy in this hotel. Mari wondered how people got undressed; she supposed there must be some screen or even curtains to be pulled somewhere, but she didn't like to sound indelicate by asking Mrs. Pollard.

"Here we are," said Ben Pollard as he opened the drive door and levered himself out.

At the same time Kane got out of his side of the car.

"Kane and I'll bring in the cases and go break our thirst,"

Ben Pollard said. "You and Mariana go and have a shower and tiz up, Ann. We'll meet you on the lawn. Right?"

"Yes, but don't have too many drinks before we're ready," Mrs. Pollard cautioned the men. "It's our party too, you know."

Mari warmed to the Pollards' goodwill.

"Please call me 'Mari'," she said to Ben Pollard. "Nobody ever called me 'Mariana' except my father—and me when I'm talking about myself to myself."

"Right," said Ben Pollard happily. "Jolly nice name too." He looked at Kane quizzically. "How come you always pick the best in girls, Kane? You never make a miss, do you?" With this he gave a jovial shout of laughter and went round to collect the cases.

Mari, as she went into the hotel with Ann Pollard, tried not to let Ben Pollard's last remark mean anything to her. He was only being funny, she told herself. It was his particular brand of wit . . . but it did sound as if Kane had quite a way with girls, and there'd been more than one of them. Well, Alice Whitford and Miss Icy-voice were two of them, weren't they?

Mari shook herself. She mustn't think of these things ; only of the way Kane had suddenly seemed so easy and as if a load had fallen from his shoulders while he was in the car talking to Ben Pollard and then turning and smiling at Ann.

Mari's spirits revived. All she needed was that bath and that drink. Come to think of it, the town hall clock hadn't chimed yet and she wasn't eighteen. How awful if Kane really treated her as a child and didn't let her have a drink. Uncle Ralph had been mad when Allen Webster had mixed her a drink in Darwin—but Uncle Ralph was hundreds of miles away now. What was the law in this country, anyway? One thing for certain, she wasn't going to *ask*.

Mari had a wonderful evening.

First she found her room in the hotel was next to Ann Pollard, and she discovered there were curtains that could be drawn across the wide unshuttered wire screens while she had a bath and changed her clothes. All the time she was engaged in these exercises she could hear the sounds of other people in the hotel. Voices rang out in laughter, glasses clinked, two

children were playing on the lawn of the inside courtyard.
conversations were not personal because, like the world of the
transceiver set, everything could be heard by everybody. It
was as if an enormous party was going on in the hotel.

When Mari finally emerged in a new silk dress, one that
Uncle Ralph had bought for her before they left England, it
was to find the Pollards and Kane already grouped round a
pretty coloured table on the lawn. The sun had gone down
and it was nearly dark. Coloured lights in the creepers at the
sides of the lawn cast a muted glow and everyone looked cool
and relaxed after the long hot day.

Kane had either forgotten Mari was " still a child," or he
himself was so relaxed away from the station and whatever
the problems were that kept him tense and preoccupied when
there, or his mind was on other things. These other things
were chiefly the camaraderie and goodwill of all around who
kept coming, one or two at a time, and bowing with a kind of
cheerful grace to Mari, then wringing Kane's hand, occasionally thumping him on the back.

Kane, standing there having his hand shaken, smiling, was
a new person to Mari.

All the greetings showed how well he was liked among the
people of Dampier ; also that he had indeed behaved like a
recluse lately, as those women on the air had inferred.

" Well, you old son-of-a-gun!" one cried, pumping Kane's
hand. " Where've you been these last months? Heard you'd
gone bush, or something. Dug yourself a hole, eh? All the
time it's been this lovely lady here!"

One after another came loping through the half-light and
grasped Kane's hand and paid small oblique compliments to
Mari.

To each Kane replied: " Have you met Mari?"

Then he would look at her intently. " Mari, this is——"
and he would perform the introduction.

Every now and again, from where he was sitting he would
look over at Mari and Mrs. Pollard and ask:

" Are you being looked after—Mari? Ann?"

When he thought the steward wasn't doing this adequately
he looked after them himself.

" Another drink, Ann? Mari, these crayfish tails are the

chef's speciality. Or what about these sandwiches? They're mangrove crab."

Mari's heart was beginning to shine in her eyes.

This is better than the coffee-bar at home, she thought. And Kane? Why, he's wonderful. Then more soberly: I'm glad I'm going to marry him to-morrow before any other girl gets him.

She saw herself walking down the street with him. Not that white dusty street outside, or even Leander Lane at home, but some fabulous street somewhere else in the imaginary world, where people stopped and looked and Mari preened herself.

Underneath her laughter and her talk she longed to tell Kane something. It was a very simple something.

" I'm in love with you."

Once, across the table, Mrs. Pollard spoke to Mari about her home in England.

" I suppose it was difficult to leave all your friends there," she said. " But then you have so many extra friends now. You won't miss the old ones. Not very much, anyway."

" My best friends were next door," Mari said. " Their son Robert was my very best friend." She laughed at the quizzical raised eyebrows. " Oh . . . it's all right," she said. " He was studying at the university and was married to a career. All the same, we did have wonderful fun. We all went to Brighton once a year, for our holidays. Robert taught me to swim. Then in the winter we used to go to concerts. I wasn't very musical, but Robert was. . . ."

Suddenly Mari saw Kane's eyes on her and she realised she mustn't talk of home too much. It wouldn't be terribly interesting to these people in spite of the kindly way they were listening to her. Perhaps she shouldn't have had that second drink.

She knew she was gay . . . excited. But then who wouldn't be? To-morrow was her wedding day.

She broke off, then said quietly:

" That's all in the past now. I've a new life here. . . ."

Still Kane was looking at her in that disconcerting way. She hoped he didn't think she was homesick, or that she was thinking of her father. That would spoil his wedding too.

She turned to Mrs. Pollard. She must say something to change the subject.

" It's fun being here," she said. " So different. Now I'll get a real suntan."

" By heavens, Kane," Ben Pollard said jovially, " looks as if you had some competition back there in the Home Country. All the same, old chap, the best man wins." He shouted with laughter and beckoned the steward to fill the glasses.

Mari's eyes wavered before Kane's.

How silly could she be? And how much more silly could Ben Pollard be, nice and all though he was. He really had a funny idea of humour. Imagine Kane competing with anybody. He just wasn't that kind.

Mrs. Pollard came to Mari's rescue, and in a minute Mari had forgotten Ben's joke.

" About that suntan, my dear," Mrs. Pollard said. " Don't spoil that lovely skin of yours. Brown faces are two-a-penny in the north. Your kind is the one we all envy."

In a minute everyone was giving advice about skin care.

" Don't go outside without a hat ! "

" Wear your hat in your sleep, then you won't forget to put it on."

" Get a straw hat ; it's cooler."

" I don't agree. Light felt is the best. It stays on. . . ."

By the time they had finished Mari knew all about hats.

In the excitement and fun of this hat talk Mari forgot the questing look that had been in Kane's eyes when she had spoken so happily of the Altons next door to her old home. She didn't know that Uncle Ralph had told Kane all about Robert and that near-miss youthful plan to marry young.

CHAPTER SEVEN

Mari was awake early the next morning. She woke up instantly with no drowsy preliminaries.

To-day I'm going to be married. To-day I'm going to marry Kane.

She hadn't remembered very much about last night. Too much had happened, and in the end she had been too tired.

Kane had asked Ann Pollard to pack Mari off to bed, and Mari had been only too glad to be packed off. It hadn't mattered that Kane hadn't said any special private kind of good night to her. There were too many people around and she had too much to say to him when they really did talk about *love*.

They would talk about it, Mari was sure of that.

Somehow, when they talked after they were married—well, they would just have to talk about love. One couldn't be married without *talking* about love.

She got up and had a bath before the maid brought in some tea. Then she wandered round the hotel in her bathrobe and found another maid who told her where there was an ironing-room so that she could iron her "wedding dress." This dress was one of pale gold chiffon, another that Uncle Ralph had bought her, with a low waist-line and a thousand tiny pleats in the skirt. She had the same white straw hat to wear, but after all she had hardly worn it. It was small, but a pretty, delicate hat. Besides, it went with her best white gloves and biscuit handbag and shoes.

Mari felt it *looked* nice.

Ann Pollard, by this time up and bathed too, insisted that Mari had her breakfast on a tray in her room. Then she gave Mari a manicure, partly because she liked doing this and partly because she said:

"You have such pretty hands, Mari. They're small, but strong, and such fine bones. Take care of them, won't you, dear? They're like an ornament."

Mari had never thought of this before, but the idea pleased her. In future she would wear rubber gloves to wash up.

"Where is Kane?" she asked a little anxiously.

"Ben's got him in hand, dear. Don't worry. He'll turn up at the church. They always do, you know. He's probably worrying himself for fear *you* get lost."

"I feel terribly happy," Mari said to Ann Pollard over the bowl of water in which her fingers were soaking.

Ann Pollard laughed.

"You look so serious when you say it. But *dear* . . . so you ought to be happy. It's your wedding day and you're marrying the nicest man I've ever known." She paused as she lifted one of Mari's hands from the bowl of water and rested it on a towel. " Well, bar Ben, I suppose I ought to say." Then she laughed again. "Anyhow, I felt the way you feel now, the day I married Ben."

Kane, well supported by Ben Pollard, was at the church, safe enough, when Mari and Ann Pollard arrived.

" So nice to be married in a church," Ann whispered to Mari. " It was darling of the bishop to allow it—seeing there was such short notice. But then he's known Kane all his life."

For one sickening moment, as Mari stood beside Kane, she did have misgivings. He was tall and silent and strange now. Neither the angry man of the station nor the friendly man-about-town of the Dampier hotel last night. He was just strange, and so very quiet.

Unexpectedly Kane put up his hand and cupped her elbow. He held her firmly and she stood easily.

That hand, holding her arm, gave her such a wonderful feeling of reassurance. It seemed to tell her, by its pressure, she was safe.

How much stronger were men than women, Mari thought in awakening awe. There was almost a pleasure, at that moment, in being the weaker sex. At home down at the coffee-bar, she had never admitted, not even in her heart, that boys were stronger than girls and that there was such a thing as " frail woman." That idea, she had thought, was as dead as the dodo.

It was all over and they were back at the hotel, drinking champagne and eating tiny sandwiches and beautiful sponge cakes filled with cream and passion-fruit. Somehow the wedding breakfast merged into lunch and the party had grown in size. This too became a festivity. Everyone talked hard. Every now and again Kane's eyes rested on Mari. She could not understand the expression in them but she was too excited, too buoyed up by the Pollards' gaiety, and one glass too many of champagne, to want to understand it now. Later . . . later!

It was three o'clock in the afternoon before Ann and Ben Pollard reluctantly agreed it was time they piled into their big shabby car and made off along the dusty track to Thursday Station ; and other stray members of the party disappeared in favour of work they were supposed to be doing some-where.

"Come on, old girl," Ben cried, touching his wife's shoul-der. "If we don't get away now we'll never reach the Mission to-night. I'm getting too old to sleep cramped up in the car. Me for a soft bed, these days. With luck we'll hit Thursday midday to-morrow."

There was more fuss and laughter, then one-for-the-road before the Pollards finally drove off, leaving Kane and Mari waving them good-bye from the hotel veranda.

It seemed an anticlimax when the last of their dust-cloud faded and died away in the grey scrub of the pindan and Mari and Kane stood side by side, no one now to wave to, and for Mari that first embarrassing moment when she would turn and look at Kane.

Mari blinked a little, as if there was dust in her eyes.

"I have a car from the garage, Mari," he said quietly. "I'll put your case in it and bring it round to the door. Are you ready?"

His voice was kind, his eyes looked down at her and into her eyes and then away. Mari felt a catch in her heart. Wasn't that the way he had looked at her out at the station? An older man looking at a child?

Surely, not now!

Somehow she would have to make him see she was grown up. Why, it was nearly two years since she had left school, been housekeeping for her father, dealing with the trades-people, doing the banking.

Yet somehow, as she waited those few minutes for him, at the table on the green lawn in the courtyard, she was at a complete loss to know how to make him see.

Presently he came back.

"Right, Mari," he said. "It's not far. The Pollards' bun-galow is about half a mile around the bay."

He opened the screen door for her as she went out, and then held open the car door. He walked round the car and eased himself into it. He leaned forward to pull the starter knob.

"We're married now," Mari said brightly. "It's about time you kissed your bride." As she said these words the full impact of the fact that she really was married came on her.

"Golly," she said. "I'm married. I'm really married." She turned her face up to him, her sea-blue eyes alight. "I'm married to you. Isn't it funny?"

"Not funny, Mari," he said. Suddenly he leaned sideways and kissed her on the lips. It was so light a kiss it might have been floating on the air. "It's serious, but we'll make out."

He started up the car and it moved off.

"Are you going to like it, Kane?" Mari asked.

They were driving into the westering sun so Kane half closed his eyes the better to see.

"Yes, if you cook steaks and make meringue pies as well as you have done so far," he said. The smallest smile was playing round his lips. He was trying to be kind. Mari felt it.

She would not give in. She would thaw him out. He was back in that reserved mood he had been in during the last two days at the homestead. The party was over, his manner seemed to say. But she would *make* him smile. She would *make* him love her.

He was this way, she told herself, because really—deep down—he was shy ; afraid of hurting someone who vaguely he felt was a stranger and perhaps still something of a child. But she would show him.

The bungalow was very pretty, sitting far back on its lawn, a great boab tree sheltering the gate and tall eucalypts standing round the house itself. A large collie dog come loping to meet them. He remembered Kane from times past and, after a first moment of doubt and inquiry, wagged his tail.

The house, like the hotel, was open ; the shutters were up, making an extra veranda shade under which tropical flowers and shrubs grew. Inside was shadowed coolness, as open to the air as if there were no walls at all.

"Oh, isn't it lovely!" Mari said, looking first round the wide polished floors of the veranda with its many pot-plants and hanging ferns, its gaily painted tables and chairs and the wall brackets that held knick-knacks and books. One corner of the veranda was partitioned off—clearly the kitchen. Inside the house were two very big rooms. One was a living-room and the other, full of cupboards, was a workroom and wardrobe-room.

"They don't have any bedrooms?" Mari said, bewildered.

Kane had already brought the cases from the car and put them down on the veranda floor.

"They sleep in what's called the 'mosquito-room'," Kane said. "Round that other veranda corner. It's exactly what it says—a wired room to keep out the mosquitoes."

He watched Mari as she went eagerly, inquiringly, as curious as a child, to the north corner of the veranda. She pushed open the wire-screen door and stood looking at the mosquito-room.

"It's lovely," she said. "This will be like sleeping right out in the open air. Except there is a roof on the veranda of course."

She looked at the wide double bed in the corner. It was the widest bed she had ever seen, and beautifully made up; the spotless covers turned back—waiting to be used.

"I suppose it has to be so wide," she said, looking at the bed, "because of it being so hot, I mean. Well—you would have to get some air some time, wouldn't you? When you're their age, I mean. It would be all right for us, though, half as wide."

Kane, his hat in his hand, came along the veranda to the screen door. He stood looking at that double bed.

"It will be plenty of room for you, Mari," he said quietly. "There ought to be another bed somewhere around for me."

Mari's heart stood still.

Marriage was only an idea, not a fact? She remembered Uncle Ralph's words.

He had given Kane the idea.

She was inside the mosquito-room now and Kane came through the door, walked to the dividing screen that enclosed another part of the veranda, which also was wired in against insects.

"What in the name of fortune have they done with their beds?" he said, looking around, puzzled, angry.

Mari said nothing.

She sat down on the double bed and watched him as he walked through the adjoining room. Then she listened to his footsteps as he went through its farther door, round the part of the veranda that looked out over the brilliant blue bay and the mangrove swamps, through the kitchen part of the veranda and back to the part that led into the mosquito-room where Mari now sat. He walked through both the inner rooms again, then back on to the veranda.

"If they haven't any children I don't suppose they have any other beds," Mari said. She looked at him steadily through the wire screen.

He was going to treat *her* as a child. Was that it? What else could it be?

Perhaps he liked two beds anyway. Some people did.

Kane walked back to the steps leading to the path, went down them and crossed the lawn to a little cottage by the boundary fence.

Presently he came back. Mari had not moved; she sat on the edge of the bed, her white hat in her hand.

"They've stored the beds up there," Kane said. "And no mattresses. They must have sent them to be re-covered."

"There's plenty of room here," Mari said quietly. "I can sleep on one side and you can sleep on the other. . . ."

He stood looking down at her. He seemed troubled, and now Mari knew her first painful thought had been right. He did not think she was old enough to be married. He did not love her enough. . . . Why had she dreamed it?

That stilted engagement! He had to get used to the " idea " planted by Uncle Ralph. He had to get used to the idea that a girl was adult when she let a man put a wedding ring on her finger.

She closed her eyes in the long, crying frustration of some-one who has been doing a grown-up job for years.

Old enough to manage her father's house! Old enough to housekeep for three men on a lonely cattle station in the heart of Australia! Yet not old enough to love or be loved by the man of her choice.

He saw her close her eyes, then open them wide to look up at him. There was mutiny as well as a quiet dignity in them. Actually, at that moment, Mari looked older than he had ever seen her look before.

Ever since she had talked about her home, and the Altons, across the small table at the hotel last night, Kane had had a recurring picture of Mari standing on that back veranda the day he had come in from the run and first seen her.

He had thought she was so young a girl, a child, standing

there in her slacks, her dark brown hair reaching to her shoulders, her chin tilted, her blue eyes challenging.

Strangely enough, sitting there last night she had had the same tilt to her chin, the same bright challenging sparkle to her eyes as she talked about her holidays at Brighton ; about *Robert* teaching her to swim ; about going to concerts in the winter because Robert liked music but she didn't. It had sounded brave and gay and very young. Now he had deprived her of all this. He was about to incarcerate her on a lonely cattle station with three men so much older than herself. She might never again swim by a blue sea or go to concerts in the winter.

" Good God!" he had groaned to himself, sitting there while Ben Pollard cracked one of his futile jokes. " Good God! What have I done? Or better still, how did I let Ralph Curtis connive at something for which none of us was ready?"

He sat down on the bed beside Mari, took her hat from her and cart-wheeled it on to a table nearby. He picked up her hand, turned it palm upwards and looked at it.

So small a hand. Why in the name of fortune hadn't he noticed how small her hand was? It seemed to be able to do so much. That polishing ; that cooking!

Mari could see the muscle of his jaw knot itself into a small hard ball.

Then suddenly he relaxed a little. He turned and looked at her, his grey eyes expressionless.

He wanted to be kind, yet, so tense were his feelings at the moment, he could only be cold.

" Mari, you are very young," he said. " Much younger than you think. If you hadn't been a child you would have thought more about what was before you. . . ."

" You are not a child," Mari said. " You must have thought about it."

" I did," he said. " Perhaps for reasons you would not understand."

Uncle Ralph's ideas . . . thought Mari.

" I understand them," Mari said aloud. " You thought you wanted a home and children. Do you mean at some future time?"

He seemed to grasp at this.

"Yes," he said. "Some future time. When you are older. When you understand. . . When you are less of a responsibility. . . ."

Responsibility? So that was it!

Mari pulled her hand away. Their eyes were suddenly battling. . . .

"I think I'll go and make a cup of tea," she said with dignity, then added, "*In a childish way, of course.*" She stood up and went to the door. "Ann Pollard said there were supplies here, so I might as well make some sandwiches too. *In a childish way*, of course. I cook dinner in a *childish* way too . . . don't I?"

Suddenly she was youthfully, very angry. She swished her way down the veranda to the open-air kitchen, without waiting for an answer.

She couldn't believe it had happened to her. She had been so happy. She had been so terribly in love with him. Yet she wasn't the kind to give in easily. She would have to show him who was, and who was not, grown up.

She put the kettle on and took the bread out of the bread-tin. Then, with bread-knife poised in the air, she remembered the trouble was something more than herself being too young. It had been Uncle Ralph's idea. It hadn't been Kane's idea at all. Of course he didn't love her *yet*.

As the knife came down on the first slice of bread, Mari had another thought herself. Uncle Ralph had not only talked about ideas, he had talked about some magic chemistry males were known to have in connection with the opposite sex.

Perhaps Kane might learn to love her. Surely that magic chemistry would work if she learned to work it the right way herself? It would make Kane see her older than she was.

Mari cut bread and thought hard.

To begin with, he wasn't going to sleep on the floor. Oh no, he was not going to do that to her. How would she hold her head up in the morning if some intruding neighbour popped in to wish them luck?

A made-up bed on the floor? Oh no, she couldn't bear that!

He was married to her. So he couldn't be unmarried. So he couldn't be married to anyone else. Not just yet, anyway.

Meanwhile she would exercise some fascination over him.
That magic chemistry, in fact.

Mari buttered bread, found some cold chicken in the refrigerator and sliced it for filling; poured the boiling water on to
the tea-leaves and took Ann Pollard's best china out of a
wall cupboard. She hadn't any idea how to exercise fascination, but she would try.

A different hair-do every night to begin with, she thought.
And what mascara did to a girl's eyes was just nobody's
business . . . *but that girl's.*

When she'd got Kane Manners in the hollow of her hand
she would give him a severe lesson. It would be his turn to be
rebuffed. Vengeance would be very sweet, Mari thought,
knowing full well at the bottom of her heart that if Kane
Manners took her in his arms all her barriers would go down
like Jericho's walls before music. There would be no vengeance. But none of this did she admit as she slapped sandwiches on to a plate and sugar lumps into a bowl.

Down there at the bottom of her heart was another vague
idea. Any moment now she might have a little cry but she'd
die rather than let Kane Manners know.

He had sent her card castle sprawling.

Afternoon tea, and later a light evening meal, would have
been a sombre affair, if either Kane or Mari had let it be that.

Kane had put on an armour of kindly politeness. It
occurred to Mari that this was how he would have acted host
to a pleasant stranger who was passing by. Mari took her cue
from him, except that she was careful to keep her conversation
very adult. She wouldn't be as excitable as she had been last
night, for instance. She would be cool-headed and very serious
about anything they discussed.

They discussed everything about the north-west, the north,
even sheep and cattle and pearl-fishing—but not themselves,
love, or marriage.

Before the evening meal Mari stood in front of the mirror
in the bathroom, a room that was down three steps from the
mosquito-room under a short covered way in an annex that
contained a bathroom like a ballroom and a wash-house like
two ballrooms. The bathroom was also the dressing-room,
Mari perceived. There were two gorgeous old-fashioned

dressing-tables that would take enough hair-brushes, combs, cosmetics and hair-oil—if Kane used such a thing—to sink a battleship.

She had quite a time of it, doing her hair and making up her face.

Mari's experiments before the full-length mirror against one wall were in order to decide on her appearance for the evening. She longed to leave out the pins and let her hair fall round her shoulders. That way she always had a sense of freedom; of a kind of sophisticated under-glamour that had been all the go back home. But somehow, from her experience of that first day on Ninna-Warra Station, Mari guessed that in Kane's eyes, instead of this appearing glamorous, and adult, it appeared schoolgirlish. It, alas, made her *younger*.

So she brushed her hair till it shone, and coiled it first this way then that way until she had it sitting on top of her head like a crown, the back beautifully swathed high—like in the pictures she had at home of her great-grandmother and Queen Alexandra.

It added inches to her height and five years to her age, Mari decided. The mascara had nothing to do with glamour, only to do with improving her eyes.

Actually Mari's eyes did not need improving, they were as beautiful as the sea, but the little black edge she put on to her lashes certainly kept other people's minds on that fact.

After dinner Kane and Mari leaned over the front veranda railings and watched a brilliant moon shed a path over the bay. The tide was in now and water curled round the feet of the mangroves up to the road that ran past the bungalow on its way to the jetty.

They talked about the sea, and the mangroves; and the pearling luggers, now floating gently on a quiet water where two hours ago they had been stranded keel-over on the beach.

At last Mari sighed from sheer tiredness.

" I think you'd better go to bed," Kane said, still looking straight ahead, only his profile showing to Mari. " You've had quite a day."

" I think so too," said Mari.

As she turned to go back into the house Kane added, " Get into bed and I'll bring you a cup of tea."

Mari's spirits rose again. So he wanted to do something for her! She would go to bed, then he would bring her a cup of tea. Perhaps he would sit on the side of the bed and have a cup of tea too. Then he couldn't—he just couldn't not—well, not kiss her good night, anyway. Could he?

The tea was brought and taken, Kane sitting on the side of the bed but a long way away because it was not only a very wide bed but also a very long one. Mari, propped up against the pillows in a pink nylon nightie, kept glancing at him over the edge of her cup as she raised it to her lips. She had an idea this might have the same effect as a Spanish *signorina* peeping over a fan.

This little device was a failure because Kane was not only silent, he didn't once look at her. In fact he deliberately looked elsewhere and concentrated his attention on his tea, and on the tip of his cigarette.

He leaned forward and put his tea-cup on the table, then standing up began to gather the spare pillows from the bed.

Mari's spirit of not giving up without a fight turned suddenly to anger.

All right! If that was the kind of person he was, that was the kind of person he could stay. If he was about to insult her glossy hair, her watered-down mascara and the pink nightie, he could insult them—but not *her*, Mariana Curtis, who was behind and inside these subterfuges for charm.

Kane had to put the pillows down to take her cup from her, and while he did this Mari grasped the pillows and held them to her. Over the top of them her blue eyes, almost coal-black now, glowered at him.

" If you're thinking of sleeping on the floor, you're wrong," she said. She took in a deep breath. " And if you think I'm going to do anything else but sleep on the very far edge of the bed—so far over I put a dent in the wall, in fact—you're wrong about that too."

Kane stood straight and tall by the bed and looked down at her. His face was troubled.

" Mari, you don't know what you're talking about," he said, some of the terse anger that was in him echoing in his words.

" Oh yes I do. It's the facts of life, isn't it? Men and

women when they get married, work together, and play
together—in sickness and in health—remember? And they
also sleep in the same bed just so they're not lonely, if for
no other reason. My mother and my father slept in the same
bed till my mother died. In fact, she died in it. . . ."

Kane's anger died, and if he smiled, it had a touch of
unexpected compassion in it.

" All right, Mari," he said. He took the pillows from her
and piled them in their proper place on the bed and as he
bent down to do this he looked over them, at her. " You
shan't be lonely on your wedding night. You don't mind if I
sleep right over on this edge?"

" So long as you don't fall off," Mari said, her own compassion for other people being made uncomfortable, breaking
through her resolution not to have her husband sleep on the
floor rather than in the only bed in the house. Oh, bother the
Pollards, she thought, nearly tearful, why didn't they leave
another bed? They might have known Kane was this sort of
person. They know him better than I do. I just don't know
him—at all!

The tears were very nearly there. She choked them back.

" No wall this side to put a dent in," Kane said. He
straightened. " Turn your light out and go to sleep. I'm going
out to feed the dog and cover up the birds. I might go for a
walk along the bay."

He picked up the cups and saucers and went through the
screen door. Mari put her hand above her head and turned
off the overhead light on the head-board between the two sets
of pillows.

Go to sleep? she thought. As if I'll ever go to sleep again!

Nature, however, was stronger than Mari's will-power. She
not only had had a long day but it had been full of so much
rise and fall of spirits, so much tension and—a little wonder
because she, Mariana Curtis, was married. Unexpectedly she
forgot her inclination to tears. She corrected that thought
about Mariana Curtis being married. She was Mariana
Manners!

She said her new name two or three times and decided it
sounded well. Nothing was worth crying about, anyway.

" Maybe, when he thinks I'm grown up . . . that's sooner
than he thinks too. I've a surprise on that score for Kane

Manners," she said to herself. Then added desperately,
" There can't be any other reason."

Like a cold douche of water she thought of Half Moon and
Miss Icy-voice.

When she was back at Ninna-Warra Station she would
listen in to that transceiver set until she too heard that voice
from Half Moon. Then she'd find out who belonged to that
voice and why Kane had to ride over and see her. She
wouldn't be prying. She would just be using her own rights.
After all, she was married to him and Miss Icy-voice was not.

Her lids drooped over her eyes. Outside she heard a night
bird crying as it flew over, and a jalopy of a car rattling
along the road round the bay; the sucking of the water in the
mangroves, as slowly but inexorably the tide went out.

Mari's eyelashes, still with their touch of mascara on
them, lay still on her cheek. She was asleep, and not one tear
had been shed yet.

Her very last thought had been—" I never felt this way
about Robert. . . ."

CHAPTER EIGHT

It was long past midnight when Mari woke. She had turned,
and in turning she struck her foot against the timber wall.
She was in a strange bed and wondered for a moment where
she was.

The moon, as bright as a winter sun, was up and flooding
the veranda room with light. Outside the branches and leaves
of one of the eucalypts, sheltering the house, cast dancing
shadows over the foot of the bed, over the wire walls, and
over the table and small cupboard that stood in a corner.

The stillness was so absolute that Mari thought for one
minute the world must have gone away—except for herself
on a tiny moon island, alone in a sea of light.

Very slowly she turned and lay on her back. That way by
turning her head, quietly, she could look at that other bank
of pillows. There were no covers on the bed. It was too hot.

Kane too lay on his back, his right arm, flung above his
head, was resting on the pillow. Mari lay quite still for a

moment, hardly daring to look. Then she saw that his eyes were open. He was looking out. through the wire wall to the moon-flooded lawn and the big boab tree at its edge.

What was he thinking of, wrapped in that silence? Even as Mari watched him he stretched out his left hand and felt for the cigarettes and matches he must have put on the table before he lay down. He brought his right hand down from over his head and lit a cigarette.

Mari closed her eyes and listened to the soft sounds he made as he smoked, the movements of his arm as he raised the cigarette to his mouth. Presently he crushed out the butt and turned to lie on his back. Mari, opening her eyes again, saw that now he had closed his own, his right arm flung back again above his head and on the pillow.

Very gently she turned towards him, as if in her sleep, and leaned her head forward so that it touched his shoulder. She let her forehead rest against him. Somehow his own ice-bound loneliness, as he had lain there staring out into the brilliant night garden, had touched her. In some small and incomprehensible way she understood there were reasons why Kane was what he was, and was doing what he did do. They must be good reasons, whatever they were, and they were not easy. They kept him awake.

As if Kane too, feeling that slight pressure of Mari's head on his shoulder, felt that communion of loneliness, the arm which he had flung above his head came gently down. His hand cupped the back of Mari's head and as softly as the moonlight stroked the leaves of the trees outside, his fingers stroked her hair.

Quietly, the lump in Mari's throat subsided and presently she fell asleep.

When she awoke in the morning, Kane was up. She heard cups rattling in the kitchen along the veranda, and reaching for her shortie bathrobe, pulled it on as she scrambled out of bed.

She ran down the steps, along the covered-way to the bathroom and quickly splashed water over her face. Then she combed her hair and switched it up into its coil again. She padded, bare-footed, back to the house and the kitchen. Kane—bathed, shaved, and dressed in a white shirt and light

rown cotton pants—was pouring boiling water into the tea-
ot. He looked up and gave Mari that smile that was half
ind, half reticent.

"You should have waited," he said. "You'd have had
breakfast in bed."

"It was my turn," Mari said. "You got the tea last night."

"Well, a man has to do something on his honeymoon."

As he said the word "honeymoon" their eyes suddenly met.
Mari smiled as if it meant nothing.

"I love tea first thing in the morning," she said. "Do you
think I could sit on the veranda steps and have mine? It
would be cooler and much nicer."

"By all means. We'll both do it. You'll find we're joined
by three cats . . . a father, mother and kitten; as well as the
dog. Incidentally neither Ben nor Ann mentioned the cats
when they said they needed someone to feed the menagerie
or them."

"So many animals?" said Mari. "I suppose it's because
hey haven't any children." Mari rescued a piece of bread
from the toaster. She drew in a breath. Talking about people
not having any children was as embarrassing as mentioning
the word honeymoon. How many more stumbling-blocks
were there to be overcome in every day's conversation?

"I'll butter the toast and put it on a plate," she said quickly.
"Do you like marmalade, Kane? There's some here in this
safe."

"Yes, I like marmalade. I'll put the tea things on the tray
and carry it out to the steps."

Kane, as they sat and had their breakfast, was very formal as
if what was in him troubled his sense of good manners. He
told her what the boab tree was, how many different kinds of
birds the Pollards had in their immense aviary; of the creeper
climbing over an old tree stump across the garden and which
only flowered on moonlit nights.

Mari listened and nodded. She concentrated hard on
remembering what he said about each thing. She had a lot to
learn and meant to learn it quickly. Soon, very soon, she
meant Kane to realise he had married someone with a lot of
intelligence, even if not a lot of years behind her.

This thought reminded her of something, and she started.

She had a large piece of toast in her mouth and nearly choked in her sudden excitement.

" I forgot," she said, looking at Kane, her eyes bright excited, pleading with him not to throw cold water on this one.

" Forgot what?" he asked politely.

" The town hall clock chimed. Only I wasn't there to hear it. All the same it chimed. Come to think of it we're eight hours ahead of England here, aren't we? I needn't have waited till midnight. Even if I had thought of it then."

Kane was looking at her, his grey eyes curious yet still reserved.

Mari had a feeling she was prattling.

" I'm sorry," she said soberly. " I suppose I should have told you about it. I didn't tell you on purpose. I wanted to prove I was grown up at midnight." She paused, then added a little sadly, " I needn't have waited, because of that eight hours, you know."

" Go on," Kane said, watching her, his eyes not yet relenting.

" Whenever I have a birthday," Mari said, " I hear the town hall clock . . . near where I live at home . . . strike midnight. Then I know, at that moment, I'm one year older."

" So you are one year older than you were yesterday?" Kane said, quietly unsmiling. Mari began the process of nodding her head then stopped suddenly.

" I'm one *day* older," she said, not to be caught out by logic. " But chronologically, for the purposes of statistics, I am *called* one year older. I am eighteen to-day, Kane." This last she said with great dignity.

Kane stood up and as he did so picked up the tray from the top step. He stood looking down at her.

" In that case," he said, " chronologically, and for the purposes of statistics, you are adult."

" Yes, adult," said Mari, watching him.

" Congratulations," he said quietly. " But for the purposes of this marriage, Mari, it doesn't make any difference. It was easier to treat you as a child, when you were a child. Now it won't be easy. I'm sorry, you'll have to make the best of it. It won't be for long."

He turned away, went into the kitchen and put the tray

down on the table, walked through the farther door of the
kitchen round the side veranda to the front. Mari heard his
footsteps stop somewhere near the centre of the house. He
would be leaning over the balustrade, furious.

He had forgotten to pick up her cup, so Mari now picked it
up and took it into the kitchen.

"What a birthday!" she said, staring at the remains of
breakfast. She said this because she felt as if Kane had hit
her and she mustn't, just *mustn't* cry. She had to play hardy.
She had to weather out some peculiar kind of storm that
she could neither see nor understand.

"Weather it out. Weather it out! Stay on the raft! Some
day it will wash you up on shore!"

Where had she heard it?

Oh yes, when her mother died. She remembered the awful
bitter anguish she had felt and as if life without her mother
was unimaginable and intolerable. It had been the doctor
who had said those words.

"*When you're on a sea of grief you're like someone ship-
wrecked on a raft in that sea. Stay on the raft. . . .*"

She remembered it now. Perhaps that was because she had
now this minute the same anguished feeling of loss. Even
being adult didn't make any difference to Kane.

"*Stay on the raft,*" she said to herself. "And I guess when
I am washed up on shore I'll know the reason. Please God, it
won't be Miss Icy-voice. Because I won't give him up."

Mari put the dishes in the sink and washed them up. Then
she went along the veranda, through the mosquito-room with
its tousled bed, and down the three steps to the bathroom.

"Heavens! They do live in a funny way!" she told herself.
"No rooms to speak of, miles of veranda, and a bathroom
and wash-house as big as half a dozen rooms."

She had to keep talking to herself, not to think.

It was very hot, so she had a shower.

When she had showered and made up . . . very slightly this
morning . . . and put on a cotton dress and her flattie shoes,
she decided to leave her hair down. That way she could toss
it when she was glad or mad. She loved doing that. And she
didn't have to do it up on her head to look like Kane's grandmother any more. It didn't work and wasn't going to work.
So she would do it any way she l'ked. It was lovely in the

pictures of Queen Alexandra, but she, Mari, *wasn't* Queen
Alexandra, alas!

Just now she liked her hair down.

When she had finished dressing she went back to the mosquito-room, made the bed, and tidied up. She had already
hung Kane's pyjamas up in the bathroom-cum-dressing-room
beside her own pink nylon nightie. *Just to punish him.* That
was childish, she thought while she made the bed, so she
went back to the bathroom, retrieved her nightgown and
folded it and put it under her pillow. When you're on a raft
you'd better not be childish. You might fall off. She would
take life as it came. Lie flat on the raft . . . and see where and
how the sea washed her up.

She pottered round the mosquito-room, the veranda between it and the kitchen, and then finally to the kitchen, just
to make sure everything was spotless. Mari hadn't lost her
instinct for home-making in her few short hours of married
life. She watered the hanging ferns, gave the three cats milk,
and then went out to look at the aviary across the lawn.

The big collie followed her and she saw that Kane had
already uncovered the birds and put fresh water and seed in
their bowls. He had done it before putting that kettle on to
boil before she had woken up.

What was he doing, leaning on the balustrade of the front
veranda, looking out at the sea? Thinking, of course, but of
what?

She wouldn't think about him. She would think of the
birds. *And the bees*, she added with her old touch of fleeting
gallant humour.

She pursed up her lips and whistled softly to the birds, not
knowing that, for all their gorgeous many-coloured plumage,
they did not understand whistling.

There were budgerigars, parakeets, a lovely green and
yellow bird Kane had told her was called a " twenty-eight "
because it made a sound like saying twenty-eight. The pink
and grey one must be a galah. . . .

She heard Kane's footsteps coming across the grass: a dried
twig fallen from the boab tree snapped under his foot.

The collie wagged his tail and gave a muffled kind of
welcoming bark.

He stood beside her, his hands in his pockets.

"Haven't they gorgeous colours," Mari said of the birds, determined to be impersonal, casual. She glanced at Kane. His eyes weren't grey any more. They were dark, angry . . . not at *her*, but at some deep troubled thought.

"I've been thinking of some alternative to this ridiculous three days in this bungalow, Mari," he said. He spoke through half-closed lips, his voice drawling.

He was tall and bronzed and very handsome standing there, his white shirt open at the throat, the sides of his trousers bulging where he had his hands in his pockets.

Out here in the morning sun, already beginning to beat down like the wrath of God through the leafery of the boab tree, the burned ochre of Kane's skin glistened, and the muscles of his throat and his bare arms, above which he had rolled his short sleeves, were powerful and tense.

"What shall we do? Go home?" Mari asked, turning back to the birds, her voice deliberately light, an effort at casualness.

"No. I think you might as well see the world, such as it is." His voice lost its restraint. He still drawled. "I think I'll take a run into Dampier and see if I can find old James. He's an aborigine who does the lawns and outhouses for the Pollards. He's utterly reliable and I think he might come and water the ferns and feed the menagerie. If I can get him I'll take you down south to Perth."

Mari looked at him in surprise.

"To Perth? But that's hundreds of miles away, isn't it? I mean . . . on the map it's the other end of the continent."

"Twelve hundred miles to be exact. We can go down on the night plane, have a day's shopping in Perth, and come back on the following night plane."

Oh, thought Mari. That will comfortably account for *the nights*. She could see it all. It might be better that way. Kane's next words, however, added something more to that thought.

"I think I owe you something better than the ramshackle furniture out at Ninna-Warra, Mari. Every woman likes to start a new life with her own idea of furnishings. . . . Am I right?"

She looked at him again and saw that his eyes were grey again. He actually wanted to do something for her.

"I hate that awful little spare room at Ninna-Warra," Mari said. "You weren't going to incarcerate me in that were you, Kane? For keeps, I mean?"

He smiled, suddenly alert, anxious to do something for her.

"I think you ought to have that top front room. My sleep-out is just outside it. At the moment it has the iron bed-stead——"

"With a white quilt that's thirty years out of date. I put it there," said Mari.

"Right," said Kane. "We'll go to Perth and you can buy what you like. Modern furniture . . . modern quilts, or whatever they are——"

"Bedcovers," said Mari. "Do you mean I can buy whatever I like?"

"Yes. Money is one thing Ralph and I are not short of, Mari."

She supposed not, with a whole cattle station of his own and half of Uncle Ralph's station.

"Let's go," said Mari eagerly.

"Let's go," said Kane, suddenly smiling. "Would you like to come into Dampier with me while I hunt up old James? You can look over the pearl-shell sheds if you like. From what Ben said last night they're building a new lugger on the slips at Sanderson's yard. Plenty to occupy you there while I hunt."

"I'd love to. Shall I get my hat?"

"Not necessary," said Kane.

"Wait till I get my bag," said Mari, "and a handkerchief." Suddenly there was adventure in the world again. And he was kind. He wasn't going to stand off in the distance, like a stranger—all the time.

She ran across the grass and found her bag, a white grass one, that looked just right in this bright sun and torrid climate. She picked up a handkerchief, and because she was suddenly a little more light-hearted she put a dash of perfume on it.

Kane pulled the car out and when Mari ran out to it she saw the collie sitting in a lordly way in the middle of the back seat.

"This is what he does when the Pollards go driving," said Kane. "He didn't ask. He just jumped in ; over the door."

"Goody," said Mari, getting into the front seat while Kane held the door for her. "I won't feel lonely while I wait for you . . . if I finish with the pearl-shells and the lugger before you've found James."

She stole a glance at him. Did he react to her suggestion she might be lonely without him? Even for a short while?

He made no sign.

"We'll drive round the bay," he said. "Then you can look at the colour of the water. If you write home and tell anyone about that, they won't believe you."

No, they won't, Mari thought. On the edges of the bay the water was yellow, then it shaded into green, then a brilliant aquamarine blue. If one painted it, it would look garish, but out there beneath that sky, now pale with heat, it looked wonderful.

Within three-quarters of an hour Kane had found James, been to the air-office and booked two seats on the night plane, and arranged for the garage to pick up the car at the airport after seven that evening.

Mari had seen the aborigines and Malays sorting pearl-shell in the big sheds, and half a dozen men working on the hull of the new lugger. She had been into Sanderson's store and bought herself an ice-cream, and while she waited for Kane she sat on the bench of the store veranda and licked it.

The girls in the shop had known who she was but had not said so. They had all smiled, flashing their beautiful white teeth against their sun-browned skins and said, "Nice day ! "

Mari had felt their eyes watching her as she had gone out. It is because I'm a stranger, she thought.

This was only partly true. The other truth was that everyone knew this was the girl who had married Kane Manners ; and every girl was curious. If Mari had only known, they looked on her as something akin to royalty.

She sat on the bench, on the store veranda, her feet stretched out before her and crossed at the ankles so that she could admire her flattie toe-pointed shoes. She licked her ice-cream and shook back her hair. Suddenly it was good to be alive. Between the pearl-sorting sheds on her left she could see the brilliant Reckitts-blue sea.

Some day that raft would wash her up on shore.

Kane pulled up the car below the veranda steps and eased himself out. He stood a moment looking at Mari. Once again she saw that odd expression in his eyes. Now she diagnosed it. It was *concern*.

Why should he be concerned for her, she wondered. She was safe with him, wasn't she? He had said so himself. He didn't want a full married life, but that was his decision. She was well, she was healthy, and she wasn't lying down and dying because she loved him and he didn't love her back. Why should he be *concerned*?

She finished the ice-cream; ate the biscuit cone, drew in her feet and tossed back her hair.

" I'm ready," she said, and came lightly down the steps to the car. " Did you get seats on the plane?"

" Yes," he said, starting up the car. " They tilt back, so I don't think you'll have too uncomfortable a night. You might be a bit tired to-morrow, and more so the next day, I'm afraid. But it might be worth it."

Worth escaping another humiliating night lying on the farthest edge of the bed? Did he mean that? If so, Mari wasn't going to let him think she thought it.

" Worth it, to buy all that new furniture and really deck out the homestead?" she said with a smile. " Jolly good, if you ask me."

" Jolly good?" said Kane, almost to himself. Clearly he hadn't heard that expression before.

Mari saw to it that the Pollards' bungalow was left exactly as they had found it. Everything shone, waste food disposed of ; the linen from the bed folded and put in the laundry box, some fresh flowers from the garden put in the vases.

The plane, a Fokker-Friendship, left the airport shortly before eight and Mari found herself airborne again, for the third time in less than a month.

The seats were comfortable bucket chairs, and after the air hostess had given them some tea and sandwiches it seemed the proper thing to do to settle down for the night. The

lights in the plane were dimmed and the passengers were
supposed to go to sleep, and the aeroplane builders had made
arrangements accordingly.

Kane made it quite clear that that was his intention and that
was what Mari should do.

She sat on the inside seat, with Kane on the outside seat
beside her. He folded his arms, leaned his back on the head-
rest and closed his eyes.

He was not sleeping, Mari knew. But it was his way of
telling her that was what *she* should do.

She glanced at his profile. When she moved, their arms
touched. He might be a thousand miles away.

She looked at the square firm line of his jaw and for the
first time realised how strong-willed he really was.

How stupid, and yes, childish, she had been last night!
Those little attempts she had made had been no more than
moths beating against a burning light, which, if they kept on
beating, would only destroy themselves. The light was too
bright and too hard.

She had a lot to learn.

CHAPTER NINE

Mari did indeed have a lovely day in the southern city. The
temperature was high but the clear, dry heat was not dis-
tressing. In spite of a disturbed night she felt light-footed,
and freed from the oppressive heat of Dampier.

She felt envious of the girls walking along the pavements
of the white and gold city. They were tall and slim-limbed
and carried themselves so freely, wide-brimmed hats on their
heads to protect themselves from the sun. They had tanned
golden skins that Mari thought were marvellous ; and she
was quite unconscious that these same girls looked at *her* with
envy. They noticed her peaches-and-cream skin, the sea-blue
eyes, that could only have come from northern softer climates.
They also, glancing under their shady hats, envied her the tall,
silent, brown-faced pastoralist walking by her side, his own
wide-brimmed, hundred-bale hat slightly aslant shadowing his
eyes.

Mari, who on the night before she was married had dreamed of herself walking proudly down some imaginary street beside Kane, was doing that right now and she didn't realise the effect it was having on others.

She measured herself beside Kane's shoulder and wondered if, at eighteen, it was too late to grow two inches.

She loved every minute of the shops. Never before had Mari had money to spend the way Kane spent it. She hadn't even dreamed of shopping like this. It was for rich people —people out of books. Yet Kane was unperturbed.

When Mari fingered and liked something, he said to the shop assistant:

" We'll take that. Air-freight, please."

When it came to whole suites of enchanting blondwood furniture and Kane said " Air-freight, please," the shop assistant looked at him, startled.

" Did you say air-freight, sir?"

" That's right. Air-freight. The M.M.A. Company will look after it. You can put a note for a special request to fly their freight plane straight out to Ninna-Warra. It's not on their route but they're very accommodating when orders come by charter."

Kane didn't do any more explaining. Mari learned that Kane said little, gave directions but never explained himself.

She wondered what he was like out on the cattle run. When she had that house right—and it would be a wonderful house when she had finished with it—she would go out on the run and see for herself. She would do this in addition to listening in to that transceiver set, morning noon and night, to hear for herself that voice from Half Moon.

Miss Icy-voice!

But she mustn't think of any of that now. This was fun, walking down the long, sultry streets of Perth, forgetting she had only known Kane for so short a while. Together, buying for the homestead, she felt a companionship, almost a conspiracy against that shabby old homestead, the dry-rot in the veranda floorboards, the dreadfully scrubbed and dowdy linoleums.

Kane said very little, but Mari was used to that now. She had only to say—" Oh, that's lovely. I could make curtains

for that gun-room or sitting-room, or whatever you call it
. . ." and, his straight-line lips easing a little into his idea of a
smile, he would look at her and say:

" We'll take it. Call it a living-room, Mari, and we'll take
out the guns. They can go in the spare room, or on the
veranda-room."

His grey eyes, though not smiling, were not serious either.
They wanted to give her something—a fine home, if he
couldn't give her love.

Late in the afternoon Kane called a taxi to take Mari for a
drive round the river.

" You will see one of the prettiest sights in the world," he
said.

Mari, alas, had visited one shop too many, walked down
the shopping area ten yards too far. The steady thrum of the
car engine, the warm soporific southern air, worked their
magic. Mari would have put matchsticks between her lids to
keep them open, for the blue, green and gold river was indeed
lovely, but this she could not do. She fought a losing battle
against drowsiness. Already her new shady hat—bought only
an hour before—was on her knee. At last, giving up, she
closed her eyes, bent her head sideways and leaned it against
Kane's shoulder. She didn't fear a rebuff. It was just the same
as on their wedding night, when he had allowed her that small
tender privilege of leaning on him. Then, he had rested his
hand on her head and stroked her hair.

No, he wasn't forbidding or foreboding. He had lent her
his shoulder for comfort. Now, as then, Mari did not care
what his motives were. She wanted his shoulder to lean on
and, adult and all though she was, being eighteen years old
and one day, she borrowed Kane's shoulder with the guileless
confidence of the very young person.

He moved so that she was more comfortable, and because
her left arm was in the way he took her hand and held it in
his own—not tightly, nor warmly. But he held it.

" Go across the Narrows Bridge and around Applecross,
come back over the Causeway," Kane said to the driver. " It's
more pleasant driving than walking at this time of day."

" 'S more restful," said the driver, taking his eye away
from the rear-vision mirror and away from the view of Mari's

head on Kane's shoulder and Mari's eyes closed in profound
sleep.

Kane had taken a room in one of the big hotels for the day,
and until evening they had not used it except to wash and
brush-up before lunch. When the taxi brought them back to
the hotel its braking and sudden stopping awoke Mari.

"Oh, Kane, I'm so sorry," she said regretfully. "I did
want to see the river."

This time he really smiled.

"You have all the rest of your life," he said, and helped
her out of the car. "I think if you go up to the room I can
arrange for your dinner to be sent up."

Mari, still a little fuzzy from her sleep, repeated his words
in her head.

Yesterday morning he had said—"Don't worry. It won't
last for ever."

What did he mean *now*?

You've got all the rest of your life?

She took the words to herself like jewels and examined
them as she crossed the wide luxurious foyer, went up in the
lift and along the passage to their room. Kane opened the
door and they went in. Mari sat on the side of the bed, her
new hat beside her.

What did he mean?

He took off his lightweight coat and went over to the wash-
basin and washed his face and rinsed his hands. He stood
towelling himself as unaffectedly as if they had been married
for years.

A small warm thought began to grow in Mari's sleepy head.

"He's getting used to being married. He's getting used to
being in the same room with me. Perhaps one day he'll get so
used to me he won't want to do without me. . . ."

This being used to one was a second-best kind of love, she
knew. But it was a kind of love. That was the important
thing.

"Would you like to have a shower, Mari?" he said over
the business of drying his hands on a very large white towel.
"Then you could lie down till the plane goes."

The bedside telephone rang.

Kane, suddenly jerked into action as if something important, even anticipated, had happened, strode across the carpet and picked up the receiver.

"Yes?" he said.

There was a moment's silence and then Kane said:

"Put them through!"

No please or thank-you, Mari noticed. This didn't sound like a cattleman with a slow outback drawl. It sounded like a man of affairs disposing of nations by the drop of a phrase.

Again there was a moment's silence and then a voice spoke, Mari, sitting on the bed only a few feet away, knew it was a woman's voice! Not intimate, but formal and polite.

Kane was speaking.

"Yes, Manners here . . . Good God, you were pretty quick picking up my whereabouts . . . Well, I'm relieved to hear your Security's so good. Yes, of course I'll come . . . Better I come to you than you come here. Will eight or eight-thirty do? . . . Not? . . . All right, I'll come right away."

He put the receiver down without any farewells.

Not very polite, Mari thought. Not very anything, when you came to think of it! But who was this woman? And how many women did Kane have in his life? It wasn't Miss Icy-voice, because although the voice, blurring a little through the phone-piece, was restrained with a hint of cautious formality, it was not a cold voice. No, it was a warm voice. Young . . .

"I'm sorry, Mari," Kane said. "I have to go out. That was a business call. Nothing of any importance to us, but I must go. Will you have your dinner here, or in the dining-room?"

"Couldn't you have asked her to dinner, Kane?" Mari said with a determined smile. "I couldn't help hearing the voice. . . ."

"Merely someone on the switchboard," Kane said. "I'm afraid it wasn't the kind of person one asks to dinner." He paused and looked down at Mari and said more kindly, "Business is like that, you know. Sometimes one has to go when one is called. This is one of those times. Will you excuse me?"

She nodded.

"Don't worry, Kane," she said. "I hope it doesn't mean

those shops are getting tangled up in all the orders and air-freights and things. . . ."

He took out a cigarette, eased in his manner. He cupped his hand over the match to light the cigarette, then through the smoke he smiled at her, a little wryly.

" You're not worrying that my cheques might bounce?" he said. " Don't worry. They never will. I can promise you that."

" To me it was an awful lot of money," Mari added, now playing his game, trying to talk of mundane things because she knew he did not want her to ask him what was the business that called him out so unexpectedly.

She stood up and patted down her skirts.

" I think I'll have a shower and go to the dining-room for dinner," she said brightly. " If I go to sleep again now I mightn't sleep on the plane. That would be an awful bore, wouldn't it?"

" I think that's a good idea," he said. He walked over to the chair and lifted his coat from where he had hung it when he came in. He put it on, straightened his tie, then picked up his hat.

" I'm sorry to leave you, Mari," he said levelly. " I won't be away long. I hope you'll excuse me."

This was excessive politeness again, but somehow Mari did know he was sorry. Underneath he was kind. She was sure of that. He had found himself landed with her: had decided on marriage as some way out of, or *into*, responsibility ; but out of kindness he didn't want her to be too badly hurt about it. This feeling for her had come after, not before, he had told her that they must get married. It meant there was something kind in him, or perhaps—oh, dearest hope—she herself was not so unattractive to him after all.

" Endearing " might have been the word to describe Mari, if she could have seen and understood herself objectively. As it was, she was too preoccupied with the dilemma of being an independent modern young miss on the one hand and a slightly love-sick girl on the other to understand in any way how a man like Kane, or Allen Webster, might look at her.

As a matter of fact she hadn't thought of Allen Webster, or

Robert Alton either, for so long she had forgotten they existed.

That was why she smiled with a delight that was really greater than the length of their acquaintance warranted when, seated half an hour later at the table which was snowy with impeccable table-linen and gleaming with silver and glass-ware, she saw Allen Webster walk into the dining-room doorway. He spoke to the head steward and then suffered himself to be led to a table in the corner.

Mari had gone downstairs a little diffident, because she had never before been in a big hotel like this. The head steward had quickly taken her in hand, led her through a positive bevy of table attendants to an alcove table on one side of the large gilded room.

For a few moments Mari had glowed in the sparkling grandeur of the overhead diamond-dancing chandeliers and the wall mirrors that showed her to herself in formal repetition—a little fresher and better-looking than she had expected —all round the room.

The stewards were so attentive that she was awed and quite unconscious of the fact that she was not just Mariana Curtis but Mrs. Kane Manners of Ninna-Warra. Quite a personage, for all her young years.

Instinct more than experience told Mari to let the table steward select her menu for her. There were foods here she had not heard of before.

"Iced rock melon, instead of fruit juice, madam, yes, but certainly. It is without reproach. Then I think fresh crayfish-tail . . . caught this very morning from the reef not a dozen miles away. . . ."

He was sparing her the French names for the Australian food.

"Or perhaps albacore? No, I think we will have crayfish. You like shell-fish, madam?"

The drinks steward was hovering around by this time.

Mari looked at him uneasily. Then because the lights were bright and the gilded walls and gilded mirrors were bright too, she had a bright idea.

She had had champagne for her wedding. It had seemed to

flow all over that hotel at Dampier. Corks popping were faster than the conversation that day.

Kane had left her to have dinner alone! Besides, his cheques never bounced. He had said so.

"Champagne," she said to the steward, her head tilted in a way meant to convey she had been ordering champagne all her life, as a matter of course.

"Certainly, madam." He scribbled furiously on a small pad and seemed to accept it as a matter of course that Mari had been ordering champagne all her life.

"Pink champagne," she amended. That ought to bring a widening of the steward's eyelids. It did not. He hastily altered his scribble on the pad, bowed and went away.

Mari refused to be deflated. She held her head high and wished that Kane would come back early enough to see her sitting, serene and mistress of the situation, drinking pink champagne. *Not missing him.*

It was at that moment Allen Webster walked into the entrance of the dining-room.

He was dressed in a white sharkskin dinner jacket with a black bow-tie, his black hair flattened down impeccably. He rolled a little as he walked; for all his handsome finery, he was still a horseman.

Mari watched him being led away to the corner table. He shook out his napkin and began to talk at once to his table steward.

Back home, in the coffee-bar, Mari had learned that if you sat quite still and did nothing when one of your friends, or Robert's friends, came in, they would come over if that was what they wanted to do.

In spite of the old-fashioned people thinking girls made friends without being introduced when they went to drink coffee and meet "the crowd," they were quite wrong. A girl sat quite still, did not look, and if someone wanted to be introduced he came back there every night until someone arrived who knew both him and the girl. Then he was brought across and introduced.

This was the "etiquette"—a word never used but its meaning understood, in the club atmosphere of the best coffee-bars.

Mari sat quite still behind her lovely table, and knew that

when Allen Webster looked about him he would see her reflection in all those mirrors round the walls. Perhaps he would remember her.

If he wanted to come, he would come.

Meanwhile she smiled with delight. A known face was not a strange face when two strangers to a city suddenly meet each other again. She hoped he would see her, and that he would come. Till that moment she hadn't realised she had been lonely and just a little frightened of the big dazzling room ; and that she would have jeopardised the well-being of her immortal soul to have had Kane sitting there beside her. All this she had been hiding from herself by a determined chin-lifting façade.

A few minutes after the steward brought the champagne bucket, Allen saw her.

Mari was wondering, at that moment, what was the right procedure about drinking champagne. Since the steward had left the bucket of ice, the bottle propped sideways at a slightly tizzy angle, without popping the cork or serving her, she surmised that he would know. At the appropriate moment he would come and perform the honours. Again, instinct warned her to leave it to the steward.

Allen Webster, across the room and from quite a distance stared in astonishment first at the vision of Mari and then at the champagne. He wrote a note, tore the leaf out of his diary and handed it to the steward, who came quick-footed across the room to Mari.

" Mrs. Manners?" he said inquiringly, protectively.

" Yes," Mari said.

" You are acquainted with Mr. Webster? He is from the north."

" Oh yes," said Mari. " I thought I saw him come in a little while ago. He is a friend of my uncle's."

" Then with your permission . . ." The steward presented her with his small silver tray on which lay Allen's note.

Mari took the note and opened it. She smiled as she read the quick screed.

May I come over—with or without Kane's permission?
                              Allen Webster, Darwin.
                                    Remember me?

Mari turned her head and smiled. Then she spoke to the steward.

"Please ask Mr. Webster if he will come and join me."

She did this with quite an air. Going to the films and watching television had proved quite a useful occupation, after all. This was how they did it in stardom.

Allen came across, preceded by the steward, who first, with a dusting flourish of his napkin, then with a deft lifting backwards of the chair opposite Mari, managed to make his arrival seem distinguished.

Allen sat down, leaned across the table and smiled at Mari.

"So you did it?" he said with a grin. "You married him? And where's the almighty man right now?" His eyes watched Mari, lighted with interest, and not a little admiration.

"Business," said Mari firmly. "We did a rush trip down to Perth to do some shopping—but of course, Kane has business too. A lot to do in one day, you know." The décor and the steward had made her feel sophisticated and just a little important.

Allen smiled again as he looked at the champagne bucket.

"Were you going to drink that lot all on your own? The whole lot?"

"Why not?" asked Mari. "Much more than that was drunk at our wedding."

In actual fact when she'd seen the size of the bottle she had been a little frightened of it. One glass, perhaps two, she had thought.

"Well, I'm glad I'm here to share it with you," said Allen. "If I remember you, as I saw you in Darwin, you were a very shy, slightly alarmed girl, drinking squashes in the company of your uncle."

"I'm a married woman now," said Mari with dignity.

"You haven't learned to drink champagne as quickly as that in Kane's company, I'll wager," said Allen with a grin. "Come clean, Mariana . . . I was introduced to you as Mariana, you know. Well, come clean, child, and tell me what's happened to you? Not trying to grow up quickly and match that ogre of a husband of yours, are you?"

Mari flushed. Here was that not-grown-up theme again.

Besides, Kane was not an ogre. He might be silent and in a godlike kind of way, be above love—love for Mari anyway—but he was her husband.

Suddenly, unexpectedly, unbidden, there was a burning feeling behind her eyes.

It was because she had remembered that behind this façade of the adult married woman dining de luxe in a de luxe hotel was a young girl who loved her husband and who at this moment was missing him desperately. *Where was he, anyway?*

She blinked her eyes and smiled.

"I like ogres," she said, picking up her fork. She went on eating the delicious crayfish from its red nest of shell. "Kane's kind, anyway." She looked up, challenging Allen with her eyes. "That's why I married him," she finished.

Allen's mobile eyebrows wavered towards his hairline, and back.

"In that case we cry 'pax'," he said. "Let's talk of other things. When do you go back north?"

"To-night," said Mari, then asked politely: "And why aren't you in the north?"

"Business," he said, mimicking her own emphatic statement as to Kane's preoccupation elsewhere. Their eyes met and they both burst into laughter.

"Covers such a lot, doesn't it?" added Allen. There was no sting in his words. Mari decided it didn't mean a side stab at Kane.

The steward arrived and, with the pomp and circumstance suitable to opening a bottle of pink champagne, began to work on the wired cork. He filled their shallow glasses, and Mari's eyes laughed across the bubbles at Allen as Allen lifted his glass to toast Mari.

"Well met," he said, "in odd places!"

"You must come to Ninna-Warra and see us," said Mari —unexpectedly conscious of her right as a married woman to issue invitations to her husband's home. Allen's eyes were suddenly narrowed, but Mari did not see this.

"I'll take you up on that," he said. "We used to have some fine horse-meetings on Half Moon. Maybe now that Kane has turned his full attention to Ninna-Warra we could stage some picnic races there. We'd have some fun out of them."

"Oh, I'd love that," Mari said happily. "As soon as I get home I'll do something about it."

She began to feel happy, thinking of Ninna-Warra as home and of having things to do like running picnic races and parties.

"We could ask everybody," she went on. "The Whitfords and the people from Half Moon . . ." Suddenly she felt on dangerous ground. Kane wouldn't talk about Half Moon.

"The Raywoods?" said Allen, his eyes watching her. "A stuck-up lot, and you can't prise them out of their shell. We've never had anything like them in the north before. But who's to know what miracles the young bride can work?"

"Do you spend all your time racing?" Mari asked, to get away from the hazardous subject of Half Moon.

"Mostly. I breed racehorses, then I race them in the north to try them out and give them experience. I race at stations that run their own private meetings. If I've got something good I try it out from smaller town-races to the bigger country towns. When I'm really running a winner I bring him to the city."

"And do you often run a winner?" Mari asked, wide-eyed at this itinerant way of working into the racing business.

"Quite often," he said with a grin. "A man breeding from stud stock down here and training him on the river flats hasn't a surprise for the other boys. They all know about any horse that's training at any time. But run him in the north first? Well, that's the way to win on long odds and spring a few surprises in the south."

They had eaten as they talked. Unnoticed by Mari, the champagne bottle had emptied. She had not noticed the steward topping up her glass and was too inexperienced to know that this was the usual practice.

Allen signalled the steward and presently another bottle appeared. When its cork popped Mari protested.

"I'm having a lovely time, Allen," she pleaded. "But please, no more. In fact I'll tell you the awful truth. It doesn't taste very much different to me from a rather dry lemonade."

For a moment Mari thought the steward, as he added a very little to the bottom of her glass, would faint. What heresy!

"I won't press you, Mari," Allen said, smiling. "As a matter of fact I wouldn't let you down." He paused, looked up at her. There was a genuine expression of liking for her in his eyes. "You know that, don't you?" he said.

Mari smiled, picked up the glass which the steward had so discreetly only partly filled, and lifted it to toast Allen's obvious kindness.

CHAPTER TEN

Her eyes were smiling over her glass when she saw, across Allen's shoulder, Kane come into the doorway.

He was looking straight across the dining-room and it was as if Mari was looking into his eyes, not Allen's.

Her heart thumped. He looked so distinguished, standing there, tall, brown, well-dressed in a dark suit he must have put on since he had come in from that business meeting.

It *had* been a business meeting, after all! He hadn't been away an hour and he had come back to have his dinner with her.

Allen saw the startled look in Mari's eyes, then the slow flush that spread over her throat and cheeks. He turned round, then rose from his chair quickly.

"Kane—by all that's lucky!" he said heartily. He went across the floor and the two men met half-way. They shook hands, Allen talking quickly, volubly, Kane half-smiling, saying so little that Mari wondered if he said anything at all.

They came back to the table together and Allen pulled out a chair for Kane as if he, Allen, were the waiter and Kane the honoured guest. Fortunately for the reputation of the hotel the waiter was there in time to push the chair in.

"What are you up to, Mari?" Kane asked quietly. "Looks like the poultry stage. What have they got? Duckling? Good, that's what I'll have."

"But sir," protested the waiter, "we have some excellent hors d'œuvre. Or perhaps you like iced rock melon? Madam found it very pleasing. Our own boats brought the crayfish in this morning. . . ."

Kane shook his head.

"I'm afraid I'm running out of time now. I'm very sorry. We have a plane to catch. Bring me some of that duckling, please." He turned to Allen. "May I share your bottle of champagne?"

"Of course. Marriages call for toasts. Believe it or not, that wife of yours has about wrecked the hotel by announcing that champagne is like lemonade."

Kane turned to Mari.

"I see you have been in good company," he said quietly. His words were so pleasant and so polite Mari knew instinctively he didn't like Allen Webster. She also knew that in spite of Allen having called Kane an ogre and having spoken of him in that off-hand way when in Darwin, Allen was a little in awe of Kane.

"Is your business all finished, Kane?" Mari asked steadily.

"Quite," he said non-committally. The steward served him, and when this rite was over Kane looked up at her again.

"The plane leaves in an hour," he said. "It takes half an hour to the airport. . . ."

"Nonsense, old man," Allen Webster said. "I have my car. I can get you there in less than twenty minutes. There's another bottle of champagne in the cellar . . . we must celebrate."

Kane was still impeccably polite, irreproachably pleasant.

"Not with an extra-precious cargo in the car," he said. "I won't risk my wife's neck with your idea of moderate speed, Allen. Thank you for the thought." This time he really smiled as he looked at the other man. "Besides, you said my wife likened champagne to lemonade. It wouldn't be much of a celebration for her, would it?"

Mari was looking from one to another. Why was Kane angry? Something to do with that business of his? Or was it because, not liking Allen Webster, he did not like seeing Mari having dinner with him?

When would she ever learn to understand him?

How odd a day it had been, she thought, when later, dinner over and coffee taken in the lounge and quick adieux made to Allen, she and Kane went up in the lift together to collect their things from the room. She didn't feel tired now, only elated. He had come back early, and now they were going home. It had been a lovely exciting day . . . but now, best of all, they were going home.

Even Mari, so given to wondering, did not pause in her thinking to reflect how quickly Ninna-Warra homestead had become for her—*home*.

In the bedroom, while she powdered her nose, she looked at Kane. He was knotting his tie.

"Why don't you like Allen Webster?" she asked.

He too looked in the mirror, to finish that tie-knotting.

"Probably because I'm a station man. I stay with my land and look after it. I make my land work for me and I work for my land. I have no understanding of a man who is never two weeks in one place and makes his money by chance."

"Oh, Kane," said Mari reproachfully, "he has to breed his horses and look after them, then travel from place to place. It must be very hard work in that climate."

"Not for Allen Webster," Kane said dryly. "How did you come to be having dinner with him, Mari?"

His eyes looked at her eyes in the mirror.

Mari felt there was injustice in this reproach—for it *was* a reproach.

"When a girl is left alone, what is she to do?"

He had finished knotting his tie and he turned round and leaned back against the wall. He folded his arms. It reminded Mari of that photograph Uncle Ralph had shown her before she had met Kane. There was something nonchalantly godlike in that gesture as if Kane was Kane and it didn't matter what the rest of the world was like. Unexpectedly the injustice of the reproach and that sudden easy yet deliberative way of standing nettled her.

His next words made her angry.

"What did you usually do when you were left alone at home?" he asked.

She turned back to the mirror.

"When Robert went to Edinburgh and left me, I came to Australia and married you. When you went out to dinner—at least I thought you were going out to dinner—why then, I had dinner with Allen Webster."

The logic of it was sound, but the words were no sooner

out than she would have given anything to take them back. They were childish. Somewhere at the back of her mind echoed lines she had heard years ago:

Men flying their white winged kites call in their birds,
But God himself cannot take back a thought, when it is
    put in words.

Another memory hurt her too. It was the ghost that had been her love for Robert. She had dismissed him with that *gone to Australia and married another man*! That was what it would sound like to Kane.

She had loved Robert, or she had had what she had understood to be love. It was a careless boy-and-girl affection that had warmed and attached them to each other, so that when it was the fashion to be married young they had thought they would be smart and do that too.

She hadn't been at all smart in marrying Kane. She hadn't wanted to be sent home to England rejected, and she had fallen in love, deeply, bitterly and hurtfully in love with him. That wasn't smart at all. She turned round.

" I'm sorry I said that, Kane," she said. " It was stupid, and for once I'll admit it—childish of me."

Very slowly he unfolded his arms, straightened himself and stood looking at her a moment. Once again she saw that strange expression in his eyes, like sad or troubled concern.

" Bring your hat, Mari," he said steadily. " I'll take the cases. It's a long flight home and I think we're both tired."

It was indeed a long flight home. They flew through the night to Dampier, and after an hour's wait took the cross-continental feeder plane to Ninna-Warra.

Once again Mari stood in the shade of the old galvanised-iron shed and watched Bob in the station wagon materialise out of a cloud of dust, coming to fetch them. This time there was no mirage to break the great loneliness of the plain.

Back at the homestead near the sundown hour, because the plane was more than an hour late, Mari left Kane and Bob at the car while they took their cases and parcels from the boot. She walked up the path, carrying her hat as she had done a long age ago when she had arrived from England. It seemed an age. A whole lifetime. Then she had been a young girl with big ideas about herself. Now she was adult—married; had travelled nearly three-quarters of the way round a vast continent, and was desperately tired.

The two dogs came to meet her, knowing her this time and welcoming her with their bounding strides and their wagging tails. Mari bent to pat their heads. Their welcome touched her.

They had known her only a little while and they seemed to like her.

She had an awful feeling she was being sorry for herself.

Then she went up the veranda steps and suddenly there was Uncle Ralph coming through the doorway. He looked at Mari for a moment, then held out his arms.

Suddenly Mari's barriers broke down, she was in his arms, her forehead dug into his shoulder, sobs shaking her body.

"There, there," he said, patting her shoulder. "There, there. Coming home when you're tired—after a long day—it is always an anticlimax, lass. People always cry when they come home."

He put his hands on her shoulders and lifted her away from him so that he could see her face. He took out his handkerchief—a clean one from his top pocket—and wiped her eyes.

"It's your home now, lass," he went on. "Come and see how two half-daft old cattlemen have tried to fix it for you."

Mari finished drying her eyes with Uncle Ralph's handkerchief and gave it back to him.

"I'm all right, Uncle," she said with a catch in her voice. "Just tired. Terribly, terribly tired and—like you said—thankful to be home."

He held the door open for her so that she could go through. Something upright and proud in his stance made Mari realise that for a moment she had to forget herself and forget that awful fatigue. Uncle Ralph was proud of something. What was it? She must notice it. . . .

"Why . . ." she said, and stopped.

The floors of the passage shone, the woodwork around the doors shone. The old-fashioned brass knobs on the doors shone right down the passage like a row of waist-high beacon lights.

"It's *polished*," she said, awed by the gleaming splendour and hardly able to believe it.

"We were downright ashamed when we saw you out with those polishing rags the first day you woke up here, Mari," Uncle Ralph said. "Bob and I reckoned we weren't going to have any more of those shinanikans. We'd do it ourselves first. Now take a look in a room here and there. . . ."

Mari opened the first door. It was the one with the iron bed and the outdated white quilt that Kane said could be her room. It shone too. Floors, woodwork, furniture and windows had been polished; but there was something more than that in this room—on the narrow old-fashioned mantelshelf above the never-used fire-place stood a vase of flowers. The vase was a squat jam jar and someone, Uncle or Bob, had painted it in a brilliant blue. The flowers were strange dusty bush flowers, here and there spiked with colour because of the odd spray of bougainvillæa put in to brighten it up. In a way it was a pathetic vase and a pathetic bunch of flowers, but it brought the tears back to Mari's eyes.

"Oh, Uncle!" she said. "This is the loveliest bouquet of flowers I've ever seen—I would rather have it than the whole Chelsea Flower Show."

And so from room to room, it was all the same. Bob and Uncle Ralph had prepared a suitable homecoming for the bride, shining floors and flowers in painted jam jars.

"That's not all, either," said Uncle Ralph. "You'd never guess, but we've cooked dinner. No, not steaks. A roast. And a good hot spanking damper so you've bread for to-morrow."

"Oh, Uncle . . ." Mari said. Suddenly she was sitting in the chair in the dining-room, wiping tears from her eyes again.

"And just you sit there—not to move, mind you, or all hell'll break loose—and I'll bring the tea right in. It might be close on dinner-time, but after that flight you've got to have a cup of tea first. Now stay put and I'll go and fetch Kane. The kettle's on the boil."

Mari stayed put. Not for a million pounds would she have spoilt Uncle Ralph's pride and pleasure. She sat looking at her hat lying on the table. It was the new shady one she had bought in Perth. Every now and again she dabbed her eyes.

"They're good and kind," she kept saying to herself. "Kane too. I'll have to try and *try*. I can housekeep all right. I can grow a garden too. But can I make them happy—well, the way Uncle has made me happy to-day?"

This last thought struck Mari as sadly funny, in a paradoxical way. Uncle Ralph and Bob by their man-made heartwarming welcome had made her happy, and yet the tears would still keep breaking over her eyelashes.

Presently Kane came down the passage. He too was making a progress, shepherded by Bob. Mari, listening to their footsteps, could imagine Bob's manner of showmanship. His face would be expressionless. He would open a door, jerk in a thumb and not look at Kane to see the reaction. He would say nothing, and Kane wouldn't say anything either. Kane would nod acceptance of what he saw, but not for a million pounds would either man look at the other.

They reached the dining-room together and came in, first Kane then Bob behind him, elongating himself to see over Kane's shoulder.

Mari's tears dried as if before a warm wind. Her eyes met Kane's down the full length of the room and mutely they too said something to each other. What it was, Mari had no idea, but it was something to do with never letting Bob and Uncle Ralph know their marriage was such a fake.

Mari got up, tripped a little because her feet were not quite steady, and walked round the table to the door where the two men stood. She stood on tiptoe and kissed Kane's cheek.

"It's a lovely homecoming, isn't it?" she said. Then she quickly turned and put her hand on Bob's arm. "Thank you, Bob," she said. Before he understood what was going to happen to him Mari leaned forward and kissed him too.

For a moment Bob looked as if he had been hit by a cloud of fairies but the dead-pan expression came back in time to save him.

"Thank yeow," he muttered. He put up his arm as if to wipe the kiss from his cheek but remembered when the arm was half-way up that that was just what his sleeve would do. He dropped his arm, stood stiffly for a moment, and then turned and went with quick, hard steps down the passage.

"He's going to take a plaster cast of that kiss, Mari," Kane

said quietly. " That was a very nice thing to do." He paused,
then added, " Thank you."

" I meant it," Mari said, and turned away to the table again.

Uncle Ralph was coming through the door, the tea-tray
held high. It was a battered ancient wooden tray but Uncle
Ralph had found a traycloth and brought out the best china—
something big and old he must have had cached away in the
store for the thirty years he had been on Ninna-Warra.

" We'll put it here, lass," he said. " You go and sit at the
side there next to Kane. I'll pour to-day."

He poised the teapot for action and looked over the top of
it at Kane and Mari as they sat down together.

" You can hold hands," Uncle Ralph advised them.
" There's nobody here going to mind, least of all Bob and me.
We kind of expect it, you know."

Bob came quietly back, and, sliding in through the door as
if not wishing to be noticed, sat down at the table on the
opposite side to Kane and Mari.

They really do expect it, thought Mari.

The same thought was in Kane's mind, for suddenly their
eyes met. Without saying anything Mari put out the hand
nearest to Kane and he took it in his own. He held it, resting
on his knee and there the clasped hands stayed while the tea
was poured, the sugar and milk put in the cups and the hot
toasted damper passed around. Mari had to eat and drink
with her left hand but she didn't mind this. It made Uncle
Ralph and Bob happy. She had only to look at the fabulous
expression that had suddenly driven away blankness from
Bob's face, and watch Uncle Ralph's puffing-billy pipe cloud-
ing the air with smoke, to know they were the two proudest
men in the world.

Any minute now they were expecting to dandle grand-
nephews on their knees.

When she had time and privacy she must remember to ask
Kane just who was Bob ; and did he have any other name.

CHAPTER ELEVEN

Next day Mari regained her old equilibrium. Those "blitz-draft" experiences, as she called her journey to Dampier, and what had followed, had done a lot to settle her feelings and make her feel more established in her new surroundings.

She felt as if she was riding out time; hoping that some day something would happen that would make that expression in Kane's eyes soften; and that perhaps he would open his arms to her.

In spite of the careful, almost rigid distance he kept, she had not given up hope.

Neither had she given up hope of resolving the enigma of Miss Icy-voice.

On that first morning, she banished the men from her kitchen. She didn't do it bossily. That she knew would never do. She simply pleaded with them as they fossicked round in their old habitual way getting their breakfasts.

"Please, darlings," she said, addressing them all, standing there in her slacks and clean white blouse, her hair tied back in a pony-tail because she had forgotten how early station men got up and, being a little late herself, had had to scramble with her dressing. "Please, darlings . . . it's *my* kitchen. Uncle Ralph! You said that was why you brought me to Ninna-Warra . . . to *housekeep*, I mean. Oh yes, to marry Kane too. Well, we're married now and we like it very much. . . ." This last she said with a smile to please Uncle Ralph and Bob, but she let the edge of her smile take in Kane too. He broke the damper-bread into pieces and did not look up.

"A kitchen is a woman's castle," she added. "*Please* sit down, all of you. You'll be surprised what a nice breakfast you'll get." This time she was cajoling them.

Uncle Ralph and Bob sat down, looking like schoolboys caught on the eve of truanting; but Kane walked outside and stood on the edge of the veranda and looked over the station square. Mari, stealing a glance at him, in between sizzling bacon and setting the table *correctly*, saw that his eyes had that half-closed, hooded look that he adopted when he was thinking as he stared out into the far distance through the white glare of the hot sun.

Breakfast over, and while Mari washed up, the three men went in their heavy riding-boots to the stables. There they must have had another of their " secret confabulations about the female in the homestead "—Mari's expression—for presently Uncle Ralph came back.

" Put your hat on, lass," he said. " This darn house is clean enough for a week, and there's cold meat left over from last night. That's good enough for dinner to-day. You're coming out on the run with us. . . ."

Mari's eyes lighted up.

" Did Kane . . .?"

" He did. Of course he did. He's gone to bring in that horse for you. Let's look at those trousers of yours. 'Pon my word, Mari, I never thought I'd see the day when I said a woman in trousers was attractive: but looking at those things right now I'd say that's the best garb you could think of to go riding. I'll get some webbing puttees for you and we can wind 'em round your instep and ankles. That way the stirrup-iron won't cut into your feet."

Mari ran inside to get her hat. It wasn't the pretty wide-brimmed straw hat Kane had bought for her in the city, but another, not unlike it, of uncrushable linen. He had said she would need something like this for station life.

She pushed the pony-tail of hair up into the crown of the hat, and put on some face cream to protect her skin.

Mari was philosophic. After all, Kane had not really deserted her last night. He had come and said good night to her. He had looked irresolute for one moment, as if he might have kissed her.

In the end he hadn't done anything but say good night, bluntly, and walk quickly through her room and out of the door that led to the sleepout beyond. This was where his bed, with its bedside table, reigned in masculine solitude.

Later, Mari heard him come from his dressing-room and then the general upheaval of his bed as he got into it. She had seen the light reflected along the veranda snuff out as it was switched off. Then she had heard the rattle of the match, the quiet muffled replacing of the cigarette on the table. She could see the intermittent reflection of that glowing cigarette tip.

He too was tired, but he wasn't going off to sleep so easily.

" Having a wife on his conscience, I suppose," Mari thought sadly, drowsily, wearily, because she herself was worn out with a day of travel and many emotional upheavals.

After Uncle Ralph had seen she was dressed adequately for riding out in the sun, he took her down to the stables.

Kane brought in the horse he had given her; not too high and not too sprightly. He helped her to mount by lifting her into the saddle, then he put the reins in her hand.

" Don't do anything but sit easy, Mari," he said. " I'll take Dandie on the lead and she'll do what I do." He gave Mari a sudden brief smile. " I won't do anything disastrous," he added.

Bob had taken her for a ride before they'd gone to Dampier; so she was not nervous.

Uncle Ralph rode madly away into the distance, a quaint hump-backed man on a wiry little horse. Bob rode off in a manner that was almost sedate . . . very straight-backed on a very big horse. Kane followed with Mari on the lead. Now and again he touched his own mount with his heel and they trotted, then they graduated to a very short gentle canter. Not once did he look round, and Mari did not doubt this was because his own sense of personal dignity forbade him to be a witness to her inexperience. She was grateful to him. It was another one of those silent kind things he did but which he expected to be taken for granted: not mentioned.

They rode two miles in this way and then came to a small hut beside which there reared an enormous windmill. Below the windmill was an engine encased in a small iron house, and beside that a water trough.

Uncle Ralph and Bob were nowhere in sight. Kane reined in and, after he'd swung off his own horse, came and helped Mari dismount.

He made no reference to her possible stiffness.

" This is what we call a ' bore,' Mari," he said. " Periodically, in the Dry and when we run out of water, we bring the cattle in here to drink. That—" he looked up at the tall windmill—" that brings the water up from underground.

Some water is stored in the tank, but mostly we regulate it to flow at a constant trickle into the trough."

He glanced at her. Mari nodded her head to show she was an attentive listener. She had much to learn.

"There are stores in the hut, if you would like to make some tea," he added. "We're mustering over on the other side of the creek to-day . . . combing the strays in out of the hills."

"I could make tea for us all?" Mari asked.

"We don't take tea till noon, Mari. Too much to do. But make some for yourself, then if you feel like it you might walk down to the creek. If you'd brought the right gear or we'd thought of it, you could have swum or fished. As it is you might like to watch the hills. You'll see the men bringing down the cattle and might see some fine riding."

"Men?" said Mari. "Are there some others besides Uncle Ralph and Bob?"

"Four," said Kane. "They live in quarters at the out-camp about six miles away. When the natives are back from walk-about we have a very big muster team; at present we're short-handed."

"I'll make some tea at noon, then," said Mari. "Till then I'd like to go down to the creek and watch. I hope something interesting does happen."

Again Kane had that shadow of a smile.

"You might be surprised," he said.

He took the saddle from Mari's horse and threw it over a hitching rail near the bore. He put a hobble and bell on Dandie and turned her loose.

"She likes it better that way," he said briefly. Then he went over to the hut and unlocked the door. He went in and opened the window on the far side and then came out, stooping because of his height.

"All okay and spick and span," he said. He stood looking down at Mari. "I think Ralph and Bob have spring-cleaned the whole station. Quite a celebration for them."

They were looking at each other, not smiling.

"I think they were dears," Mari said. "I wouldn't like them to be hurt because you and I . . . you and I . . ." Her voice tailed off.

He turned away to pick up the dangling reins of his horse.

"They won't get hurt, Mari," he said, with a touch of irony. "They're tough and they'll rationalise any situation so they don't get hurt—too much."

He swung up into the saddle.

"You'll be all right," he said. "One or other of us will keep you in sight and I'll send one of the dogs back."

"Kane," Mari said. "What is the rest of Bob's name?"

"Smith. They're all Smiths outback, Mari. Ralph picked him up half-crazed with thirst, and with a lost memory, about twenty years ago. Since then Bob's never left the station. . . ."

"Oh," said Mari, suddenly saddened. "Hasn't his memory ever come back?"

Again there was that touch of irony in Kane's voice.

"I imagine it has," he said. "But Bob likes it best this way. I'd take him as he comes, Mari. He's utterly trustworthy."

The horse, rearing to go, pranced a little and Kane reined him hard.

"Will you be all right?" he asked.

Mari nodded.

"Right as rain in the gully," she said.

Kane looked surprised. That was an expression she had picked up in a very short while.

Suddenly they both smiled. He dug in his heel and his horse cantered away. Two minutes later, as Mari watched, he broke into a gallop. He rode away around the loop of the creek to cross somewhere behind a small hillock of broken stone and tussock grass.

Mari sat on the trunk of a fallen tree, lying across the creek, and watched the men riding on the distant hillside. Two and three at a time the cattle were coming out of their hiding-places, hunted down by a fast horseman. Often she could hear the cries of other unseen men, and an occasional crack of a stockwhip from the far side of the hill.

At ten minutes to twelve by her watch she went to the small hut and found tea and sugar in bins by the wall. Also some tinned jam and some not-so-very-stale damper.

Not much of a lunch, she thought. To-morrow they would do better than this. She, Mari, would cut them lunches . . . or make them something. She'd think about it when she got back

to the homestead and remember to ask Kane if she could
have the keys to the storehouse.

Nothing startling happened in the muster that day, and early
in the afternoon Kane had to go back to the homestead.

" I guess that's enough for one day, Mari," he said. " I'll
take you back with me now. Bit by bit you'll get the hang of
riding . . . and the way we do things out at a muster."

They went back to the homestead, still in that single file,
Mari's horse on a lead behind Kane. At the stables he swung
off his horse and helped Mari dismount. She felt stiff now and
somehow had dwindled in size. She was sure she had bow
legs, and that her knees were nearer the ground than when she
set out.

She didn't want to be shorter ; she wanted to be taller,
somewhere up there, nearer Kane's ear.

As they walked up to the house in silence she wondered why
Kane had had to come home, but she would not have asked
him.

When they went into the homestead she asked him for the
store keys. He took her into the office, while he reached for
them from a high shelf behind the door. As he did this,
almost with the same gesture, he switched on the transceiver
set.

Do we get news at this hour? Mari wondered. She had
been on the point of asking this, when she realised that Kane
had not only handed her the keys but was holding the door for
her as if he expected her to go.

" Thank you," said Mari. " Is it all right if I use anything
from the store?"

" Yes, anything." He was still holding the door, implacable,
she felt, in his intention that she should go. As she turned
he added one of those curious, softening, kind things that
came from him at unexpected moments: "Everything's yours
in the store now, Mari. It's your home."

He turned his back, and bending forward juggled with the
dials on the radio. Clearly he expected her to go. This was a
gesture that made a dismissal of a regiment of soldiers sound
silent.

Slowly Mari walked away down the passage. How near she
was to him one moment, and how far from him the next.

She had barely arrived at the kitchen door when she remembered her intention to cultivate suntan—slowly. Suntan was something not achieved in a day. She would go and cold-cream the dust off and then suntan-cream a layer of charm on.

She sat on the back veranda and unwound the puttees from her legs. Her feet were dusty and hot, so she slipped off her shoes too. Then she padded, barefooted, up the passage to that top room.

She was passing the office door when she heard Kane's voice speaking to someone on the air. He was finishing saying something.

". . . about five-thirty last night. Thought I'd let you know. Over."

There was a click of the dial and a second's silence. Then a woman's voice.

"Thank you for calling. It was kind of you. Finish now. Closing . . ."

Miss Icy-voice?

Mari was uncertain. It was a clear, cool voice, like water in a lake on a hot day. But not icy, surely. What was it? Mari tried to capture that sound again.

Then she remembered she was standing still in the passage. I'm eavesdropping!

Horrified, she ran up the passage to her room.

Kane didn't want me to hear. He showed me the door. And I listened! Bewildered at catching herself thoughtlessly listening, puzzled that Kane should not want her to listen, curious —because after all he was married to her—Mari almost belaboured her face with cold cream.

Half an hour ago I was so happy, she thought. Now I'm not. Why did he want to come home to talk to *her* on the transceiver? Five-thirty last night? That was when we came home. He wanted to tell her he was home. He felt he had to tell her.

Mari wiped the cream away with a paper tissue. She dug into the pot and put on another layer . . . too lavish and very messy. The cold cream became tangled in her hair above the hairline.

But was that Miss Icy-voice?

The voice wasn't really icy to Mari. She tried to recapture the sound, and as she did so her heart sank a little lower.

Being absolutely and scrupulously honest, Mari had to admit to herself it was a nice voice. It was cool, and clear, a little clipped. It was a voice Mari had heard a hundred times in the West End of London.

Perhaps that's why he likes her, she thought. She's something *different*.

To-morrow . . . any time Mari wasn't out on the run, she herself would listen and listen. One day she would pick up that voice for herself. One day, when she really heard it, she might know why Kane was so silent about, yet so preoccupied with, the girl who lived on Half Moon.

" And that," said Mari to her image in the mirror as she wiped off the last layer of cream, " would not be eavesdropping. That would be the legitimate rights of a legal wife."

Mari put a dust of powder on her face, and went back down that passage to the back veranda. There was no sign of Kane, nor sound of the transceiver set in the house. As Mari picked up the keys of the storehouse from the veranda table where she had left them, she heard the sound of a horse galloping away from the homestead. She opened the wire door and stood on the wooden steps and looked out through the homestead trees. Kane was galloping away, making a good-sized cloud of dust as he went down towards the creek bed.

He hadn't said good-bye. He had good manners, so he must have been very much preoccupied with that radio conversation, Mari thought.

Mari, her shoes back on her feet, thought about this as she crossed the square to the storehouse.

It must have been a very important conversation, was her last sombre reflection on the business.

After that she had too much to do and, having been out on the run for two-thirds of the day, too little time to do it.

Ten days passed in this way. Twice Mari went out on the run with the men, the second time there was no lead on Dandie. Mari was learning to ride by herself. Twice at night, by brilliant moonlight, Uncle Ralph took her out and let her try her hand at driving a car.

Soon she became wholly absorbed in station life. She wondered a little at herself that there could be never a moment of dleness, never a moment of loneliness, when there was no one but herself and a handful of station men for thousands of square miles.

Then on the next day—it was a Tuesday morning, though for the life of her Mari couldn't have said what day in the week it was—everything changed.

First of all, her vigilance on the transceiver set had some reward, though not the one she was waiting for.

She had listened several times to the open session, though not volunteering to say anything herself. She was not a very shy person, yet oddly enough she was too shy to do that. Each time she made an attempt, her voice just wouldn't come. So she gave up trying. Some day someone would call her and then she would have to reply. She would be *in*.

She had heard all the gossip, the most interesting part being about herself. She and Kane had flown to Dampier to get married. The Pollards had arranged it all. My dear! The hotel just swam in champagne! There was a wonderful ding-dong! Kane had flown her to Perth and was lavishing everything on her. Did anyone know when they'd be back?

Mari smiled to think there was something they—those voices on the air—didn't know.

All the births, engagements, christenings and accidents were reported ; recipes were exchanged and new wardrobes were discussed.

It was wonderful fun, Mari thought, listening in. It was like reading her weekly magazine back home. Any minute now she would hear a crochet pattern. This thought made her laugh. Who ever would have thought of *hearing* crochet patterns !

She sat in front of the transceiver set, hugging her slacks-covered knees. If only Miss Icy-voice would come in !

Then suddenly a voice did come in. It was vaguely familiar, but not the cool, lake-like voice Kane had talked with.

" 9KY coming in," the voice said. " Is Ninna-Warra on the air? Please be quiet, all the rest of you, and let's hear if Ninna-Warra's there."

" Empty air," a sardonic voice said. " We tried them twice last week and again yesterday. Old Ralph's out on the run looking after the cattle while Kane's away."

Is that so? thought Mari. Twice last week? It must have been when she'd gone out with the men. And yes . . . she was out trying to do something in that garden all yesterday morning.

"Well, that's all you girls know," said the familiar voice. "Kane's been back over a week. They didn't have a honeymoon."

"'Scuse me . . ." Mari tried to say. She coughed to clear her voice.

"Was that someone coming in from Ninna-Warra? Look, be quiet, you girls, and let's listen. Come in Ninna-Warra, if you're listening."

"Yes, I'm listening," Mari managed to get out at last. Her voice squeaked and she imagined the listeners thinking—*my goodness, he did marry a child, after all.*

She coughed again to clear her throat. It was a very funny thing to be so frightened of a box. That's all this jolly transceiver was—call it what you will.

"Come again?" said the familiar voice.

"This is me," said Mari. "Mariana . . . Manners." She brought the last out triumphantly, thankful she had remembered in time not to say—Curtis.

The familiar voice was suddenly a little cool, as if now having got Mari she wasn't too enthusiastic about it.

"This is Alice Whitford from White Trees. Welcome home, Mari. I believe you and Kane really are married?"

There was such a silence on the air, except for Alice, that Mari knew everyone else was listening with held breath.

"Of course we are married," said Mari airily. "That's why we went to Dampier. It was a lovely day . . . and we had champagne for lunch."

There was laughter like a faint angel choir all around.

"One for you, Beryl," someone said.

"Don't interrupt. Go on, Alice," another said.

"How's Kane?"

"Marvellous," said Mari. "He's out riding. When are you coming to see us again, Alice?" she asked brightly.

"That's why I'm calling," Alice replied. "Your best admirer, next to Kane, of course, flew in last night. He left his horse-plant with us before he went south. You know who I mean. Allen Webster. He said you've promised us some

picnic-races over there at Ninna-Warra. Is it still on, and have
you fixed a time?"

There was a chatter of approval from the air voices at this
idea. It gave Mari time to think.

She had forgotten about that conversation with Allen. In
fact she had forgotten about Allen altogether. She hadn't
mentioned the idea to Kane or Uncle Ralph, and now she
wasn't at all certain how Kane would like it.

"I'll ask Kane to fix a date to-night," she said, then added
cautiously: "He just might be busy mustering . . . or something."

"He's got to go across and muster Half Moon for them," a
voice put in. "I heard him putting in a call late the other
night about that."

"Oh, do let's have a race-meeting over at Ninna-Warra,
Mari," a new voice said.

Half a dozen voices began to speak at once.

"Hallo, Mari, how are you? When are we going to meet
you?"

"Hallo, Mari, welcome to the north. We're dying to see
you."

"Hallo, Mari, stir that stick-in-the-mud Kane up and let's
have a party. . . ."

The sardonic voice came through again.

"Not so stick-in-the-mud when he can get married less
than a week after he meets his fiancée for the first time."

Again there was that soft chorus of laughter like a choir of
angels somewhere laughing softly in the next room.

"Please be quiet," said Alice Whitford's voice again. "And
let's get this race-meeting business straight. Mari . . . are you
listening? Allen's here and he wants to know date, time and
place. . . ."

"Oh dear," said Mari frankly. "I forgot to tell Kane about
it. Will Allen be very disappointed if we put it off for a little
while?"

"We all will," half a dozen voices seemed to say, each in a
different way.

"Allen won't be in this area that long," Alice Whitford
said. "You stir Kane up to-night when he comes in, Mari.
And don't let Kane wall you up in that hermit life he's taken
to lately himself . . ."

"We're not going to let you, Mari," another very pleasant voice put in. "If we don't hear from you, you'll hear from us. We'll pack the rear-end of our cars and all turn up at Ninna-Warra. The men can bring their racers over in horse-boxes."

CHAPTER TWELVE

Time must have been up on the open session, for suddenly a friendly male voice cut in.

"Time's up, open session. The doctor wants to come in now. Switch off, girls, all except 3KY. Come in, 3KY. Are you there, Mrs. Cookson? Doctor Heals wants to speak to you. Over."

The good-byes and last messages were cut short, for somewhere, back there at headquarters, the operator had turned his dials. Now there was only the doctor on the air.

Mari switched off and sat, her feet stretched out before her, pointing the toes of her shoes in to one another and regarding them seriously. She wasn't thinking of her shoes but of how she would break the news to Kane. They were about to have a party on Ninna-Warra. If she didn't give one then they'd all come and give one themselves.

It was at this moment she heard the droning of a plane overhead. She had heard the small plane that came over and dropped the mail, and knew this one was different. This plane was big or was flying very low.

Mari ran out, down the path to the gate. The plane, gleaming silver as its wings caught the sun rays, did indeed seem big. It was flying very low and presently it circled and came back across the homestead. Mari saw a tiny white parachute floating down to the earth in the horse paddock.

She ran out across the square, scrambled through the wire fence, and chased the tiny white handkerchief with its small carrier bringing it slowly and gently to rest on the grass.

The plane had flown out to the east before it once again made a wide circle back, and by this time Mari had un-screwed the top from the metal casket and taken out the note.

The message had been scribbled with a thin ballpoint pen.

Freight for Ninna-Warra. Bring down the utility. Five
thirsty men ready for five gallons of tea. Okay?

The plane came over again and Mari bent her head so far
back, in order to see it, she nearly fell over. Someone inside
the pilot's cabin was waving a white handkerchief to her.
Mari waved joyfully back and started to run for the homestead.

Uncle Ralph had given her two lessons in driving the
station wagon. She knew how to start and stop and the prin-
ciples of driving in top gear. But dear heaven! How did she
get the utility backwards out of the shed?

Her beautiful furniture, her curtains and tea-towels and
carpets for the passage and living-room had come. Not to
mention a new dress and two new pairs of slacks. Cotton
ones . . . God be praised. Five thirsty men wanted tea, and
Mari was going to drive that utility truck down to the airstrip
or die in the attempt.

" And I'm not going to die," she added.

She raced into her room and clapped the white linen hat
on her head, then to the kitchen, and put the biggest kettle on
at low heat. She snapped her fingers for Laddie, the kelpie dog
left at home to mind her, and together they raced to the big
galvanised-iron sheds that housed the station cars and trucks.
The small utility was parked in by the jeep. So it had to be
the big utility truck.

" Jump up in the front seat," Mari told Laddie, " and for
goodness' sake don't talk while I think. I need *concentration*."

The first time Uncle Ralph had taken her out to give her a
driving lesson Kane had remarked dryly: " The best way to
learn to drive is to have to go somewhere urgently. Then get
in and drive." He'd been joking. To Mari's courage-of-youth
it had sounded like sense.

She started up the truck without any difficulty, but she
stalled twice after she had found the reverse gear and before
she got the truck rolling out smoothly.

" All right, Laddie, I heard you the first time," Mari said.
The dog, tongue lolling, sheer joy oozing through his short-

haired skin, had given a muffled woof with each jerk. "Let's take it slowly. Panic never got us anywhere in a hurry."

The dog's tail agreed, with a thump, and presently Mari had the truck well out from the shed. Then followed a few minor fumbles while she moved the gear out of reverse and into first. Then turning the steering-wheel cautiously, as she gradually moved forward and round, Mari was on her way. She apologised to Laddie each time she took a bump instead of the smoother course down the wide red track and across the paddocks to where the big silver metal bird was lying, near the iron shed, waiting for her.

Men were already out of the plane, its side open, lifting parcels and small wooden crates. They gave a cheer when she pulled up the truck . . . with just a little too much brake.

"Say, Mrs. Manners," the pilot said, "anyone 'ud think you've never driven a truck before the way you slammed on those brakes. Good job you didn't take the plane in your stride."

An hour later they were all sitting on the homestead veranda relaxing, feet out before them, cigarettes in their hands and airline caps on the floor by their chairs.

They had brought up most of the precious crates in the truck, had had tea and sandwiches, tinned fruit and Mari's cakes, and heard the tale of Mari never having driven a truck before.

Mari didn't know which of them had laughed most as she reported the things she had said to Laddie, and the things Laddie had said to her.

"But I got there," she said defensively as they looked at her half in admiration, half in amusement.

"You sure did!" one said. "All but the plane and all."

Mari, still conscious of that order . . . five gallons of tea . . . was certain they had not had enough. She was thrilled to have so much company, each member seeming to treat her as if she was either a *prima donna* or this year's most amusing hostess. She had gone back to the kitchen and boiled up more kettles of water and had just brought out the replenished teapot.

She stood looking at them, her feet slightly apart, the teapot in her hand and her best white wide-brimmed straw hat on her head.

She had been telling them about her buying spree in Perth. This was because she had bullied them into bringing everything from the plane they could cram into the truck. She couldn't open the crates to demonstrate the beauty of her purchases because of the necessity to provide those five gallons of tea . . . but she had gone into her room and brought out the new hat, her best one, and shown it to them.

" The loveliest hat I ever saw," she said.

They had roared with laughter, not at the hat but at the supposition that a girl from London had found the loveliest hat in the antipodes.

Mari had put it on top of her head for safety while she had taken in the teapot and replenished it. She was unconscious of her slim slacks-clad figure, and the pony-tail of hair that hung under the gala-party hat. She was only thinking of how happy she felt with this all-male audience which was so appreciative of her tea-making and had pronounced her sandwiches and cakes the best they'd ever eaten.

She stood there, her back to the veranda steps, her feet apart, her hat on her head and the teapot in her hand.

" You've only had three gallons so far," Mari said reproachfully and they greeted this with a burst of laughter.

At that moment Kane came along the path, his brown dust-covered figure suddenly taking up all the distance between the veranda floorboards and the roof. He looked at the scene with a restrained kind of astonishment.

Mari turned and smiled at him—from under the hat, and over the teapot.

" I have company," she said. " They brought my things from Perth."

Slowly the five men were straightening themselves from the veranda railings, or climbing to their feet, according to where they were relaxing when Kane appeared.

" Hiya, Kane! How are you doing?" the pilot said and he came forward.

Kane seemed to ease suddenly, and a minute later he was smiling, shaking hands, then chatting with all the men. Mari put the teapot on the table.

" I'll go and get another cup and saucer, Kane," she said.

She would make some more sandwiches too, but she didn't mention this.

Kane looked at her speculatively.

"Were you going somewhere, Mari?" he asked.

"Going somewhere?" Mari looked astonished. "Where would I go?"

"You have your hat on."

Suddenly Mari felt abashed. How silly she must have looked. She had forgotten her hat, and in any event she would never be able to explain to Kane *why* she had it on. How silly it must have looked with her white cotton blouse and slacks and flattie shoes. Not to mention the way her hair was done.

She took the hat off. "I'd forgotten it. 'Scuse me and I'll get that cup. . . ."

She ran inside, and, standing in her room in front of the mirror, put her hat on again. How funny it looked. No, not funny . . . silly. If Kane had been there when she'd been telling the airmen about it he would have known it wasn't silly. But now . . . coming in like that . . .

Somehow Mari felt she had reverted to childhood again and Kane had caught her being childish.

Why couldn't she learn to do her hair up and keep it up?

Only the thought of those crates and those many brown cardboard boxes, piled up below the veranda steps, kept her spirits up. Mari hadn't known that air-pilots were not necessarily expected to help the men unload a plane and deliver the goods to the station doorstep, but this pilot had been ready to do anything chivalrous for a very charming little person who had been unafraid of trucks, lonely station homesteads, and who thought heaven was here because she had some new furniture and a carpet for the hall.

About time someone arrived, he had thought privately, to brighten up that barn of Ninna-Warra.

He also had wondered where on earth Kane Manners had got himself this peach. But then, he had supposed, Kane Manners with his looks and his reputation as a crack horseman and cattleman might be reckoned to get himself the pick of peaches anyway. He was that kind of a feller.

Another hour passed and the airmen had gone back to their

plane, this time Kane driving them down in the station wagon.

Mari had been a little subdued and a little more formal while they drank fresh tea with Kane, then she had excused herself on the plea that something had to be thought about dinner to-night.

When she heard the sound of the plane zooming towards the homestead again she ran out on to the station square to wave farewell. She could see the handkerchief waving again inside the pilot's cabin and others from the small portholes in the side of the plane. She was not to know that the pilot had taken off with the wind instead of into it so that he could fly across the homestead for that farewell salute.

Kane, who knew all the usages of flying in the north, was thoughtful as he drove back to the homestead. He had a picture in his mind of Mari standing there on the veranda, the teapot in her hand, her big hat on her head, and the men laughing in sheer delight at her company. He pushed his hat farther back on his head, whistled silently between his teeth His eyes, half-closed because of the dust haze, were without expression.

He put the station wagon back in the shed; walked round to the horse-yard where he had left his horse. He stood thoughtfully a moment, swinging the ends of the reins in his hand. Then he put his foot in the stirrup, mounted and rode away down to the creek bed.

Mari, from behind the wire screen of the back veranda, watched him go.

If only he had come up to the house and said good-bye to her first, it would have added happiness to a very full day.

That evening Mari was carefully dressed, her hair more matronly than Kane's grandmother.

He smiled at her when he came in. He was on his way to the bathroom and was hanging his hat and stockwhip on the veranda pegs when Mari came through the kitchen door. She hoped he would admire her appearance, she wanted him to feel happy about the prospects of doing-over the homestead now the wherewithal had arrived: and be crazy about the aromatic smell of a very good dinner that was stealing from the kitchen. She hoped, but wasn't very sanguine. Somehow she sensed Kane had not exactly approved of the

fun she had been having with the airmen on the front
veranda. Perhaps they all ought to have been more dignified!

Kane latched the whip on to the wall peg and turned his
head.

"You drove that truck down to the airstrip?" he said.

"Yes," Mari said. "Well . . . you see . . . someone had to
go and get them. We couldn't leave the crates down there in
the sun and we couldn't *not* give them tea, could we?"

He looked at her, as if trying to take her in, not her words.

"Did you hit anything?" he asked.

"Oh no. The truck's quite all right, Kane. I didn't even
put a scratch on it."

His face relaxed, not because of the absence of scratches on
the truck but because he saw that Mari misunderstood his
question.

"A scratch or a bump doesn't mean anything on a station,
Mari," he said gently. "We've ways of fixing those things
here. I would have been worried if I'd known you'd taken the
truck . . . or any car for that matter . . . with so little experience. You might have had an accident."

"I didn't," said Mari reassuringly. "I'm sound in wind
and limb, and so is Laddie. He came with me. He gave me
unwanted advice, in fact."

Kane took the makings of a cigarette from his pocket.

"Weren't you nervous?" he asked. He looked up quickly,
his grey eyes curious, penetrating.

"No," said Mari, surprised. "I knew *how* to do it. Uncle
Ralph told me. And you said, Kane—the best way to learn to
drive a car is to have to go somewhere urgently, and get in
and drive. Besides, there isn't any traffic on a station, is
there?"

Kane struck a match and lit his cigarette. Through the
smoke Mari could see he was smiling. He wasn't angry about
the truck. He was pleased because she'd driven it down to the
plane. He had had that puzzled look because he hadn't
thought she'd have the sense to do it. It still didn't occur to
Mari that it took courage.

Now was the time, Mari thought, to cash in on the fact that
for once he was pleased.

"I have one of those new dresses on," she said. "Do you
like my hair this way, Kane?"

He quickly put up his hand and drew on his cigarette.

"Very much," he said. He turned away, as if to go for his shower, not easy or willing to get into such a personal conversation.

"Kane. . . ." Mari pleaded. "I've had such a marvellous day. It wasn't just the airmen, and all my things coming." She drew in a breath. "I talked on the air to-day. I wasn't game to do that before. It took real courage."

Driving the truck was nothing . . . talking on the air was everything. She wanted Kane's approbation.

He stopped still, suddenly. He turned and looked at her.

"Who did you talk to?" he asked abruptly.

"Alice Whitford. All the voices. Kane, they want to come over here to meet me. Allen Webster is over at White Trees with his horses. We could have a race-picnic, or something . . . that's what you call it, isn't it . . .?"

Her voice tailed away in the face of the sudden deep anger in Kane's eyes.

He threw his cigarette on the ground and put his foot on it.

"They invited themselves?" he asked incredulously. "They know I don't entertain on Ninna-Warra. Or did *you* ask them, Mari?"

Mari felt her balloon of happiness slowly deflating.

"It was my idea first," she said quietly. "I asked Allen Webster when I was having dinner with him . . . in that hotel. I had forgotten about it. . . ." She stopped, then went on quickly, "And I would like to meet my neighbours," she persisted stoically.

Driving the truck and talking on the air was nothing to *this*. She lifted her head and looked at the kitchen door.

"*Oh!* That's my pie burning!" she wailed as she turned to run.

Kane caught her by the shoulder and spun her round. He held one shoulder, the knuckles of his hand turning white where he gripped it in his anger.

"Listen, Mari. I am sorry to disappoint you. I thought you understood there would be no goings-and-comings on Ninna-Warra. That was why I married you. With you single, free, I had no hope of running the cattle and watching where you were, of keeping you a *prisoner*. . . ."

The fateful words were out, and Kane, realising himself

their portent, suddenly took a pull on his anger. He dropped
his hand from Mari's shoulder.

Mari was so shocked she couldn't think of what to say. She
drew in a breath.

" Excuse me, Kane . ." she said at length. " My *pie* . . ."

" The damn' thing can burn," said Kane, speaking quietly,
drawling with controlled anger. " I'll have to explain this
thing to you once and for all."

" After I've taken my pie out of the oven," Mari said with
dignity. " Excuse me, please."

She walked away to the kitchen.

The word " prisoner " kept ringing in her head. Why should
he want to keep her a prisoner? Why keep himself a prisoner
here on Ninna-Warra?

Yet he went to Half Moon. Next week he was going to
Half Moon to muster their cattle for them!

Mari took the pie out of the oven and set it on the rack to
cool. She stood looking at it with eyes that didn't see the edge
of charring on the crust.

That girl on Half Moon! Everyone on the air knew that
Kane was married. That girl must know too. He'd spoken to
her on the air himself. He wasn't open for competition.

She heard Kane come along the veranda and into the
kitchen doorway.

" Mari," he said quietly. " Come out here and sit on the
veranda. I'm sorry I was so abrupt with you. I want to
explain something to you. . . ."

Mari pushed her hair back with one hand. She turned
round, half sad, half defeated.

" All right, Kane," she said. " I'm sorry I have to have a
thing explained to me twice." She had reached the door by
this time. She looked at him with sad sea-blue eyes. They had
a curious effect on Kane, for he was no longer angry. Once
again he had that troubled look of concern.

" Sit here, Mari," he said. He held one of the casual cane
chairs while she sat down. He pulled an upright chair for
himself. He sat at the side of her, his chair drawn forward
so he could see her. Unexpectedly he picked up her hand,
turned it palm upwards and sat looking at it.

Mari made no attempt to draw her hand away. She herself
sat looking at it, then at his dark head, bent because he was

looking down. His hair was very dark, and thick too. It made Mari feel as if she wanted to take her hand away from Kane and touch his hair. This she couldn't do because he had said exactly what she was . . . a prisoner.

He looked up and caught the expression in her eyes, but she did not change it because he was looking at her. Mari believed in the truth and he could read it in her face, if he wanted to. It wouldn't get her anywhere, anyhow. Not now.

"Mari," Kane said steadily, "are you listening to me? Then take that far-away look out of your eyes and pay attention. What I've got to say is important."

She nodded.

"I'm listening," she said.

"When I leased out Half Moon I did so on the undertaking I would keep Ninna-Warra free from visitors and close it as a through-route from other stations. Do you understand what that means?"

"Yes. I was a visitor so I had to be turned into something else to make my presence acceptable to the people on Half Moon. But why, Kane? Are they so important? Why did you have to lease it? Was there such a lot of money to make out of it?"

She couldn't quite believe Kane had sold his freedom, and his neighbours' right to drive their stock through his stations, for money. And she didn't believe it.

Kane's mouth was a straight line.

"There was money in it, Mari," he said at length. "Shall we leave it at that?"

"No," said Mari. "I don't believe you would do all that for money. You're not that kind of person."

He curled, then uncurled, the fingers of her unresisting hand.

"Nevertheless . . ." He stopped short and looked up at her. "Thank you for having faith in me," he said unexpectedly. "That was rather nice of you, Mari."

"I'm a nice person," she said, unsmiling.

It was Kane who smiled this time, wryly.

"I should exchange the honour of confidence," he said. "The fact is, Mari, the Raywoods are experimenting over there at Half Moon. They're the kind of people who don't want interference, don't want interruption, and have no interest in social relationships whatever. You must believe me when I tell you that."

He paused. Mari watched him unwaveringly. That much might be true, she thought, but in a minute he would tell something that wasn't quite the truth. It would be because he didn't want her to know what that truth was. But she would pretend to believe him. Otherwise life here, which to-day had seemed such fun, would be intolerable.

He spoke very slowly now, the quiet drawl steady with purpose and meaning.

"I leased out Half Moon by contract on that undertaking. I am responsible *at law* to maintain that contract, whether you like it, or I like it, or the people of the north like it. *And—that—I—shall—do.*"

For love? Or money?

"I see," Mari said aloud.

He closed her fingers and held her hand curled, in his own hand.

"You have a thousand square miles of station run here, Mari," he said. "You may roam every inch of it. I will do everything in my power to teach you everything you want to know about a cattle run, and see that you join in everything. If you are interested in it, and like the way of life, you need never have a dull moment. Ralph, and my men, have a full life here. They don't need outsiders. . . . But you may not go off the run," he went on. Then added, "And I won't let anyone from outside on it."

There was silence on the veranda. It was sundown and everything on the station was wrapped in that sundown quiet. Not a leaf in the eucalypts stirred, not a tree-nut dropped. The dogs, lying prone out there on the gravel square, their noses on their paws, did not stir. They too seemed to know and understand that Kane meant what he said.

"Is that clear, Mari?" he said quietly.

She nodded.

He released his grip on her hand, let her fingers uncoil, and lifting her hand held it against his cheek.

Then abruptly he let it go and stood up.

"If I don't have that shower Ralph will be in to beat me to it," he said.

Mari stood up too.

" And my dinner will be spoiled," she said quietly.

They stared at one another, then Kane turned on his heel and walked away.

Kane shut the office door that night when he tuned in on the transceiver. Mari knew it was to tell the Whitfords . . . and the people of the air . . . that there would be no party on Ninna-Warra. And he would do it in no uncertain terms.

CHAPTER THIRTEEN

Mari, in her excitement at the arrival of the airmen and the air-freight, had overlooked the small canvas mailbag.

It wasn't until breakfast the next morning that she knew there were letters for her. Apart from the radio telegram about her father's death, this was the first news she had received from home.

She was up very early these days and had come to love the pale grey light that followed the false dawn ; and the scent of the dried grass and fallen gum leaves which was strongest before the powerful sun took everything, including colour, out of the garden.

She was always in the kitchen before the men now, break-fast really on the way by the time they appeared. Mari, with a certain pleasure in beating the clock, always timed her sizzling bacon or carefully grilled steaks for sunrise.

How exact those men were! They were never early, never late. She could hear the parade to the bathroom, the thump of boots as they were pulled on, the last-minute pacing of a room where one or other moved from wardrobe to mirror to door. Then, as the sun came up—a yellow streak, then an orange blaze on the east window of the kitchen—they came in.

They came in spruced and alert, fresh from showers, their hair a little damp ; Bob, with early-morning dust on his shoes because he slept in his own cottage across the gravel square. They carried with them the air of world-management as they came in. A cattle station was a world of its own. Their world.

True, they didn't talk much in the mornings, but then there wasn't one of them that talked much anyway. They worked

hard out on the run all day, they came in at sundown fo
dinner, and everyone was in bed early.

The men had learned to appreciate Mari's cooking and tak
pleasure in her shining house. Mari kept flowers—strange
odd, colourless bush flowers—in those painted jars. Not fo
the world would she have had Uncle Ralph or Bob think thei
vases fell short of the loveliest and most artistic. One by on
she might replace them, but not now. It would be some tim
in the future when one by one Uncle Ralph and Bob ha
forgotten them.

On this morning, the day after the arrival of the freigh
plane, Mari found two letters waiting for her on the kitche
table.

Mari had gone to bed first last night and had turned ou
the light but had not gone to sleep until long after she ha
heard Kane go to bed. But he would never know that.

She pounced on the letters with joy, quickly slit the envel
opes open with the bread knife, then turned to put on th
breakfast before giving herself up to news from home. Mai
and the early-morning feeling, made it impossible for Mari t
go on feeling angry with Kane, or any creature. Anger ha
gone with sleep.

The kettle had come to the boil and was turned down on th
low heat, the steaks were on the griller, the bread cut ready fo
the toaster, before she dared to pull the letters from thei
envelopes.

In a stillborn kind of way she hoped one would be fron
Robert. She knew now that she and Robert had never really
known what love was. They had been " steady "—a substitute
for love—and they had believed in its false identity. Some
echo of that past affection could still be heard in the deepe
part of her heart. She wanted to know that all was well with
him and that he wished that all would be well with her.

She was disappointed. The first letter was from Mrs. Alton
Mari read it quickly.

Mrs. Alton was delighted that dear Mari had found the
right man. Of course she had known all along that Mr. Right
would turn up ; that the feeling between her Robert and Mari
was nothing more than boy-and-girl friendship. How right
they had all been, hadn't they? She did hope dear Mari was
well. Robert was still with his uncle in Edinburgh and was

getting on famously in the bookshop. He wrote twice a week. He was getting on with his study too . . . making ready for the opening of term! It was so sad about her father. The house next door with the new people in it didn't look the same. . . .

The second envelope contained a joint letter written by some of Mari's friends. It rejoiced at her marriage but said how sorry they were dear old Mr. Curtis had gone. Would Mari write and tell them all about a cattle station?

All? thought Mari, part gladdened, part saddened, by her mail. I wish I knew.

Kane was coming through the door for his breakfast as she put her letters back in their envelopes.

"You found your mail, Mari?" he asked.

"Yes, thank you," she said. "One from my friends and one from the Altons next door."

Uncle Ralph had come through the door now and he heard this last.

"Those people next door!" he said gruffly. "No nonsense from that young man of theirs, I hope." He looked at Mari under bristling eyebrows. "That young-fellow-me-lad's missed the bucket. If he'd wanted you, Mari, he should have been a shade faster on the draw."

Mari could have laughed.

"Why, Uncle Ralph . . ." she said. She had been going to say, "You jolly well saw to it he wasn't faster on the draw," but she caught sight of Kane's face. He was watching her, not exactly intently, but as if what she said, or was going to say, mattered.

"Never mind about Robert now," she said soberly, and turned back to the stove.

"Mari," Kane's voice said quietly from behind her, "I'll stay in this morning and open up those crates for you."

Mari whirled round.

"Thank you, Kane," she said. "That's kind of you. But please not. You'd hate to lose a day's work on the run, and we can do a bit each night. If you'd just open the one that has the sewing-machine I could get on with the curtains. They take the longest."

"No need to stay in," said Bob, who spoke once in a blue moon and then only if it was to say something very important. "The natives will be in. They're on the track now."

Nobody asked Bob how he knew. Generally it was the natives only who knew—by some strange bush instinct—about an event hours before it happened. Bob, who must have lived all his life in the outback, probably with natives, knew as much as any of them.

Neither Kane nor Uncle Ralph questioned him, so Mari knew he must be right. They were all getting on with their breakfast and only talking in flashes between long gastronomical silences.

" You'll have some help now, Mari," Kane said. " I'll stay in till they arrive. Then I'll introduce you."

Breakfast over and the washing up and kitchen sweeping done, Mari went out to the front veranda, where Kane was already ripping the boards from the tops of the wooden cases. The sewing-machine, first unpacked, stood shining and new in its pristine glory, on the table where yesterday she had served tea to the airmen.

" Oh, isn't it a darling!" said Mari joyfully. " Now I'll be able to make my own clothes as well as do curtains and things."

Kane looked up.

" You make your own clothes, Mari?" he asked.

" Of course," she said. " I've done that since I was fifteen. I had to. I didn't have very much money, you know. Only pocket-money."

" Pocket-money as a reward for housekeeping?" Kane said quietly, wrenching a board away from the case. He looked up at her. " Were you and Robert going to marry on *pocket-money*?"

" You don't understand," Mari said. " You can do it if you live at home. Two can live as cheaply as one."

" On pocket-money?" asked Kane again.

" Yes, on pocket-money. You see . . ." Suddenly she realised Kane was looking at her and the expression in his eyes was sardonic.

" I expect that is what is called ' marrying for love '?" he asked.

" Well, it's quite a good excuse for getting married," Mari said flatly. Then she realised this conversation was getting on to dangerous subjects. Fortunately, over Kane's shoulder, she

could see a file of natives, coming over the far rise of the
paddock towards the homestead.

"Here they come now," she said.

Kane turned round.

"About time too!" He put down his tools, and without
speaking again went down the path, through the gate and out
towards the paddock.

He'd gone to meet them in spite of his exasperation!

The natives began to shout and wave joyously. Quite
clearly they were excited at seeing the boss coming towards
them, and at being home again: walkabout over.

Once again Mari had quite a day of it. First there was a
ding-dong about giving the natives stores of flour, sugar and
tea from the storehouse ; new gingham dresses for the women
and girls, short drill trousers for the boys and long drill
trousers and shirts for the men.

"What did they do with their old clothes?" she asked Kane
as she helped him at the long trestle table set up near the
storehouse for this purpose.

"They give them away to their relations out in the bush.
Half this flour, tea and sugar will go the same way. That's
their tribal law."

Later there was great camp-fire building down along the
creek bed, much singing and laughter-making. By midday
the men had put on their new working clothes and big
sombrero hats, caught their horses in the outer horse-paddock,
and ridden away with Kane. The women stayed with their
children down by the camp, waiting for Mari to make the first
approach.

They were shy at first but full of kindness and goodwill,
when Mari did at last go down to make a closer acquaintance.

She thought the children marvellous, and said so. The
lubras shrieked with delight at this verdict and then one
brought out her greatest treasures. Even on walkabout she
had carried them, stored in a kangaroo-skin dilly-bag and
hidden in a rock crevice somewhere near their hunting
grounds. These treasures were vivid-coloured paintings done
by a youth . . . now initiated into the tribe and very much the
subject of the recent corroborees on walkabout.

Mari thought they were the most colourful paintings she had ever seen. When she came to think about it, the brilliant greens and blues, the glaring yellows and reds, were the true colours of the broken hills beyond the creek.

One painting in particular caught her attention. It was a steep, rock-strewn slope, like a desert glacier, leading up into a wide gap in the hills between sheer, unbroken rock cliffs. The only evidence of life was a single pencil-slim white-trunked tree.

That lonely tree, sparse of leaf and incredibly white against the brilliant rock background, was very striking to Mari.

"That fella Half Moon," the proud mother said to Mari.

"What do you mean, Half Moon?" Mari asked, looking up. Those magic words were calculated to catch her attention anywhere.

"Youi, Missus. This track bin way-up Half Moon." She pointed to the wide rock-strewn rise between the rock cliff in the picture, and giggled. "Half Moon bin way up on top, Missus. Plenty flat up there. All good cattle country."

"Is that the only way up?"

"Youi. All roun' Half Moon those fella rocks." The lubra pointed to the cliffs on either side of the rock road. "Plenty blackfella climb up, alla-same plenty hard. Too much trouble. . . ." She burst into a shriek of laughter and her companions joined her.

"No good-fella cattle come down there," she said. "Only come down that fella Big Fall."

"Big Fall?" queried Mari.

Again the finger pointed to the rocky track.

"That fella Big Fall. Cattle come down there a'ri. No other track from Half Moon."

"And the other stations on the other side of Half Moon?" Mari asked.

"Two tracks in there from White Trees," the lubra said. "Some time Bill Whitford bin brung cattle in there and bin come out down Big Fall. No more. Boss, he close up those tracks other side Half Moon. Big grass up there, Missus. Alla-same very rich place Half Moon."

Mari handed back the picture.

How strange it all was, she thought. There on the top of a

wide plateau was grass; beautiful cattle country. There were
two ways in from the Whitfords' station on the other side, and
only one way—Big Fall—out on this side. Kane had given it
up, and closed the way to the station owners beyond.

All for money?

It couldn't be. Somehow, something about Kane belied the
idea.

As Mari went back to the homestead she thought about that
picture with its formidable gateway from a track so steep and
rocky that no one would want to run up and down it just for
fun. The single tree stood finger-pointing by the side of the
track like a signpost.

"That fella ghost-gum," the native woman had said. Then
she had pointed to clumps of gums along the stock route
across the plains. "That fella ghost-gum alla-same," she had
said.

Mari could see the reason for the strange name. The white
trunks of the trees stood out, an anachronism in a world of
brown, grey and red.

The homecoming of the natives had woken the homestead to
a new life. The women and their children, dressed in their
new colourful ginghams, came up to the homestead to see
what went on with those crates and parcels still littering the
front veranda. They shrieked with delight as each article
was unwrapped. They fingered the materials and lovingly
stroked the new furniture. The children, desperately shy, kept
cover behind their mothers' skirts, but their eyes rounded so
much that Mari thought they might pop right out at any
moment.

Kane had warned her not to hustle anyone into helping her.

"Give them time to get to know you," he said. "In spite
of their fun-making and giggles they're a very shy people.
Just be friendly, then one morning you'll find one or two of
them waiting on the back veranda when you get up. After
that you won't have any difficulty."

Mari actually didn't have any difficulty from the very next
day. The new blondwood furniture and the carpets were too
much for the younger women. They wanted to see where it
was to go, and by eleven o'clock that day Mari had the old

furniture out on the side veranda and the passage carpet and living-room carpet down. By mid-afternoon the new furniture was in its place. Many hands made the work quick and easy.

True, Mari had had difficulty in moving tables and chairs through the host of gingham-clad bodies pattering all over the homestead, but everything was worth it in the end, for the excitement and admiration of her new friends knew no bounds.

Next morning Kane, seeing Mari's immediate success with the homecomers, gave her some more advice. It was still dark when she had got up, and there were three young women waiting for her on the veranda.

"You gibit me broom, Missus. I sweep up all that mess," one said.

"I make alla-same pretty good bread, Missus," another said, laughing merrily as if this was a funny thing to do and not a useful one.

"You gibit me cloes, Missus. I wash um," said a third. So they'd worked it all out down there at the camp! Here came a housemaid, a bread-maker and a laundress!

Kane, also up very early, had come through the passage at the sound of voices.

"All right, you girls," he said. "Scatter! Missus will talk to you after breakfast."

"Yes, Boss!" They fled happily in a cloud of giggles across the station square.

"They're wonderful friends and allies, Mari," Kane said. "Once they know you, and take to you. But I'm afraid you'll have to train them. Before you came they had the run of the homestead and did things their own way." He paused and then added, "Not always *our* way."

"I know. Uncle Ralph told me," Mari said. The grey light was stealing across the eastern sky and she could see Kane's tall, lithe body silhouetted dark against the lightening sky outside. "That's why he brought me," she added. She had been tempted to go on and say, *He wanted a housekeeper*, but she felt that the time had arrived when Uncle Ralph's ambitions in the home had better be forgotten. After all, they had come true, hadn't they?

"It mightn't be easy," Kane went on. Then suddenly his face creased in an unexpected smile. "I expect I'm wrong.

Anything's easy to a girl who can drive a truck down a bad track after her second lesson in car driving."

Mari was surprised that that little feat had extracted admiration from Kane. Apparently it had. She flushed, mostly because she was pleased but partly because his sudden smile had stirred again a sense of longing, and a hidden imp of loneliness.

Sometimes Mari had the thought that all the fun of running a homestead, all the excitement of occasional rides out on the run, all the pride in her cookery, were together one big front to hide something else inside her. That something was a capacity to be unhappy if she didn't work madly at the business of being house-proud and station-curious.

This was one of those moments of being aware of something behind her own façade. It was because of Kane, standing brown and tall, his spurs jingling as he moved his feet, his smile suddenly creasing his face under that dark cap of hair.

" We'll manage," she said hastily, and fled to the kitchen. She didn't know what Kane thought about her reaction to that moment of kindness, and just now she didn't care. She had to slice bacon, halve tomatoes and trim chops for breakfast at a great pace.

" Kitty . . . she's the middle-sized one with the gap between her teeth," Uncle Ralph said at breakfast. " She's a good rider, Mari. You can take her anywhere on the run."

" More'n likely she'll take Mari," said Bob. This was the first time Bob had used Mari's Christian name. Till now he had avoided calling her anything.

Mari, in the ensuing days, found that Uncle Ralph's words were true. When she and those three girls weren't sprucing and decorating the homestead she and Kitty were out riding. The native rode barefoot and barebacked on a horse of her own. She took Mari all along the creek beds, to the billabong for a swim and up amongst the hills where they found tiny hiding-holes of fern and soft-coloured flowers in the rock crevices where water oozed from tiny underground springs.

Then came a day when a violent thunderstorm suddenly turned the gravel square into a sheet of water. Next day, when the water had dried out, there were green shoots of

grass on the paddocks and in the shabby, neglected garden.
Two days later, beside the path near the gate, Mari found a
tiny star flower, growing face open to the sky but close to the
earth.

It was the first flower Mari had seen other than the strange
prickly grey-green bush flowers and the brilliant bougainvil-
læas, growing fairly near the homestead. It was like a flower
at home, except that its tiny stem, frail-looking at first, proved
to be wiry and almost unpickable. Not that Mari had tried to
pick the flower, but she had tentatively felt out the strength
of the reed-like leaves that had appeared so miraculously with
the flower.

She had not forgotten the primroses and violets and other
modest flowers of her own home, but suddenly this small
flower, so pale a blue it was almost white, seemed to her to be
the sweetest of them all.

Half a dozen times a day Mari went to look at it, afraid the
scorching heat of the sun would kill it.

"What is it, Kitty?" she asked.

"That fella Drage," Kitty said. "Boss call him 'desert
daisy.' Him won't die longa time now. Lil' bit of water every
two-three day. Alla-same not too much, him die."

Mari guarded and nurtured her flower as much as she
polished and nurtured her home. Each time she went out
riding she went to look at the flower first. When she came in
she looked to see if all was well with the desert daisy before
she went into the homestead. She had shown it to Laddie,
the kelpie dog, and cautioned him never to walk there. Laddie
understood perfectly, especially as Mari had put a tiny barricade of small sticks around the plant. She didn't have to
worry about Laddie's possible misdemeanours when she and
Kitty were out riding. Laddie went with them, and would
never have been parted from his mistress without a command
from his master. Kane, and the dog he had given Mari, had
minds that thought alike.

It was on Sunday night, after late tea, that disaster befell the
desert daisy, and all but broke Mari's heart.

Kane had gone down to the gate to let the dogs out into the
square and Mari had run down the veranda steps to join him
because Kane had forgotten to give Laddie the one command

that meant he might leave his mistress. Laddie had stood irresolute on the path, looking first after his master, then uneasily backwards at his mistress sitting on the veranda.

Mari, looking up, saw Kane's retreating back and Laddie's indecision. She had jumped up and run down the path, calling Laddie as she went.

"It's all right, Laddie," she said. "You can go. Kane just forgot to tell you specially. . . ."

Kane had nearly reached the gate when he realised something was going on behind him. He turned round, as Laddie, released from bondage, bounded at his master. It was almost as if he had to throw his whole weight at Kane to remind him that he too had to give the word of command. Kane, beset by two dogs jumping up at him, stepped back. The tiny stick barricade around the desert daisy cracked and crumbled under his boot, his heel rested on the face of the flower.

"Kane!" Mari cried. Suddenly she was at him, pushing him away, pummelling his chest with small clenched fists.

"My flower . . ." she was trying to say, but the words choked with sudden desperately unhappy sobs in her throat.

Kane, not comprehending what had happened, caught her fists in his two hands and held her tight. Mari struggled to free herself.

"You've killed it . . . you've killed it," she cried, still unable to see the flower for Kane's tall, wide-shouldered body.

"Steady, Mari!" he said, his voice suddenly commanding, sharp and staccato.

Mari leaned forward, her head hitting Kane's shoulder. Her whole frame was wracked with sobs, the tears ran wildly down her cheeks.

Uncle Ralph, thinking something catastrophic had happened, came down the path.

"Mari . . . Mari girl," he said, puzzled, stooping and twisting sideways to try and see into her face where it was hidden against Kane's chest. "What's the matter, lass?"

"My flower," she sobbed. "He's got his foot on it."

Kane dropped Mari's wrists and one arm went round her shoulders tightly. Her head still stayed buried in his shirt, one freed hand was clenched, beating a slow desperate tattoo against his shoulder. Kane, still holding Mari tightly in the circle of his arm, stepped aside. He turned his head and looked down at the ground. The little blue-white flower was indeed flattened. It lay sick and stricken in a shambles of broken sticks.

Uncle Ralph bent down and peered at the flower.

" I don't know so much," he said judicially. " It might come all right again. Takes a lot to kill those daisy things. They look weak, but by golly, they're strong. Last out the Dry they will, if they get a drop of rain at the right time."

Kane caught Mari's wrist again and attempted to lift her away from him so that she could collect herself . . . and to see himself why so small a thing should cause such a breakdown in Mari.

He was not a flower-conscious man, but he was prepared to understand that flowers were things that meant a lot to women. But Mari's tears, her heartbroken sobs, were something more than the near-destruction of a flower!

Mari would not be lifted away. She could not bear to show her tear-stricken face to Kane or Uncle Ralph or even the two dogs, sitting, tongues lolling, the picture of misery themselves. She found herself clinging to Kane, where a moment ago he had had to hold her forcibly.

" Now look here, Mari." Uncle Ralph said in his most avuncular voice, " you've too much sense to be crying over a flower that maybe's not going to die after all. Just pull yourself together, lass, and have a look."

Mari lifted her head and gradually disentangled herself from Kane's arms. Somehow, she didn't know quite how, she had Kane's handkerchief in her hand. She wiped her eyes, and, still keeping her head down-bent, looked at the flower. She knelt down and lifted the crushed leaves that radiated from its tiny earthbound stem.

They, by being lifted, lifted the small face of the flower with them.

" It was so sweet," she said. " It was tiny and newborn and fresh and young. . . ."

She looked up at Kane and said with bitter, sad reproach: " I hate you!"

CHAPTER FOURTEEN

Suddenly Mari too understood what it was all about. The flower was young and newborn and it had been hers. It had been a compensation for something else unuttered in her heart.

Marriage was only the opening of a book, and the next chapter should have been the hope of children. Mari suddenly was aware of all the biological complications of getting married. Once she had opened the book, she wanted to go on and turn every leaf, know every chapter.

Her marriage with Kane would be childless if she could not somehow win his love. There were signs of winning his kindness—but then he was that kind of man—but absolutely no signs of winning his love at all.

She straightened herself and stood up.

"I'm sorry. I beg your pardon for saying that," she said huskily and turned and went back to the veranda.

Kane let the dogs through the gate and followed Uncle Ralph back to the veranda.

"Excuse me, I have a headache," Mari said. "I'm going inside." She went through the front door, then into her room, which was already transformed into something feminine and attractive by the new curtains, the pretty blond-coloured furniture and the latest thing in frilled candlewick bedcovers.

She stood in front of the mirror, horrified at her streaked and tear-puffed face.

"Not that it really matters," she said. "My face hasn't done a thing to help me since I came here."

Disappointed with her face, regretful for her behaviour, ashamed of her tears, she belaboured her skin with cold cream, more as a punishment than as a caress.

She wiped the cream away with a tissue, then remembered she had performed this rite with her dress still on her. She slipped her dress off, and in doing that, somehow managed to take off her other clothes without quite knowing what she was doing. Her thoughts, sad and chastened, were elsewhere. When she found herself in her bathrobe she decided she would go to bed anyway. It was not yet dark, but she couldn't go back and face Uncle Ralph and Kane on the veranda. Bob, thank goodness, had followed his usual practice and gone to his own quarters in the little cottage on the other side of the station square.

Mari padded down the carpeted passage to take her bath. For the first time since it had arrived, Mari failed to notice or feel a thrill of pleasure in the carpet under her feet.

The bath over, she went back to her room, put away her toilet things and hung out her towel to dry, then lay down on her bed, full-stretched on the cover. Mari, had she had her mind on things, would have lent out her immortal soul on lease rather than lie on her bed without turning back that beautiful, much-loved but very new bedcover.

She lay staring at the ceiling, thinking such muddled thoughts that she would never have been able to put them into words.

It wasn't just " all over a flower," she kept telling herself. It was much, much more. It was so *young*, and *new*. And it was Kane who did it . . like what he has done to *me*. But what has he done to me? Was it his fault that I came any-way?

There was a sharp tap on the door, and Mari, turning her head, saw Kane there.

He came in, taking acceptance for granted.

Mari did not stir. She was too emotionally tired, ashamed, though she wasn't sure she cared any more.

Kane sat on the side of her bed and picked up her hand. His eyes had that distant. troubled concern that Mari had seen once or twice before. She turned her face so that she could go on looking at the ceiling. Yet she did not take her hand away.

That would have been a childish thing to do.

It did not occur to Mari that Kane too might have under-stood the implications of her love for that flower, and that he too was troubled. If she had, she would have said to herself, " So what?" It didn't make any difference to the fact it was a barren marriage and this was Kane's decision.

He loved Miss Icy-voice over at Half Moon. To-morrow was Monday and he was riding over there to muster their cattle for them. He would be away a week. He would have dinner at *their* dinner-table, and eat *their* steaks . . . but not a meringue pie as good as one Mari could cook.

As a plain statement of fact, she hoped they'd be very bad cooks over there.

Childish? Yes, she knew she was childish. Maybe Kane was right, and the Altons too. She was too young to be married.

A thin shining edge of tears glistened along her lashes. Mari closed her eyes to force them back.

Not again, she told herself. We've had enough hysteria for to-day.

Kane had waited a long time in silence, watching the clouds in her troubled face. When he saw her effort to quell back those tears he put her hand down on the bedcover beside her and reached in his pocket for cigarettes and matches.

" Mari," he said, not looking at her but watching his own fingers closely as they wrapped rice paper round fine tobacco. He slitted his eyes because though he was watching his fingers he was thinking about choosing his words carefully. " I'll get the men to dig a flower garden for you. This time of the year we get occasional thunderstorms, whiskers of the first cyclones. They soften up the ground ready for the Wet."

Mari still looked at the ceiling, and meanwhile Kane had made his cigarette. He cupped his hand over a match to light it.

" When the Wet comes," he went on quietly, persistently, as if he were talking to a child who needed instruction, " the whole aspect of the plain changes. The grass comes up overnight and there are flowers as far as you can see." He paused and added more kindly, " Desert daisies, mostly."

Mari flickered her eyes, but still she said nothing.

" It is more than flowers you want, Mari," Kane said suddenly. Now her eyes went quickly, wide-open, to his face. " You want a home and a husband and children. I'm sorry I thought of you as a child. It was because you are so slight . . . and yes, in spite of your eighteen years . . . just a little naïve. But you are a woman all the same, and those things . . . your very young figure, your pretty soft face and even that naïvety . . . make you a very attractive woman."

Mari's eyes were dark and questioning. What did he mean? She was not so naïve as all that! Was he going to tell her that mere physical attraction was enough to call a special relationship in marriage *love*?

Oh no, Kane! she wanted to say. I learned about that sort of thing before my hair was long enough to put up on my head. We aren't children when we're sixteen or seventeen in *our* age. Maybe in yours, or your grandmothers' . . . but in our age we know what is what and what is not what . . . whether we look young and act naïve or not. You'd be surprised, but what we want is *love. In our age, anyway.*

Kane saw the expression in Mari's dark blue eyes. He smiled a little grimly.

" I was thinking," he said slowly, drawling in that effective, hard-bitten way that he used when he was saying something he meant to get through, and stay through. " I was thinking you've been tensed up ever since the mail came last week."

Not tensed, thought Mari. *Only excited because of my furniture and my curtains . . . and Kitty coming riding with me.*

" I don't think it was your friend's letter," Kane went on steadily. " I think it was the letter from your neighbour. I am sorry I was somewhat derisive about marrying-on-pocket-money. Perhaps you were right when you said nothing matters if you marry for love. Are you listening to me, Mari?"

She nodded. It occurred to her he had no idea how he was hurting her. On the other hand he might be doing that to make her understand more clearly how he felt. Sometimes you had to hurt to kill. Perhaps he sensed she had fallen in love with him, and wanted to kill that . . . very dead.

" If . . ." he said, dropping his words one at a time, like stones in a pool. " If you went back now, would this young man, this Robert, be free to marry you? I would of course set you free. Please be frank with me, Mari. Is he too tied to his studies, or do you think his parents have too strong a hold on him?"

" It doesn't matter which it is, Kane, we wouldn't get married anyway."

She couldn't bring herself to say that Robert's silence proved he had changed his mind, and the things that had happened to her had certainly changed hers.

" I see," he said. He stubbed out his cigarette on the tray on her table and picked up her hand again and held it palm upwards. For a moment there was something in the way he held his bent head, something suddenly whispering in the air that filled it with an unexpected urgency.

If only he would . . . if only he would!

All her barriers would be down. She would throw herself in his arms because she wouldn't be able to help it. A greater power than herself would be in command.

She half lifted her head from the pillow. Kane looked up and caught her eyes. He put her hand down and stood up abruptly. His eyes were quite dark.

He went to the door.

"I'll bring you a cup of tea before I go to bed," he said from the door. "It might help you to sleep better. I'm afraid I'll be gone to Half Moon when you get up in the morning, Mari. I hope you'll be all right while I'm away." There was a sudden softening in his face as he added, "I'll leave Laddie to look after you."

He went out and Mari lay on her bed, the fingers of her hands curling inwards so that the nails bit into her palms.

Stay on that raft. Stay on that raft. Some day the current will wash you up on shore.

Her hands relaxed and she turned her head into the pillow.

"Yes, but *what* current?" she asked herself sadly.

Later that night Kane came in with the promised cup of tea. Mari had taken off her beloved bedcover and folded it up. Even in the midst of what she called "dire distress" she could not bear to spoil her new possessions. Her room was lovely and she loved it. She wasn't going to have it spoiled by the fact she'd had a childish cry over a flower that Uncle Ralph had said would probably recover.

Mothers probably cried when their children had measles . . . but the children always recovered, and probably were happier for some temporary coddling.

Mari felt so much better after that cry that she decided she was up on that raft after all. There wasn't a storm brewing in the heavens or on the sea that could shake her off.

She had combed her hair, plaited it, and pinned the two plaits like a coronet over her head. That way the lumps of hair wouldn't stick into her head and keep her awake.

She had creamed her face again, more as an apology fo
the way she had done it before than bcause she thought he
face really needed it. She had added some night-cream just fo
luck.

Kane had said she had a nice soft skin.

What a lost opportunity, not to have looked coy!

Mari had reached the smiling stage. The idea of coynes
having any but an adverse effect on Kane was very funny.

I'm not doing too badly, she told herself as she slipped int
her bed, under the single cover of a sheet.

She reached up and turned off the light, then lay staring ou
of the veranda door at where the moon, early up, was alread
beginning to flood the place where Kane slept.

She couldn't see his bed but she could see the sleepout floor
It was part of him. Somehow it gave her comfort.

Oh no, she would never go home. She would never fall of
that raft. She would never leave him. Not ever!

The emotional upheaval of that tearful outburst had its reaction, however. By the time Kane came in with the tea, Mar
was asleep.

He put the small round tray on the bedside table and then
leaned over Mari to switch on her overhead light. Mari la
with her head turned into the side of the pillow, outside the
pool of light. Kane stood looking down at her for a minute.
Then he bent once again and his fingers touched her hair.

"Tea, Mari?" he said gently.

She stirred but did not open her eyes. He bent farther and
his lips brushed her forehead. Mari's eyes flew open, then
she turned her head to look up at him. He stood smiling at
her, his eyes inscrutable except for that smile . . . which didn't
seem to mean quite anything to Mari.

Then he bent down again and kissed her again on the lips.
It was one of those gentle cloud kisses, like the one he had
given her on the day when they were married. It was so sweet
that Mari closed her eyes while his lips lay on her lips. When
he lifted his head she opened her eyes. He smiled at her and
she watched him as he went to the door.

She hadn't said anything because there were no words that
would not have spoiled that kiss.

It was a gesture because he was going away to Half Moon to-morrow, perhaps. But to Mari it was very sweet.

For five days after Kane had gone to Half Moon, Mari was very busy. There was still so much to do to make the homestead into a home that sometimes she thought it would take years. She painted all the cane veranda-furniture with bright enamel paints, she made curtains for Uncle Ralph's room, the office, and that regrettable little spare room she had so hated when she had first come. That, she decided, would be a sewing-room for herself. The machine was kept busy whirring there while the other rooms in the house were being dressed up.

The hardy little desert daisy survived . . . with only two of its petals withered from the bruising it had had under Kane's heel. Meanwhile another bud had appeared and within hours it too was open, its star face looking up to the pallid blue sky.

One of Kane's stockmen, Tim Wetherby from the outcamp near the boundary, had gone with him to Half Moon along with Bob. The stockman's wife had died some years before and he always kept his small son with him at the outcamp. Andy, about eight years old, was now sent up to the main homestead to be looked after while his father was away. The natives were supposed to be looking after Andy, but Mari found herself with a new companion.

What his father hadn't taught Andy about bush-lore, the natives had taught him. Mari was very shocked to find he had had no formal education at all. He could read a little—having learned from the labels of jam and fruit tins and from occasional old and treasured newspapers passed on from boundary rider to boundary rider. When Mari tried to explain to him some of the rudiments of arithmetic she came up against a blank wall of bewilderment. Twelve pennies in one shilling, twenty shillings in one pound, meant nothing to a child who not only had never used money, he had never seen it. A tin of biscuits was something his father put down to his account at the station store. It didn't need money.

Mari decided she couldn't change the social usages of a whole race of people overnight and it might be more useful to

Andy if she took him driving. The manner in which an engine worked was more important to a small boy in Andy's position in life than a very useless pound note surely?

So driving she took him.

Kane had said she might use the station wagon . . . as she had graduated from trucks that were much harder to drive . . . and now each afternoon Mari backed the station wagon out of the shed, swung it round, like a veteran at this manœuvre packed it up with Andy, Kitty, Laddie, and a picnic basket and set off down one or other of the many tracks criss-crossing Ninna-Warra.

This to Mari was great fun. She felt, with that wagon-load of Kitty, Andy and dog, that she lived in a full world. She was crowded with people and there were a thousand things to learn about the station.

They drove from one bore to another; they took the magazines and stores out to the outcamp; one day they went fishing in the pool above the creek.

She had driven quite fearlessly many, many miles away from the homestead, feeling that each turn of the track, each small hill to be surmounted, would give her another view and show her another world. It hardly ever did this. There were only three worlds of Ninna-Warra—the grey-grassed plain with its red earth; the trees and water along the creek bed, and the broken rocky scrub hills which the men daily combed to bring the cattle in to brand, and earmark with the station clips.

Uncle Ralph was out all day, and since dinner was always ready when he came in at sundown he had a vague idea, if he thought about it at all, that Mari had been in the homestead all day. He could see curtains falling like waterfalls of flowers from the windows . . . that must have kept the lass very, very busy while Kane was away, he thought.

"Real little home-maker!" he repeated at regular intervals, addressing his puffing-billy pipe when he wasn't commenting to himself.

"She's not missing Kane too much either. Well, all to the good. A station wife's no wife at all if she doesn't understand a cattleman's like a sailor—away from home a good deal of the time."

Mari did miss Kane. The whirring machine and the long explorations with her "family" in the station wagon were her ways of doing something to stop herself missing him. She was not worrying so much at his absence as that the absence from Ninna-Warra meant his presence at Half Moon. And that meant Miss Icy-voice! She would not let herself think about what he had for dinner, or whether he slept in the homestead or in the quarters with the men: or what they used for conversation.

By eagerly mapping the terrain of Ninna-Warra she didn't give her mind time to think of anything else but the station. Strangely, it gave her a lot of pleasure. She liked Andy, loved Kitty, adored Laddie; and anyway she had company. She had fun.

She never listened in to the transceiver set. Since the evening when Kane had shut the office door while he froze everyone on the air away from the idea of a race-meeting on Ninna-Warra, Mari had been too embarrassed to renew her unseen acquaintances.

How could she tell *them* she was a prisoner, not a wife!

She had changed her mind about listening for Miss Icy-voice. Now Mari didn't want to hear her. Her voice might turn out to be nice, lake-clear and silver—a joy to Kane's ears!

It was on Saturday morning, the sixth day since Kane had gone, that Mari decided that to-day there'd be an all-day picnic.

There was something about the air of the homestead that made her feel really lonely when she got up early that morning.

Breakfast over, she started cutting slices of new-made bread, and chops from the "side"; packing small tins—one for each of them—of fruit; filling a basket with store apples and oranges and sending "the girls" scattering in search of a big billycan. To-day she would not have Thermos tea; she would have a real camp-fire. Andy and Kitty had never liked the Thermos tea, anyway.

"What for you go all day, Missus?" Kitty said. "You get plenty tired."

"Uncle Ralph is staying at the outcamp to-night so we don't have to cook dinner, Kitty. We can scramble a meal and go to bed as early as we like."

"Ralph know you go out all day?" Kitty asked, anxious.

"No. Why should he?" said Mari lightly. Then, because she was grateful for Kitty's concern, she smiled at the dark girl. "Besides, I'm with you, Kitty. Nothing can happen to me on Ninna-Warra when I'm with you."

Kitty beamed.

"An' that young fella Andy. Youi, that young fella pretty good out there in the bush. He darn near pretty good as blackfella."

She giggled and then ran barefooted across the station square to tell Andy to "clean his one-face and git that lazy Blue Grass fella fill up the station wagon. He better bin git goin' fast. Missus goin' way out round boundary to-day, for sure."

They all piled into the station wagon, Laddie and Kitty in the back seat with the picnic basket and the billy, Andy—because it was his turn to-day—up in the front seat with Mari.

Mari hadn't the slightest nervousness or trouble in driving a car now. She felt as if she had been born at the wheel. She wondered vaguely what her father would say if he could see her with her dark blue cotton slacks covering her legs as she stretched them forward to meet the clutch and accelerator, her cotton blouse with collar turned up so the sun wouldn't burn the back of her neck, her white linen hat, now a little brown, at a very outback angle over her eyes.

"Do you know what the man who went to a zoo for the first time said when he saw the giraffe, Andy?" she asked.

"No. What did he say, Mari?"

"He said—'Shucks, there ain't no such animal.' That's what my father would say if he could see me driving this car across this track and dressed up the way I am."

Andy was silent a minute, then he looked at Mari reproachfully.

"You used bad grammar," he said. "You told me not to say 'ain't'."

Mari smiled down at the small boy beside her.

"You haven't any sense of humour, Andy. And what, just for the record, is *grammar*?"

"I dunno," said Andy.

Mari burst out laughing. She saw a pothole in the track just in time to swerve the wheel and escape it. She swung back on the track while Kitty from the back seat wailed:

"You look out, Missus. You break ebry fella neck that way."

"I'll look out," said Mari soberly, having learned her lesson in careful driving for the day.

"Where we goin' up this bad fella track?" said Kitty. "This way all pothole. Boss not bin fix this road longa time. He doan use it some more."

"I want to see what's over the hill. Over there it's blue along the skyline. Perhaps it's trees. Isn't there any high bush on Ninna-Warra, Andy?"

"That's not blue," said Andy succinctly. "That's Half Moon. It's way up high. . . ."

"Half Moon . . ." said Mari under her breath.

If Kane had mustered the cattle on Half Moon and was bringing them down the Big Fall to Ninna-Warra she might meet him. Uncle Ralph had told her there was only a small mob on Half Moon, the progeny of the cattle Kane had left behind in the scrub. When he had mustered them he would bring them on to Ninna-Warra, to be branded and ear-clipped ready for the big drove west.

"Kane said he'd be away a week," Mari said musingly. "It's six days to-day. That might mean he's brought his cattle right to the boundary of the two stations."

"You more-better drive somewhere else," Kitty said from the back seat. "Boss plenty mad if any fellow go over Half Moon these days. He tell ebry black fella on the place fire-eatin' jinji up that way now. Mos' lak he oney means ebryone stay away, Missus."

"We won't go on to Half Moon," Mari said easily. "Besides, I'm the 'Missus,' Kitty. I can go and meet my husband if I want to."

Can I? she wondered. *My husband.* How sweet those words sounded!

Mari put her foot on the accelerator partly so the car could take the rise at a faster pace, partly to accelerate herself out of that momentary half-sad tenderness. She couldn't afford to feel that way . . . *ever.* That way she hurt herself.

CHAPTER FIFTEEN

They drove for just on an hour and then stopped to open a bottle of lemon juice and a bottle of cold water to mix with it. Everyone wanted a drink, including Laddie. He had water alone. Nothing sour for Laddie on a day that promised real fun! This was the farthest he had been out from the homestead since his master had set him continually at his mistress's heels.

Refreshed, they drove on for another hour. The blue that Mari had seen on the skyline was still blue, but it was the shadowed outline of hills. There was nothing yet in that soft colour to indicate the rough passage of the Big Fall or the broken cliffs of the rock that guarded it. Mari had learned enough now about the effects of distance and the continual haze that rose from the hot red ground to know that appearances could belie reality. She knew that, close up, that blue would disappear, but she was burning with curiosity as to what she would see.

She was not disobeying Kane in coming along this track. He had forbidden her to go off Ninna-Warra. He had not said she might not go to the gates of it.

Already she had learned that long before one saw a mob of bullocks one saw their dust clouds so while she drove, her eyes were narrowed under the tilted brim of her hat, longing to see a dust cloud.

The sameness of the landscape had reduced everyone in the car to silence long since, so Mari could concentrate on wishful thinking.

A quarter of an hour passed, and then Mari saw the brown ball of dust in the air which she knew was caused by something moving. Her heart leapt, and then gradually subsided to near-disappointment.

"Andy," she said, "that's not cattle is it? It's something moving fast."

Andy, who had been lying with his head lolling on the back-rest, sat up straight.

"That's a car," he said. "A big car."

Short scrub had grown into sparse taller scrub as they had travelled nearer the hills. The land on either side had grassy patches, real green in colour. The earth was sandy brown instead of red.

"Are we getting near Half Moon?" Mari asked.

"Pretty near," said Andy, who never committed himself to exactitude. "They've had more storms out this way. The grass is shooting better than back on Ninna-Warra. There's waterholes along about two miles. They'll be full."

Mari drove a little faster now as if she wanted to get nearer, quickly, to that moving car. Supposing it was Kane coming home by car? Andy's father had driven over by one of the station cars because he had taken the mustering plant out two days earlier.

The nearer Mari came to the moving ball of dust the more anxious she became. Perhaps she shouldn't have come, after all. Perhaps he wouldn't be pleased to see her.

Her indecision caused her to slow down, whereas five minutes ago she was pressing her foot on the accelerator.

She was almost relieved when Andy spoke.

"That's White Trees' car," he said. "I guess that's one of the Whitfords comin'."

"Which one?" Mari was half relieved, half in despair.

"That Alice coming," Kitty said flatly.

"How do you know?" asked Mari. "You can't possibly see."

"That way Alice drive that big fella car," said Kitty. "Bill Whitford he drive 'nother way. Boss Whitford he drive 'nother way more."

Mari, in the midst of her disturbed thoughts, had time to marvel at the knowledge of the natives. Who else, at that distance, would know who was driving a car?

Ten minutes later the two cars neared each other. The track in this part ran towards a clump of trees seeming to sprout out from behind a hillock of broken stone.

Then Mari pulled the station wagon to the side of the track and braked. At the same time Alice passed her, then swung her car round to come up and park behind her.

The two girls got out of their cars at the same time. Alice slammed her door and came to meet Mari.

They were almost like twins, standing there. Alice wore

the same clothes as Mari had on, blue cotton slacks, a white blouse and a jaded white linen hat. Mari's first thought was that she had bought the right things when she had been in the southern city and Kane had told her to get herself something for riding and driving in the outback. Her second thought was that Alice was not smiling. She wasn't very happy about seeing Mari.

"Hallo!" Mari said, determined to smile herself. "Were you coming to the homestead, Alice?"

"No. I was driving over from Rollins' station north-west of Ninna-Warra and I thought I'd have a look-see what's going on at Half Moon. Once they were never on the air; now they don't seem to get off it. Something's stirring them up there. By the way, what's been happening to you?"

She looked at Mari curiously, not very friendly but not exactly at arm's length.

Mari thought the truth was the shortest cut to an understanding. "I've been frightfully busy refurbishing the homestead, learning to ride and learning to drive a car. Besides . . ." She hesitated, and then smiled ruefully. "I was a little embarrassed about the picnic-races that didn't come off. Was Allen very disappointed?"

"No. He'd had a wager with Bill, my brother. Three to one against. It didn't stop us trying to pull it off, though. You haven't made much difference to Kane, Mari. He still likes the hermit's life."

"I think it's because he's so busy," Mari said in defence. "He works very hard, you know."

"He always did," Alice said shortly. "It didn't stop him being neighbourly in the old days. It's those people at Half Moon. They seem to have a leg-rope and halter on him."

Mari's heart dropped as it always did when this thought came uppermost in anybody's mind, including her own.

In spite of this she managed to get a light note in her voice when she answered Alice.

"Nonsense. He's only over there mustering for them. It seems that when he left Half Moon there was still a lot of cattle in the scrub. And they've had children. I suppose the new stock really belongs to him. . . ."

"But you don't know?" Alice put in. "Well, what's wrong with us going and finding out?"

Mari flushed.

Coming along the track to Half Moon was one thing, but going right up there and finding out what went on was quite another thing. That way she might meet again Kane's anger as when she had suggested people should come to visit her on Ninna-Warra.

Andy was out of the car and Laddie was on the point of vaulting through the window of the back seat. Mari turned hastily towards them.

" I've passengers," she said, relieved there was an excuse to change the conversation. " We were going to have a picnic lunch and it's about time we had it now. Kitty will know if there is a waterhole round here. . . ."

Alice followed Mari back to the station wagon.

" Hallo, Kitty," she said, putting her head in the window and smiling at the dark girl.

To Mari's surprise, Kitty was all beaming smiles. It was clear she *liked* Alice.

" Hallo, Alice, you bin long time comin' to Ninna-Warra. Where you bin, all this longa time?"

" Not invited," said Alice frankly. She fell into Kitty's form of pidgin-English. " What you fella bin doing no come over White Trees? What that fella Kane bin doing shut up longa time Ninna-Warra?"

Kitty smiled, but even Mari could see she was wary. She wasn't likely to say anything about her Boss that wasn't something good.

" That fella Kane musta got him two million bullocks, Alice. It tak him all day musterin'. All time, alla-same musterin', that fella. . . ."

" Two million bullocks!" said Alice in exasperation. " He must have taken to duffing. Last time they had a tally on Ninna-Warra they barely mustered fifteen thousand." She suddenly changed her tactics. She turned the handle of the door. " Come on out of that car, Kitty, and we'll show Mari where to find a waterhole."

She turned, but Andy was in first with this important piece of information. He pointed to the trees sprouting from behind the hill.

" Over the other side," he said. " That's where the kadjibuts are growing. They always grow in deep clefts. That's only the tops of them you can see."

" Then let's picnic at once," Mari said determinedly. " Look at Laddie. He's starving."

" You mean you-all starvin', Missus," Kitty said, getting out of the car. " Come on, gibit basket. We-all start eatin' 'fore you starve yourself thin."

Giggling, delighted, followed by an active small boy and a bounding dog, Kitty led the way across the dry ground and up the hill.

Mari and Alice followed.

" I'm awfully glad we met, Alice," Mari said, trying to be friendly and neighbourly. Actually she *was* glad, but she was still worrying about what Kane would think.

" Let's eat first and talk afterwards," said Alice. " I'm hungry myself. Then we can go and have a look-see at Half Moon. With you in attendance, Mari, I won't be afraid of being thrown off. You have an excuse to go and see Kane. You are at least *married* to him."

Mari wondered if Alice said this last in a sceptical way. She must only be guessing. She couldn't *know*.

Thinking about this took her mind from worrying about Alice's suggestion that they go up to Half Moon. When they'd had lunch would be time enough to think about that.

Mari was beginning to hate the sound of the name Half Moon.

True enough, over the hill the immediate aspect of the land changed. The hill descended, on the other side, into a deep cut, like a ravine, in the hillside. The trees, immensely tall with foliage only in their crowns, were growing straight up out of this ravine.

They clambered down and presently came to the bottom, where a small underground stream welled up from the rocky floor, flowed in a miniature creek for about a hundred yards, then lost itself down the dry, barren hillside beyond.

They sat down and opened their baskets—Alice had brought a small carry-all from her own car—while Andy and Kitty made a camp-fire in a bushmanlike way.

In no time the billy was boiling and they were all drinking scalding tea, holding barbecued chops between slices of bread and butter, and chatting away in high spirits. Alice, in the radiance of Kitty's smiles, had either forgotten or forgone her earlier reticence with Mari. In no time Mari was telling her about her former home life, and Alice was describing White Trees to her.

Andy had taken Laddie for a walk along the short creek bed and he could be heard clambering about amongst the rocks, making enough noise for a dozen small boys.

"Those rocks slippery and that-fella Andy not used to rocks," Kitty said. "He's plenty good on a horse an' twistin' any cheeky young bull's tail but he just no used to rocks. I guess I fetch'im."

Kitty went off in pursuit of Andy while Alice and Mari packed up. When this was done and Kitty, Andy and the dog were seen coming back, Alice said: "Let's get going or we'll never make Half Moon before it's time to head for home." She looked at Mari sideways. "Of course I wouldn't be invited to stay on Ninna-Warra, if I was too late, would I?"

She saw the dismay and uncertainty in Mari's face.

"Don't worry," she added briefly. "I shan't invite myself. I'll wait till I get a card with gilt edge on it from Kane."

"Oh *please* . . ." said Mari. "Of course you must stay if you are late."

Suddenly she felt angry with Kane. How could he put her in such an embarrassing position as this? As if it could possibly matter that Alice, an old friend, had driven herself on to Ninna-Warra and might even come back to the homestead and stay the night.

"I insist," Mari added.

"I won't be as late as all that," said Alice. "Come on, let's up to Half Moon."

Mari hadn't the courage, or the degree of unfriendliness, to say she wouldn't go with Alice.

Besides, Kane had only said she was not to go *off* Ninna-Warra. He hadn't said she wasn't to go to the limits of its boundary. He had said she wasn't to mention Half Moon; probably because he was sick to death of being reproached for leasing it out to such unfriendly people as the Raywoods.

Mari, as she packed her "family" back in the station wagon and then got in and started up and turned the car to follow Alice's car, thought more happily of this as a solution.

Once Kane had signed a contract he couldn't get out of it when he found out just what the implications were. Now could he?

That was it. He signed . . . and then he was caught.

Really, she had been making mountains out of anthills!

The cars had been travelling up an incline when Alice had to change down into second gear to negotiate a bad rocky stretch and Mari followed suit. Beside the track was a wide path of hard beaten brown earth. Andy told Mari this was the cattle pad.

The buff of hills that was the boundary-line of Half Moon had materialised into that barren cliff the native boy had painted. It was a formidable sight—an impassable barrier, Mari thought, until she saw that the track they were on led to a wide gap.

There by the gap was the single pencil tree. The landmark of Big Fall. Beyond Alice's car Mari could see that the white quartz-strewn road led up and into the gap. Somewhere up there were the grassed plains of Half Moon, the place Kitty had said was " very rich."

At the bottom of the pass Mari swerved her station wagon off the track and came to a stop. Alice pulled up, got out of her car, and came back to the station wagon.

" What goes on? " she said.

" I'm a novice at driving," Mari said by way of excuse. She had to give Alice some reason for not driving right into Half Moon. " I'm sorry to show the white flag," she added ruefully, " but I'm just not game to drive up there. . . ."

" Well, get out and let's all walk," said Alice, making a concession. " After all, time is getting on and I've far to go. From the dust blowing about up there I'd say they've got the cattle pretty near Big Fall. We might meet them at the top."

" I don't think . . ."

" No, don't think. Just come on. I'll lead the way with Andy. That kid's not afraid of any climb. Are you, Andy? "

Andy was out of the car before Alice had stopped speaking. Laddie was through the rear seat window and panting to go.

" As far as the top only," said Mari firmly. " Then I'm going home. I've dinner to cook—a family to look after."

She prayed Alice wouldn't ask where Uncle Ralph was. She

wanted above all for Alice to think she, Mari, had to go home
and cook Uncle Ralph's dinner.

It was a long, hard climb and there wasn't breath for conversation. Andy scrambled way up ahead of the others,
periodically making forays to the left or right according to
where he saw something different and interesting to a small,
adventurous boy.

"You get off those fella rocks," Kitty cautioned with what
little breath she had to spare. "You ain't any good on rocks,
Andy!" The boy's legs were spindly thin and looked as if they
might crack as easily as a dried stick.

Several times they all had to stop for breath. The climb
was steep and the way littered with small jagged stones.
Looking to the right and to the left, Mari decided that this
track was at least safe compared with the sheer fall of cliff
and broken boulder on either side.

"How did they manage to find this pass?" she asked in one
of their rests.

"They didn't find it. They made it," Alice said. "Dynamited it out. The plains up there were too rich to be left
unsettled for want of a track. This is it."

"And the other side? The White Trees side?"

"Dynamited too."

She said no more, and Mari knew that Alice was thinking
sorely of those gaps that had been dynamited open so the
cattle from White Trees and the stations beyond could be
routed through Half Moon then across Ninna-Warra.

It had been a "law of the country" that a station owner let
his neighbours drove their cattle through his territory. Kane
had broken this "law" and so left his neighbours bewildered,
unable to be exactly unfriendly because formerly they had
liked Kane, even loved him.

Mari glanced at Alice as they trudged on up the uneven
track.

Was this the case with Alice? Was this the root of her
curiosity about Half Moon? Why had he done it?

Yes, why had he done it?

Mari was certain it was not because of unfriendliness,
because she knew in her heart that Kane, in spite of his aloof
manner, that cold-hooded-look in his eyes, was sometimes a
kind man.

Money or Miss Icy-voice!

Mari knew she didn't want to know the answer. It was better not to know because that way she wouldn't be hurt.

Andy had ranged away amidst the boulders on the right side of the track.

"Alice, I've had it," Mari said. "I'm worrying myself sick over that boy. I can't keep him in order, and neither can Kitty. If anything happens to him . . ."

"Don't be silly," Alice said with determination. "That kid's been roaming over a station all his life. Nothing could *happen* to him. We're nearly at the top now. Come on."

She stopped and looked up.

"Whacko!" she said. "Dust, and what a pall! They've got the cattle mustered up there and we'll see something."

Mari looked up—the opening in the rock wall was only twenty feet away. It was so thick with dust it might have had a curtain drawn across it.

Even as they stood and looked they could hear the "Hoo-hoo-hoo" of men calling to the cattle, the occasional crack of a stockwhip.

"What luck," said Alice. "We might get a second swig of tea. They'll never start the down-drove over the Big Fall without a smoko to start it off."

Mesmerised by that dust curtain and the distant muffled sounds of men rounding cattle into one compact mob, Mari followed Alice.

Only to the gap, she told herself firmly. That'll be the boundary. I won't be bullied by Alice into putting one foot over it.

At the moment she was thankful Andy had scrambled away out of sight amidst the boulders to the right. In a minute, when she got to the top, had one look, she would have a good excuse to go back and would have to look for Andy.

Mari felt sick at the thought of subterfuge, but how could she tell Alice she herself was a prisoner? That Kane had forbidden her to put one foot off Ninna-Warra?

It was something she just couldn't confide in anyone. It would make Kane look an ogre—it would tell the truth about herself.

They were at the top now. Alice had rounded the butting boulder wall on the left and stood, because of that boulder, just out of sight. Mari pressed on and came up beside her.

The cattle were a hundred yards away mobbed in a bunch under some trees. The dust was dying down because now the mustering was over and the cattle were being quieted by the dogs. Three stockmen were dismounting from their horses by the trees and nearby was a jeep, standing in the shade. A young woman was sitting at the wheel, leaning forward so that her arms rested on the steering-wheel, as if she had been watching the scene for a long time.

Even as Mari watched, Kane rode up from behind the trees, dismounted with that easy swing of his, let the reins of his horse dangle over its head and came forward to speak to the girl in the jeep. He leaned in the window and Mari could see he was smiling.

There was something young and fresh and easy in that smile. It shone, lighting up his whole face.

The girl's head was turned away from Mari now, but Mari had seen her profile as she sat leaning on the steering-wheel, waiting for something. Waiting for Kane?

She had the face of a young woman, perhaps twenty-four or -five, with clear-cut features, a firm but attractive mouth and chin. Her hair was fair where it showed under a little white cap, very much like the caps the air-hostesses wore on the planes. She had on a white tailored blouse attached at the neck by a loose-knotted blue tie. In fact, to Mari's unhappy eyes what she did look like was the magazine posters of a very, very pretty air-hostess—the kind who had brains and ability as well as good looks.

One of the stockmen who had dismounted earlier came up to the jeep and began to take a billy and tea things from the back of it. Kane opened the door for the girl to get out.

"Come," said Alice. "If tea's on, I'm in it. Now I'm going to meet that Raywood girl, willy-nilly."

She walked forward through the dust haze towards the group under the trees.

Mari was rooted to the spot. Then suddenly, from down the Big Fall and well to the right of it, came a child's scream.

"My golly—that Andy boy!" said Kitty, who had just puffed up behind Mari.

Mari swung round.

"Oh no!" she cried.

Kitty had started back down the way, and Mari came stumbling and slipping a little on the small stones in the track, her heart in her mouth.

Dear God, I must have wished it on him, she thought, wildly. Kane, the girl, the cattle muster behind her, were forgotten. She only thought desperately of getting to Andy, and of her own dreadful contribution to his fall by having thought she would make just this possibility an excuse for not following Alice right across the boundary on to Half Moon.

"Don't let anything have happened to him, *please*," she prayed. In her mind she saw Andy lying broken and maimed at the foot of some hideous rock pile.

She slipped badly in the down slope of the track, but righted herself. Kitty had swung off to the side and was scrambling down and over the dreadful rock surface of the cliff beside the Half Moon track. Kitty's bare feet and bare hands seemed to cling to the rocks like limpets. She went across them without a fall.

"Jes' you wait, Andy," she was calling. "This fella comin'."

There was no answer from the child.

Where was he? Did Kitty know with that infallible instinct for locality that natives had?

Mari started over the boulders as Kitty had done. She slipped badly as she scrambled, slowed down by a wild kind of seeking for footholds that Kitty had known instinctively were there. Mari's shoes wouldn't grip.

She leaned against one of the rocks and took off her shoes. After them came the socks. It was Kitty's bare feet that were giving her a hold, Mari thought.

She scrambled on down the rocks, falling frequently. On the smooth rocks her feet did hold, but not on the jagged ones. They cut into her soft soles—feet that had not known a lifetime of walking on bush and rock as Kitty's had done.

Both Mari's forearms burned painfully where they had been badly grazed in successive slips. Her feet ceased to hurt; they were numbed temporarily by the cuts.

"You there, Andy? You young fella fool?" Kitty was calling.

What a way to speak to an injured, perhaps dying child! Mari thought, feverish with anxiety.

A stone rattling down from above told the lubra Mari was following. Kitty stopped and waved Mari away.

"You go back, you one big fool, Missus. You mighty like git killed," she screamed.

Mari did not answer.

Kitty would get to Andy first and Kitty would know best what to do, but it was Mari who had wished it on him.

Not wished it on him, she pleaded with herself. I had only been planning to make an excuse to go and look for him. But he was my charge. I brought him. I shouldn't have let him go off by himself.

Mari was still climbing down when she was aware that Kitty was no longer rattling stones. She was standing still— at the mouth of a crevice in the hillside—her soft aboriginal voice murmuring and scolding at the same time. Mari had not dared take her eyes from her own footholds.

Then suddenly she was there, standing on a flat rock beside Kitty, who was stooping over the small boy.

Andy was sitting on a rock nursing his foot, and beside him, tongue lolling, eyes occasionally moving from Andy to Kitty, was Laddie.

"You let me feel that foot, Andy," Kitty was saying. "I guess you damn-all broke it."

"Andy . . ." said Mari, still catching her breath from that frightening climb downhill. "What did you do? Are you hurt?"

Laddie gave a yelp, and then, looking at Mari, began to whistle sadly through his nose.

Andy turned an indignant and pain-controlled face to Mari, then the expression on his face altered. He went quite white and his mouth opened.

"Mari . . ." he said. Then gulped.

Kitty straightened and turned.

She showed the whites of her eyes and her mouth opened and shut as if for one moment she didn't know what to say.

"Missus—Missus——" she wailed.

Laddie alternately woofed and whistled as an accompaniment.

Mari was suddenly aware her feet were no longer numb;

they were screaming with pain. She looked down and could see the blood welling from the lacerations. Her arms and hands were grooved with brilliant red scratches, and where she had wiped one arm across her face the red trademark of those wounds had been left like a weal.

"Yo sit down—right here," Kitty ordered, forgetting Andy. "My goodness, when the Boss see that—he'll break one fella big hell loose. Look what you bin done, Andy—you young fool."

Crooning and moaning, Kitty helped Mari to sit down.

"What is wrong with Andy?" Mari said. "Kitty, you must attend to Andy."

"I dare say he broke his leg," Kitty said sanguinely, taking Mari's handkerchief from her and trying to wipe the dust and rock-grime from the wounds.

"Oh no! Andy, how bad is your foot?" Mari cried, trying to brush Kitty aside.

"His foot damn all right," Kitty said mollifyingly. "I jes' done tell 'im that to teach 'im one-fella lesson. I tol' him—'Don't you gin go over those rocks'."

"It was my fault," said Mari. "I should have kept my eye on him. I was thinking of other things too much."

Half Moon and what she would see there! Alice and her strong-minded determination that Mari should go up through the gap!

"What is the matter with his foot?" Mari insisted.

Kitty stood aside.

"I tink it sprained an' he got a big swelling," Kitty said complacently.

Mari closed her eyes with relief. All down that long slide and scramble she had had a picture of Andy's thin legs . . . so like a stick that might snap easily.

Small rocks were suddenly rattling and pouring, a minor avalanche, down the cliffside to the left of them.

"Here comes the Boss," said Kitty. "Now we's sure for it."

Fifty yards farther beyond Kane, Mari could see his horse. He had ridden down the Big Fall track to about level with where they were now sitting.

I should have run down that far, then cut across, Mari

thought ruefully. How like a man to have brains about a rescue.

Another horseman dismounted on the track and then Bob too was climbing across the rocks towards them.

Kane swung himself round a boulder and stood on the flat rock beside Mari and above Andy.

He seemed more concerned about Mari than about the small boy. The difference between the two—the two faces—was one that Kane could see and Mari could not. Andy's colour was good and his eyes alert and just a little alarmed. Mari's face was white—except for that red smear. Her arms, hands and feet told their own gruesome tale.

" I done tell her go back," Kitty said ruefully.

Kane stood, the dust of the muster ground in his clothes and in his face, his eyes grey and unreadable.

" How badly are you hurt, Mari?" he asked quietly. Mari might have thought his voice sounded gentle if she hadn't known for a certainty it couldn't be. That quietness was only hiding his anger. He was like that. . . .

" I'm only scratched," she said. " It's a bit sore, that's all. It's Andy that's hurt, Kane. Would you please look at his foot?"

" Yes. But I'll look you over first, if you don't mind."

Bob swung himself round the boulder and Kane spoke to him over his shoulder.

" Feel that kid over, Bob, will you? Then lift him out to the track. You could take him up to Half Moon and get Daphne to drive him up to the homestead."

Bob didn't answer because he never did answer. He just did what was necessary. At once.

Mari, in the midst of her pains and aches, had a thought that hurt more.

Daphne. So that's her name and that's what he called her! She closed her eyes and did not realise that Kane, in bending, was going to lift her up.

" Where's the station wagon, Kitty?" Kane asked, as he gathered Mari in his powerful arms. Strangely, Mari did not feel she was heavy. She felt feather-weight. It must be the ease with which he lifted her.

" 'S down bottom Big Fall, Boss," Kitty said. " Guess I'll

git along an' git out that med'cine box. You always done
keep med'cine box in the back uv ebry car, Boss."

"Okay, Kitty," Kane said. "Take Laddie with you. Give
Bob a call to take my horse back up to Half Moon. I'll drive
the station wagon home."

With extraordinary ease Kane managed the rocks on his
way back to the track, then steadily down the track to the
wagon.

Mari looked up at him. She expected to see him very
angry but was surprised to see, when he took his eyes from
the track to look at her, they were quite kind.

"All right, Mari?" he asked.

"Yes. Please put me down, Kane. I can walk quite well."

He smiled grimly.

"Not on those feet," he said. "They look as if you've cut
the soles off them, Mari."

"I haven't, Kane," she pleaded. "They're only scratched."

"We'll see about that when we get back to the car."

They went down the hill.

"Why aren't you angry, Kane?"

He glanced at her.

"I'm not angry, Mari," he said. "It was a rash but brave
thing to go over those rocks after Andy. I'm only concerned
for how much damage you have done to yourself."

"I meant about our going up to Half Moon," Mari said.
She hesitated, then added, "I wasn't going *in* to Half Moon,
you know."

There was a strange expression in Kane's eyes. One
moment there seemed a cloud, the next moment it cleared and
he was very nearly smiling.

"It doesn't matter so very much now," he said. "I think
things will change from now on. Things *have* changed. It
will make a difference to everyone."

Mari blinked her eyes. Was she mad, or only suffering
shock from much bruising and laceration? Kane looked
different. He looked as if he was suppressing something—
happy.

Had Kane and this girl Daphne—the one in the white
blouse with the lovely, calm, confident profile—come to some
conclusion?

The girl had been waiting for Kane in that jeep. He had

smiled at her—the way Mari had never seen him smile since she first met him.

It was too fantastic to think that Kane had gone as far as using a false marriage to win Daphne. And yet . . .

He didn't have to get married to do it, thought Mari. He could have pretended he had another girl. Or even got engaged. But married? What a mess to untangle first!

It was all fantastic, and not realistic enough for a man like Kane. Yet Mari was certain, with the instinct of a woman in love, that this change in Kane had something to do with that girl—Daphne.

Perhaps her voice was warm now. She wasn't Miss Icy-voice any more.

Mari closed her eyes.

Kane put her down on the rug Kitty had already spread on the ground. Mari did not open her eyes; not because she was in physical pain, but because her thoughts were infinitely more painful.

She knew they were fantastic thoughts, but she could think of no other explanation.

She kept her eyes closed because she didn't quite care what happened to her now and she didn't want to have any more conversation with Kane. Even if he didn't say anything, his eyes would say it for him. Mari couldn't bear any more.

Kane was changed. She knew it by the muscle fibre of his strong arms, and the tender way he began now first to bathe then to dress her wounded arms and feet. It was a tenderness of one removed—perhaps felt for someone else and which she now, by accident, was receiving.

Had she fallen off that raft, after all?

Her eyes flew open and she looked at Kane. He smiled at her.

" That feel better?" he asked.

No, she wouldn't give up. If she had to scale Half Moon's worst cliff walls she would get inside there and get to know *Daphne*. This time no orders from Kane would stop her.

Suddenly Mari saw great virtue in Alice Whitford. She was a *trier*. She didn't lie down and cry. She too wanted Kane and she hadn't let him keep her off Ninna-Warra; or Half Moon, for that matter. She'd come uninvited.

Comrades in arms.

Mari started to laugh with the kind of laughter that brough
tears to her eyes.

"She truly am bad," Kitty said, looking down at Mar
compassionately.

"She's had a lot to put up with," said Kane briefly
"Apart from you and young Andy."

He bent and lifted Mari in his arms again. She made a
half-hearted attempt to free herself. She could walk, she
wasn't ill, her two feet weren't as bad as Andy's one foot
Yet she liked being lifted. She liked that strong feel of Kane's
arms, and she liked even better that somehow, in those few
short yards to the car, he managed to carry her so that her
head couldn't help resting on his shoulder. He held her tight
pressed to him, as if he wanted it that way.

He wasn't angry; he was happy, yet she, Mari, had dis-
obeyed all the rules.

What *was* going on, anyway?

CHAPTER SIXTEEN

The next day was the day of all days.

It began when Kane came into her room to dress her cuts.
He threw back the sheet covering and sat down on the side
of the bed, his back to her, and began to examine her feet
first.

Mari, a little fuzzy in the head from the sedative and
tetanus injection Kane had given her the night before, lay and
watched his back, for that was all she could see.

Very gently he removed the lint dressing from the soles of
her feet.

"Good," he said. "Now leave them there exposed to the
air while I have a look at your arms. Then I'll bring some
fresh dressings."

He turned round and altered his position on the side of the
bed so that he was facing her. He did not look at her as he
took first one arm and then the other and removed the dressings.

"Good!" he said again. "Don't cover them till I'm back
—air is good for drying out suppurating wounds."

Except for speaking to her he had treated her more as an inanimate body than as a human being.

He was no sooner out of the door than Mari reached for the comb she always kept in her beauty box on the bedside table. At lightning speed she flicked the comb through her hair, and then, after listening to make sure Kane was not yet on his way back, she quickly dug her fingers in the cold-cream pot and smeared it over her face. Seconds later she had wiped the tissues over her face, rolled the tissues into a ball and hidden them under her pillow. With two minutes to spare Mari lay back on her pillow, closed her eyes and pretended to go to sleep again.

Kane did not knock at the door. He came in as if he owned her room.

Just like a married man, Mari thought. *Thinks he owns his wife's bedroom.*

He carried a small round tray and must have put the heavy layers of Vitin ointment on the lint strips before he brought them in. He put the tray on the table and again, sitting on the bed, back to Mari, dressed her feet. Once again he turned round and sat, this time facing her, and dressed her arms.

Only when the whole job was completed did he look at her.

He smiled. It was a beautiful smile and wrung Mari's heart.

" Good morning!" he said.

" Good morning," Mari said in a very subdued voice. She was accustomed to battling for Kane, not being overwhelmed by kindness from him—with a smile too.

He leaned forward, put his hands on either side of her pillow and, resting on them, looked down at her face. Suddenly he bent forward and kissed her on the lips. It wasn't a passionate kiss, or even a loving kiss ; it was, however, more than a cloud kiss, and Mari loved it. When he lifted his head she wished he would do it again. Her sea-blue eyes looked into his.

" You smell nice," Kane said thoughtfully. " It must be the cold cream." His eyes flicked over her face as if taking everything in. " And you've done your hair . . ." he added.

Mari flushed and tried to look cross. Even if he had guessed, he shouldn't have mentioned it.

He was smiling, and the only thing she could do was smile back.

"Kane, you seem very bright this morning," Mari said for want of a better word to use. "Something very nice must have happened to you over at Half Moon yesterday."

"Something very nice did happen," he said. "Yesterday and the day before and the day before that."

"Will you tell me?"

He shook his head. All the time, his hands had been on either side of her pillow and he had been leaning on them, looking down at her.

"I can't do that," he said. "But it will break any minute now. Be patient, Mari. . . ."

Once again he leaned forward and once again he kissed her —very gently.

He stood up, straightened himself, and tucked his shirt in his trousers.

"I have to go out and bring that mob in from Big Fall, Mari," he said. "Ralph is busy sizzling some breakfast for you." He went to the door, turned and lifted his hand.

"See you at sundown," he said.

See you at sundown, thought Mari. If only I could hear him say those words every morning for the rest of my life.

Uncle Ralph brought Mari her breakfast—the tray held high and proudly—like the day when she and Kane had come home from Dampier. It was a well-cooked breakfast and Uncle Ralph was very pleased with it. Mari was too kind to pretend she was anything but the invalid, needing attention, and grateful for it.

All the same, she waited impatiently to hear all the heavy-booted footsteps die away across the station square. It was still too early for the girls to come up from the quarters down by the creek. Bob, who had turned up late last night, merely showed his face in the doorway as he went past.

Mari couldn't help something of a tearful smile at the attentions of her masculine family. Bob never had the words, nor the facial expression, to say what he thought. But his nice brown dead-pan face in the doorway had been enough. It was his way of saying "Good morning."

Mari let silence reign in the homestead for ten minutes

before she started to get out of bed. She put first one foot and then the other on the floor. It wasn't too bad. They didn't hurt very much, even when she stood up. Kane had put dressings on like velvet sponges.

She found she had to hobble a little on the side of her feet, though that didn't matter so long as she could get about. Mari was far too healthy to contemplate a day in bed with complaisance.

Ablutions in the bathroom weren't easy, for she dared not get her dressings wet—for fear of Kane's displeasure—but somehow she managed to feel clean and washed. Dressing wasn't so bad, because her arms were the least painfully scratched.

She did her hair in the pony tail because that was easiest, and anyway Kane wouldn't be in till sundown.

See you at sundown!

The sweetest words ever said. No! She would never let him go. She would fight for him. She was still on that raft.

If she could make herself more beautiful—always be kind and sympathetic when he came in tired at sundown. . . .

Yet he had said *See you at sundown* as if that meant the beginning of something, not the end of it.

On the way to the kitchen Mari heard the news session come full blare on the transceiver set. Kane must have left it on, and full on too. He must be mad, or did he think she liked listening to the news from her bedroom?

Mari switched off the set a trifle petulantly.

She didn't want to hear anything for fear she might hear Miss Icy-voice with a voice that had thawed out. If she could have stamped down the passage on those wounded feet, that was what she would have done. Instead she ricocheted along the carpet from the outside of one foot to the inside of the other.

She was on the point of telling the native girls, rather shortly, they were late, when she was saved from this unkindness by the sound of a plane flying overhead.

The girls precipitated themselves out of the back door and Mari could make the distance to the front door much faster than she would have dreamed ten minutes earlier.

She stood out on the veranda and watched it circle overhead. It was the Flying Doctor ambulance. Mari could see

its white-painted sides with the big red cross amidships. The
pilot in the cabin waved and Mari could see the nurse waving
at one of the portholes.

As the plane went low over the home paddock it dropped a
small parachute. Already the girls were scrambling out,
through the wire fence, to capture it.

Once again the plane circled, the pilot waved, and then it
winged its way towards the north-east.

Mari waited till the girls brought in the mail basket—for
that was what the ambulance had dropped.

Usually the small cross-continental plane dropped the mail.
She thought perhaps the ambulance doing it to-day might
mean something important.

There was a lovely sheaf of letters for herself. One from
the Altons and a host from her girl friends and two of
Robert's erstwhile friends all agog with excitement and goodwill over her marriage.

Mari couldn't open Kane's or Ralph's letters to see if they
were the important ones. The only other thing the basket contained was a newspaper. Mari didn't realise it was to-day's
paper, because she had lost count of days and dates long ago.
On a station they didn't mean a thing.

She sat on the front veranda, her bandaged feet stretched
before her, and read her letters avidly. Then she flicked open
the newspaper.

How odd papers were in a different country, she thought.
So unfamiliar!

She wasn't very interested in the front page because Mari
wasn't terribly interested in politics anyway.

Australia had a vast uranium find; in the largest area of
pitch-blende in the world. Mari didn't know what uranium or
pitch-blende was, so she wasn't interested.

Mr. Sandys was having talks with the Government. Now
that was something. Mr. Sandys belonged to her. He came
from the same place she came from. Mari read about those
talks with care.

She turned the page. There was a lot about Sydney but she
thought it couldn't possibly be as beautiful as Perth.

That lovely river! And she had slept when the car drove
along it!

If only she could have that day back again. That was the

time to have won Kane. Somewhere she had read that it was
the first three days of marriage that mattered.

If only she could have those first three days again. She'd
have a better try this time.

She thought of Kane stroking her hair as he lay on his back
beside her, on that wedding night, and a lump came in her
throat.

She should have done something about *that—then.* . . .

The day wore on and the only thing that was odd about it
was that the natives seemed strangely restless. Down at the
quarters along the creek bed there seemed to be a hubbub of
excitable noise. Kitty and her two companions in the house
laughed and whispered together. In the end, after lunch, they
fled back to the quarters to join in whatever it was that was
going on there.

"They know something. They've heard something," Mari
thought. "It's probably something happening hundreds of
miles away. Uncle Ralph said the natives *always* know ; and
nobody knows how they know."

Thankful to have the kitchen to herself she got on with
making the dinner.

See you at sundown! There was a sweetness in that, and if
she let herself be a fool she would believe also a secret promise. That was what she wanted the words to sound like, she
supposed.

Anyhow, just for the cause, she would make a wonderful
dinner.

The men loved roast beef. It would be roast beef and it
would have everything—a wonderful warm brown gravy, a
stick of celery here and a stuffed tomato there, with nicely
browned onions, not to mention roast potatoes. She would
have some Yorkshire pudding too—she'd always been good
at that—and anyone who didn't like it could have horse-
radish sauce or mustard.

And lemon meringue pie.

That was one secret she had prised from Kane's stonewall
heart. He liked her lemon meringue pie.

It was sundown when Kane came in. He was different
from what she had expected. He had moved a big mob of
bullocks to-day—all the way from Big Fall at Half Moon to
the Number Twelve bore. That was five miles, but then he

had had to go right out to Big Fall to do it. And all the way back. He ought to have been tired.

He came striding across the gravel square. As he stepped up on the back veranda he took off his hat. Mari had come to the door to show him she was not a bedridden invalid.

" Mari . . ." he said abruptly, ignoring her stoic heroism in being up instead of being in bed. " Did you listen in to the news?"

" No," she said. " I turned the set off."

Suddenly Kane looked exasperated.

" I should have told you to listen," he said. " I was expecting important news."

"The ambulance came over with the mail," Mari said. " Perhaps the news is in one of the letters. They're piled on the table on the front veranda with a newspaper. The paper, as usual, will be weeks old and there's nothing much in it."

" I'm afraid the ambulance won't be bringing me the news I want, Mari," he said.

He hung his hat on its usual peg on the veranda wall and then, standing silent, began to wind the lash of his fourteen-foot stockwhip round the handle.

It was funny, Mari thought, but she had never seen Kane do that before. He always wound up his stockwhip as he walked across the square. He always finished this at the moment he needed a spare hand to open the wire door.

It seemed as she stood there as if Kane was controlling himself. When he finished furling he hung up the stockwhip and turned to Mari.

" How are the wounds?" he asked.

His eyes were kind, though showing their tiredness now. Mari was grateful for his interest but couldn't help noticing that it had come second to his interest in " news." She was being childish again, and she knew it. Disappointment makes anyone childish, she thought. Me most of all.

" Can you smell my dinner, Kane?" she asked, forcing brightness.

He smiled.

" I can," he said. " Thank you, Mari, for going to that trouble."

He was concentrating on her again, looking at her eyes

intently. He took two steps towards her, and taking her chin
in his hands looked right down into her eyes. He bent his
head and kissed her lightly on the lips! Not lovingly, not
passionately, but with something more than cloud softness in
it. He lifted up his head and stood looking at her, his own
eyes dark—the old look of concern in them.

"Bravo, Mari!" he said, then he dropped his hand and
walked away in the direction of the shower-room.

"I've lost my chance again," thought Mari, exasperated.
"When he kissed me I should have put my arms round him
and *clung*—like a *vine*."

Yet in her heart she knew she was far too shy, too innately
reticent herself to do anything like that. Kane had to say the
first word—perhaps he never would.

Yet he had kissed her three times this day.

Mari touched her lips with her fingers. What did it all
mean? If only she *knew*—for sure. . . .

They had Mari's dinner in state. Uncle Ralph and Bob
were tired, but not too tired to appreciate it. Kane said all
the polite things necessary about the roast and had two
helpings of the lemon meringue pie. Yet he seemed preoccupied. Yesterday he had been happy, this morning kind
and tender, sundown disappointed and inexplicable, to-night
preoccupied.

Mari was bewildered because one thing she had learned to
believe about Kane was that he had a very even temper. It
took a lot—such as Mari inviting people to a race-meeting, or
Uncle Ralph bringing a strange girl to live on Ninna-Warra
—to rouse him to a cold and formidable temper.

He certainly has something on his mind, Mari thought
sorrowfully. *And it's not me.*

After dinner Kane sat at the transceiver set trying to get
through to other stations, but for once an electrical storm
hovering to the north made it impossible to get the trans-
missions. Nothing but static came across the air.

Mari, having finished in the kitchen, had a bath—minus
the soles of her feet and her forearms—and went to bed.
After all, she wasn't quite as normal as she thought. That
scratching about she had had yesterday had taken some toll
of her.

Half an hour later Kane knocked at her door and came in. "I'll do those dressings again now, Mari," he said. "Can you put up with it for ten minutes?"

Mari nodded. Actually she didn't want to put up with dressings, but it brought Kane near her and she loved the gentleness with which he did the dressing. And who knows? He might kiss her again. This time she would put her arms round him!

Kane had finished bandaging her feet and all but finished wrapping the last bandage on her arms when Uncle Ralph— with a short rap on the door—came in. He had the newspaper that had come in the mail basket that morning. There was something triumphant about the way he carried the paper—like the way he had carried the tea-tray when he had brought Mari's breakfast to her.

His puffing-billy was emitting clouds of smoke from the corner of his mouth and he said nothing as he put the paper, front page open, on the bed where Kane could see it.

Kane's fingers stopped tying the knot of the bandage as he read the headline. Uncle Ralph stood by the side of the bed and watched him.

Mari thought Kane did a funny thing. He simply closed his eyes for a long time. Then he opened them and looked at Mari.

"It's out!" Uncle Ralph said, waving an arm almost as if he was waving a flag. "It's *out*, Kane."

"Yes," Kane said quietly, still looking at Mari and not at Uncle Ralph. "It's out."

Suddenly he stood up.

"That *damn'* transceiver!" he said.

"Bob's trying to get through to Half Moon now," Uncle Ralph said placatingly. "Now take it steady, Kane. It's all over. Maybe you can come to life again."

"Excuse me," said Mari meekly. "But what's out? What's all over?"

Kane bent down and kissed her. This time it was a real kiss —hard—full of mixed relief and longing.

"Darling, you said that paper was weeks old. Of course the old Doc sent it in! Why didn't I think of it? He was the only other person in the north who knew. He had to know, because he had to go there occasionally. . . ."

" Go where? Know what?" pleaded Mari.

" Go to Half Moon, darling; know it was a Government Mining and Research Survey and not a damned cattle station any more. . . ."

Bob's voice came down the passage. For once even he was driven to words.

" She's through, Kane," he said. " Can do now. You got the code?"

Kane bent and kissed Mari again, then turned to the door. At the door he stopped and turned and came back to where Mari was lying bewildered and trying to think out the meaning of what was said.

" Mari," Kane said quite quietly, " I'm sorry I kissed you like that. Put it down to excitement and relief, will you? I've known for a fortnight they've found uranium and miles of pitch-blende on Half Moon and known all this week the Government was about to announce the news to the public. I've had to keep it to myself or the stock market would have rocketed. I've got to go and talk to Half Moon now, but just try and understand why I had to keep you, or anyone else who came on Ninna-Warra, a prisoner. I thought marriage was the best way to tie you up. . . ."

Mari lifted herself on the pillows.

" Put me down as one of the heroes—or should I say heroines?—sacrificed to exploration, will you, Kane?"

Uncle Ralph, who had sped out in the direction of the office, came posting back.

" Hey, we're through, Kane! Come on before someone else cuts in."

Kane went back to the door.

" See you later, Mari!" he said.

Yes, and finish off apologising for kissing me, Mari thought, and telling me you married me because it was one of the "things" you do because you're a hero. One of the back-room boys, or something. And now you've gone off to talk to *Daphne*. Miss Icy-voice, who just happens to be a very pretty person. Except for that funny cap she wore. All right on an air-hostess, but not on a cattle run, even if it is a Government Survey Station.

Mari thought she knew a lot about what was right to wear

on cattle runs, this season. Hadn't Alice Whitford worn the
same clothes she herself wore?

Away down the passage Kane's voice went on talking and
other voices were talking back. Presently Mari realised he
was tuning in to other stations, other excited voices were
talking. The office, the passage, and even the air stealing
through the open door into Mari's room, seemed full of
excitement and happiness.

Everyone was busy forgiving Kane. They were all inviting
him over, and yes, he was busy inviting people over to
Ninna-Warra too. Australia would be a rich country. It was
better than finding oil, it seemed.

Mari put up her hand and switched off the overhead light.
Only the light reflected down the passage and the moonlight
flooding the floor of Kane's room softened the darkness of
her own room.

Mari put her hand under her cheek and, through lowered
lids, looked out across the veranda.

She had put out the light and that would tell them she had
gone to sleep. But she knew she wouldn't go to sleep. She
was the only sad one in that atmosphere of happiness radiating for thousands of square miles around—from station to
station.

Half Moon was open to the stock route again!

Mari heard Uncle Ralph, then Kane, stamping up the
passage and back again. She heard Bob close the outer door
of the side veranda as he went down to his own cottage.

Presently all the lights in the homestead died out except the
one in the room off the veranda: Kane's dressing-room. Mari
saw the light from its open door flood Kane's sleepout, then
switch off. He did not need a light to go to bed, the moon was
giving it to him in plenty. Mari, watching that moonlight
flood through the door, heard the sounds as Kane stopped by
his bed. There was no sound of the usual upheaval as he got
into it. Instead his feet, not slippered, came on down the
veranda, and he was standing in Mari's doorway. He carried
in his arm—a pillow.

He came on in and bending over the bed said, " Move
over, Mari. It's too big a night for me to spend it alone." He
smiled down at her. " I need you, darling. I want to talk. . . ."

He needed her! He had called her darling for the second time in two hours!

Ice melts before sunlight and Mari's heart thawed and softened.

A strong man needed her . . . and, dear God, how much she needed him!

"It's not a very big bed," she managed to say. "Not as wide as the Pollards'."

Kane thrust his pillow into place and a moment later was lying full length on the side of the bed. He swung the arm nearest her above his head and let it rest on the pillow. It was just as he had done that night in Dampier. Mari lay still, filled with a terrible mixture of hope and fear. Was this the moment? What if she let it slip through her hands again? What did she say? Do?

Alas, she was silent as she was stiff: forlorn as she was, somewhere, deep inside her, wildly happy that he had come to her.

"What—what," she said at length, "is uranium, Kane? Why did it have to be such a secret?"

One-armed, because he had the arm nearest Mari flung back on the pillow above his head, he took cigarettes and matches from his pyjama coat pocket, lit a cigarette and put the box and packet on the bedside table.

He lay on his back, smoking a cigarette and looking at the ceiling.

"Uranium!" Kane said quietly. "Isotopes for medical treatment! Power to drive machinery! The greatest radio-active power in the world is in uranium. Power for good . . . God willing. I had to hope they'd find it and I had to keep their secret."

He drew on his cigarette and there was a long silence.

"Mari . . ." he said. "It is a wonderful thing to think that up there on Half Moon there is uncountable wealth for the good of the people of this country . . . and all countries." He repeated softly, "*On Half Moon*." His station.

He lay in silence for a while. Mari didn't move either, for fear she would break some spell that lay over Kane—indeed over them both.

At last he turned his head while he stubbed out the cigarette on a tray on her table. Once more he was lying on his back looking at the ceiling, talking as if to it.

"Then you came," he said. "What was I to do with you? You were so young, and then so homeless. . . ."

"And Uncle Ralph put an *idea* in your head," said Mari.

Kane laughed. It was a very low laugh and there was some of that old irony in it.

"He sowed a seed in rich ground, Mari. It was so easy for me to let it grow."

"Chemistry?" asked Mari. "Or just to keep me out of the way of Half Moon?"

Kane turned his head and looked at her.

"Chemistry?" he asked, incredulous. "What do you know of chemistry, Mari, even of the human body? Dear child, you didn't even know what uranium was!"

"Just putting two elements together . . . like any female does. And the way we did it in test-tubes at school. Oh yes . . . I did do a little bit of general science when I was at school. Only we hadn't got as far as that stuff up there on Half Moon."

Kane turned his eyes back to the ceiling. Mari lay, her head on the side, and watched his profile. He hadn't answered her.

"Do you like coming in here, and lying on my bed? And talking to me, Kane?" she said very softly.

"Like it?" He neither moved, nor looked at her. "I like it, Mari, because I love you," he said quite simply. "And to-night I wanted to be near you. When I saw you that first day, standing on the back veranda—those absurd slacks, that mass of hair round your lovely youthful shoulders, your blue eyes challenging me—I thought you were the loveliest thing I'd ever seen. But oh, so damnably young! Like a child!"

Mari lay in a quicksilver of astonishment. No words would form in her head.

"What was I to do with you?" he went on. "I couldn't leave you running loose round Ninna-Warra because of the secrecy of that project up on Half Moon. I couldn't woo you and win you in the traditional way. You were too young. It was too callously unfair. I had to marry you to protect you, Mari. From *me* . . . as well as from running loose in forbidden territory. Then I had to take care of you; and not affront you with the feelings I had for you."

There was a long silence in which neither said anything. Neither stirred. Mari who had been so full of plans to win and hold her man was suddenly speechless and incapable of the movement of one hand. In spite of all her brave words to herself—her fine modern ideas of how modern girls should be allowed to behave—she suddenly knew that all the time she was desperately shy. Deep down, she was not confident. It was all a front.

Kane, put out your hand and touch me . . . she cried in her heart.

Kane lay on his back, looking to the foot of the bed. He had not heard that mute cry.

"So now?" Mari managed to say at length, her voice wavering.

"So now," said Kane, "I love everything about you, Mari. I love your sense of humour, your wonderful capacity to make the best of everything, your sheer dogged purpose in doing a good job well. Even damn-all polishing floors."

He turned his head and looked at her. The moonlight was playing over them and there were only pale silvered faces and dark pools for eyes, that each could see.

"But most of all I love you, Mari, for just what you are. A slim-jim of a girl in slacks, a white shirt, and your hair tied up in that silly knot behind your head. You stand, with your feet apart, and look out of those eyes of yours as if the world was your oyster. Did you know that, Mari. *Is* the world your oyster?"

Mari shook her head on the pillow. There were tears in her eyes.

"Daphne?" she managed to say at last. "I saw her—up there on the top of Big Fall. Miss Icy-voice, they called her on the air. She's prettier than I am. . . ."

Kane half-lifted his head from the pillow to look at Mari.

"Daphne Raywood?" he said, slightly incredulous. "She's nice-looking in her way. And incredibly capable. Runs her husband—he's the senior testing officer up there. Officially she runs the switchboard. Does all the decoding messages. As a matter of fact, from a managerial point of view she just about *is* the Survey Station. Put uranium down to her."

" Oh," said Mari. After a long time she added: " I love th
homestead to be nice, but I hope I'm not *managerial*. . . ."

She didn't know what she hoped, she was unbelievabl
relieved to know that Daphne Raywood, Miss Icy-voice, wa
safely and happily married to someone else.

Kane's head went back to its former position on the pillow
He didn't answer her. His hand, the one on the pillow abov
his head, dropped down and rested on Mari's head an
gently, tenderly began to stroke it.

Mari's head leaned forward and touched Kane's shoulde
just as it had done that night at the Pollards' bungalow whe
they had first been married.

How did she tell Kane she loved him too?

She hadn't any words, and wonder of wonders, she, Mar
was too shy to utter them anyway.

She moved her head and her lips were touching Kane'
shoulder.

What he was thinking he would never know himself, bu
suddenly he was aware of those warm lips. In them was
message as soft and kind and true as the moonlight floodin
the world outside and sending flickering patterns of deligh
over the floor and over the bed.

Kane turned. One arm wrapped round Mari and one han
cupped her head.

" Mari?"

There was still no answer, only her head burrowing into hi
shoulder, warm lips saying all that had to be said.

" Mari darling!" His fingers entwined in her hair an
pulled her head backwards. Then his mouth was on hers.

This time there was nothing of cloud softness in that kiss
His arms crushed her to him.

Time enough another day to explain away Robert Alton—
and the sweetness of that young love and the passion of thi
true love. The one might have grown into the other, but thi
was here *now*. For ever.

Sixty miles away on the veranda of White Trees, Alice Whit
ford lay back in a cane chair. The geologist beside her settle
back in his chair, and between the two chairs their hand
hung, clasped together.

" Of course, Dad and Bill minded about the cattle no

oing through," Alice said. "But I was just plain selfish. I
ainded about you being shut in there at Half Moon. I just
ouldn't make myself believe you'd turned stockman—let
done a recluse one. Geologists see so much of station life,
ome of them do take to it. But . . ."

She laughed.

"Two recluses!" she said. "You and Kane. It was hard
o believe, and I don't know why I did believe it."

"A hundred marks out of a hundred for Liaison," the geo-
ogist said. "I must say we had our qualms when Kane went
erserk and married that girl. . . ."

"She's all right," said Alice protectively. "She's mad about
im, and he's mad about her, although he's always reserved
bout showing his feelings. That way your precious survey
ecret was safe. Neither would ever let the other down."

He leaned forward and kissed Alice on the lips.

"Here's to love then!" he said. "And much of it!"

Romance in the tradition of Lucy Walker

IRIS BROMIGE

AN APRIL GIRL. Philippa and Rupert's love was fragile thing, needing encouragement to grow. B something in Philippa's past held her back—and Lucill Pallys was quick to take advantage of it.

THE QUIET HILLS. Christine and Rachel were friends very good friends, so they thought—until handsome an charming Neil came between them. But was he afte Rachel's money, as Christine accused—or did Christin want him for herself?

THE MASTER OF HERONSBRIDGE. Hoping to prov her independence, Charlotte left her wealthy parents t work for the Staverton family. But soon she was inti mately involved in their traditions, their rivalries—an their romances.

ONLY OUR LOVE. Linda was sure her hated relative were deliberately disgracing her, but she wasn't sure i her beloved Angus would see it that way.

THE TANGLED WOOD. Alison thought she had chance for a new life—but an inherited feud with he nearest neighbors threatened her newly found confi dence and her hopes for love.

THE STEPDAUGHTER. Bridget was no kin to th wealthy and tightly knit Rainwood family, and so sh never felt completely accepted—especially when the began to spread rumors about the man she loved—th man who'd married her cousin.

THE YOUNG ROMANTIC. It seemed as though Robi knew all about what she did before she even had tim to tell him herself. Something—or someone—was un dermining their engagement—and she was totally help less.

THE ENCHANTED GARDEN. Julian's garden had always been Fiona's refuge when her world became to harsh. She loved him dearly, but to him she was just child—and Fiona thought the only way to bring him t his senses was to leave him.

THE CHALLENGE OF SPRING. When Tony died Delia took refuge in her grandparent's peaceful countr home, hoping to fill the void. But soon she realized sh was in love with their neighbor, Gavin Dilney—a lov whose destiny hinged on someone else's despair.

To order by mail, send 80¢ for each book (covers postag and handling) to Beagle Books, Dept. CS, 36 West 20t Street, New York, NY 10011.